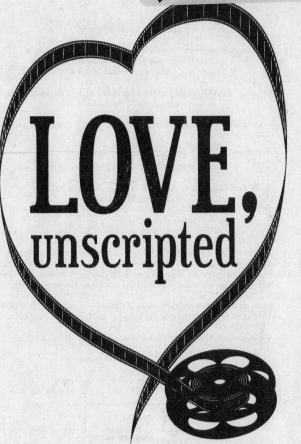

LOVE,
unscripted

OWEN NICHOLLS

REVIEW

Copyright © 2019 Owen Nicholls

The right of Owen Nicholls to be identified as the Author of
the Work has been asserted by him in accordance with the
Copyright, Designs and Patents Act 1988.

Excerpt on p. 258 from 'Mia' taken from *First Love* by Emmy the Great,
used by permission of Emma-Lee Moss

Excerpt on p. 200 from 'Ghostbusters' courtesy of Columbia Pictures

First published in Great Britain in 2019 by
HEADLINE REVIEW
An imprint of HEADLINE PUBLISHING GROUP

First published in paperback in Great Britain in 2020 by
HEADLINE REVIEW
An imprint of HEADLINE PUBLISHING GROUP

1

Cataloguing in Publication Data is available from the British Library

ISBN 978 1 4722 6 3148 (Paperback)

Typeset in Bembo Std by CC Book Production
Printed and bound in Great Britain by Clays Ltd, Elcograf S.p.A.

MIX
Paper from
responsible sources
FSC
www.fsc.org   FSC® C104740

Headline's policy ... ts and
made from wood gr... sses are
expected to c... l.

LOVE,
unscripted

OWEN NICHOLLS is a screenwriter and author. His first novel *Love, Unscripted* was chosen as part of the Escalator Talent Scheme run by the National Centre for Writing. He lives in Norfolk with his wife and their two sons.

To Nina – my real love

Prologue

When we were eleven, Leon Woodward told me about his plan to kiss Sally Carter.

He would take her to the cinema to watch Disney's *Aladdin*, a film he'd already watched three times in order to work out the exact moment a girl of Sally's disposition would be most susceptible to a spontaneous lunge in which his lips pressed up against hers.

He chose the moment the Princess first saw Aladdin for who he really was. It worked so well that the week after, he took Sally's best friend Hannah Jenkins and did the same thing.

Even at a young age, I thought this was a dick move. For two reasons.

First, I liked Sally Carter. She was funny and kind and had nice hair and didn't deserve to be the first guinea pig in Leon's sexual blitzkrieg on every girl in school.

Second, I really liked that part of the film. To me, it seemed wholly unfair to interrupt a pivotal scene where two characters' true selves are unveiled for the first time with something that could easily wait until the end credits.

But then Leon kissed a lot of girls in school.

And I didn't.

1

I'm still thinking about Leon Woodward kissing Sally Carter when the fire starts. It isn't a big fire, just the melting of an inch-long piece of plastic, but the smoke sets off the alarms. I pull the film from the projector and stamp out the flames as an extremely anxious and very sweaty Seb comes running into the booth.

'Ah shit, what happened?' he asks, with an exasperated tone I assume has less to do with the problem at hand and more to do with the paperwork he'll have to fill out later.

'The gate got stuck, the lamp was on, A plus B equals man fire,' I explain.

'Nick, you have to strike the lamp after you've got the loop running.'

I scratch at the hair on my chin and cheeks. The two weeks' growth of a boyfriend in a coma.

'I did know that. Sorry.'

It's not like I have a particularly bad memory. I can recite the entirety of the Pacino/De Niro coffee-shop conversation from *Heat* and can remember the exact order in which the eleven jurors are turned by Henry Fonda in *Twelve Angry Men* – it's Juror #9, Juror #5, Jurors #11, #2 and #6 at the same time, Juror #7, then Juror #12 and Juror #1. Juror#12 changes his mind but switches back with Juror #10 and Juror #4, leaving just Lee J. Cobb breaking down in the final reel as Juror #3. But I can never retain certain key information about the inner workings of the projectors. A small part of me thinks they might lose their magic if I know exactly how they work. If I ever mention this to Seb, he'll probably fire me.

'I'm sure Humphrey . . . it is Humphrey, right?' Seb asks.

I nod. It was my idea to name the projectors after my celluloid heroes, and Booth 3 houses both Humphrey and Katharine, Screens 6 and 7.

'I'm sure Humphrey will be fine.' Seb says. 'And you?'

I know what he's getting at.

'I'm fine.'

He gives me the international face of 'Really?'

'I'm absolutely fine. It was just a little fight.'

His eyebrows rise enough to add an exclamation mark to the 'Really?' And a 'Really?!' is harder to brush off.

'Because Ellie said—'

'You spoke to Ellie?'

He shouldn't have spoken to Ellie.

'She rang me. She wanted to make sure you were okay.' He pauses, not for dramatic effect, although it has that result. 'She told me she'd moved out.'

It's true. She moved out a week ago, but I convinced myself she'd move back in quickly enough that I wouldn't

4

need to tell anyone. I was approximately two days away from dressing up in her clothes and waving at people from the window in order to convince friends and neighbours everything was still a-okay.

'It wasn't a little fight,' I confess.

Seb's 'Really?!' face collapses into one of such pity it's all I can do not to well up. We both suggest a cigarette break at the same time.

'I think the fire's gone,' Seb assures me.

'That's what she said,' I reply.

2

4 November 2008 – 23.21 GMT
Obama 0
McCain 0
270 needed to win

I first met Ellie at a 2008 election night party held by a mutual friend of ours who just happened to be a libertarian. Normally I would baulk at being near anyone who would describe themselves as such, but Tom had a big house, good weed and an encyclopedic knowledge of Asian cinema. That he was the only person in south London who wanted John McCain to win wasn't quite enough to counter these excellent qualities, and the fact that he'd only invited thirty or so twenty-somethings, who were all sane non-libertarians, was typical of him. He hated people agreeing with him, loved confrontation and would almost exclusively start arguments with the phrase 'I'm just saying'.

He addressed a crowd of five.

'I'm just saying, you lefties all fawn over Obama, but policy for policy he has more in common with Cameron than Brown.'

A clueless twenty-something in a beanie hat took the bait.

'So you want another four years of the same regressive Republican agenda that took the UK into two wars?'

Ellie entered my life half watching David Dimbleby informing us the polls for Kentucky, Indiana and Georgia would close in forty-nine minutes, and half watching Tom take on the hipster. A wry smile crossed her face; she knew full well what he was doing. It was that smile that got me. I'm a sucker for any kind of smile, but a wry one just floors me.

Her smile was one of the first things I remember really liking about Ellie. The second was the way she tucked her hair behind her ears. There was a surety in the action. Maybe it was because as a teenager I was teased about my sticky-out ears. I even grew long hair to cover them. To see someone purposefully putting theirs on show made me want to yell out, 'Good for you!'

I didn't. Obviously.

That in a certain light she looked like Holly Hunter when Holly Hunter was in her mid to late twenties – so *Broadcast News*-era Holly Hunter – certainly didn't inhibit my attraction. They shared the same quizzical eyebrows and flawless skin. Plus, she had Kate Winslet's neon-red hair from *Eternal Sunshine of the Spotless Mind* and wore the most nondescript zipped-up grey hoodie and navy jeans, like she was paradoxically trying not to be noticed yet screaming, 'Look at me!'

It took me forever to make my move. I became paranoid

I'd been staring at her and she'd noticed and was now wondering who this weirdo creep with massive ears and . . . Wait . . . were we wearing the exact same hoodie?

It was a sign.

I grabbed two beers from the kitchen and went for it, handing her one and observing, 'You must have seen Tom do this before to smile like that.'

She squinted slightly, viewing me with the requisite amount of scepticism with which you should view someone who comments on your smile, and took the drink.

'He certainly has a need to be disliked,' she said, elongating the vowels in 'need' – an Elliesque idiosyncrasy I have since found both adorable and infuriating in equal measure.

We watched as Tom stepped his attack up a notch with a one-two of questions on the difference between the House and the Senate, and a much more aggressive than passive investigation into his opponent's previous UK election-viewing habits, to which the hipster could only respond with a shake of the head.

Tom was obliterating his foe with a smile in his eyes. I could see where this was heading and gave my insight to Ellie.

'If that guy mentions hope or change, he's done for.'

And just like that . . .

'So,' he said, a little too smugly, 'you don't believe in hope? You don't believe in change?'

Tom erupted.

'Fuuuuuuck you!'

The hipster was taken aback by this outburst and looked around for help, but none was forthcoming. On the contrary, if there'd been popcorn, it would have been opened and passed around for the crescendo.

'I will happily have a debate with you about the rights and wrongs of universal healthcare, military spending or the antiquated penal system of America. But I am fucked if I'm going to stand in my own home and try to form a cogent argument over two-bit slogans. Jesus Christ. Hope. Change. You moron. Those posters might as well have said "Kittens" and "Puppies". Nobody is against hope. Or change. Everyone loves change as long as it's vague enough. I had genuine respect for you when you were arguing the ins and outs of foreign policy. But this. This is beneath me.'

The doorbell rang and Tom – without missing a beat – patted the victim on the arm and departed to answer it. But not before giving me and Ellie a wink on the way.

'He's good,' she said in a way that made me a little jealous, again bringing several extra vowels to the word.

'He almost convinced me to join his anti-tax group when we were at university,' I said, stopping for a sip. 'Before I remembered I like roads and hospitals and libraries and that I'm not an arsehole.'

'Is that where you know him from? University?'

'Yeah. You? You're not part of his anti-tax group, are you, because if so, I didn't mean the thing I said just then about them all being arseholes.'

She let out a short, sharp laugh, her brown eyes twinkled and my heart soared.

She followed the laugh with 'I'm tempted to say yes to see how quickly your principles fly out the window.'

'As Groucho said, "These are my principles and . . .'''

'". . . if you don't like them I have others.'

When I went to clink beers, the move was not reciprocated. Perhaps she just didn't see me do it, but the minuscule rejection brought a cold sweat to my neck.

'I was friends with his sister when we were little. When I moved to Clapham, she passed me his details so I'd know someone locally. He has a point about why we're so interested in another country's election, though,' Ellie said, erasing my social anxiety over the missing clink. 'Did you stay up for the last election in the UK?'

'Nope,' I said.

'So why this one? Why are we all so besotted with this guy?'

I hadn't contemplated until that very moment why we were all (except Tom) so excited at the prospect of Barack Obama becoming the 44th president of a country the vast majority of us had no actual affiliation with.

'First of all, it's him,' I said. 'He has an allure. An allure so strong that a straight male from the south of England can say "he has an allure" without even pausing to wonder why he's using such a romantic word.'

At this Ellie flashed a grin that blew the wry smile clear out of the water.

I continued, spurred on by the grin. 'But I've always loved American politics. It's what America pretends to be that's appealing. Truth, freedom, liberty. All that jazz. In a country that's still sort of young . . .'

She looked deep into my soul and offered, 'The possibilities are endless.'

3

'We'll always have Barack,' I say to Seb as I put out my second cigarette. But the line and its relevance are completely lost on him.

'What's that?'

'Me and Ellie. We met at the 2008 election.'

'Oh right. Is that three and a half years ago already?'

Since he became a dad, Seb has become hyper-aware of time passing, and can often be caught forlornly noting ten-year anniversaries of albums he remembers buying with a similar refrain. He's recently been promoted to projection manager, which is fine by me. He's my friend, he works hard, and even though I've been at the cinema three years longer than him, I don't really want the extra work and stress the promotion would mean.

'Two thousand and eight? Wasn't that your *Before Sunrise* night?' he asks.

I'd actually described it as my *In Search of a Midnight Kiss* night, but Seb still hasn't seen that film, and when I explained to him that *In Search of a Midnight Kiss* is a lo-fi American indie about two people who meet and talk all night and get to know each other and fall in love, he kept saying, 'Like *Before Sunrise*' and it was clear he'd married the two things in his mind.

I don't feel like correcting him, because he's being incredibly supportive of my current relationship status. Considering he's only just come back to work after the birth of his second child – and exists on three hours' sleep a night – him giving even a solitary shit about me is superheroic friendship.

When I first met Seb, if someone had told me he'd one day be responsible for the lives of two actual human beings, I would have found the quickest way to have him castrated. But seven years is a long time, and the twenty-three-year-old Seb with huge hair and a ginger Gandalf beard who used to leap across the tops of parked cars high on LSD has been replaced by a trimmer, tidier version who goes for weekly runs and takes his eldest to toddler yoga.

'You know you can call me any time, Nick. If you need a chat,' he offers. 'I don't sleep.'

I silently nod my appreciation.

'I better go do the handover with Lizzie. You staying down here?'

I nod again, and Seb leaves me alone on the fire escape, smoking.

It's getting on for five, and that means shift handover. I'm on a mid shift, working from one until nine. Seb did the open shift, nine to five, and Lizzie is on the close, five until midnight. She'll be print-checking the new Judge Dredd film tonight, *Dredd (2012)*, making sure it's put together properly and isn't scratched to shit. The state of some of the films we get from other cinemas makes you want to weep.

We're a little behind the times. It's 2012, and most cinemas are gearing up to be one hundred per cent digital. We just have two digis, which replaced projectors Cary and Ingrid, named for Grant and Bergman. When all eight screens go digital, there goes the job as we know it. I have faith that since we're a small(ish) indie(ish) cinema, the powers that be will keep it true for a good few years yet.

For me, 35mm has a proper feel to it. Sure, it may cut the crap out of my fingertips, and I know that in later life I'll have a hunched back from carrying films from booth to booth, but it's real. It matters. Digital cinema is just code and bits. And digital cinema means no print check. No getting to see the latest release sometimes way before the general public.

And real film will always remind me of Ellie.

She's etched on every inch of this place. When I look at the bench where we put the reels together, I see her hanging out with me on an evening shift as I wind on film. When I look out of the glass port down onto Screen 4, I remember the time that to keep ourselves entertained watching one of the many crap late-noughties Woody Allen films, we tried out every seat in the auditorium to see which one was the comfiest.

Having an entire cinema screen to yourself and your loved one is arguably one of the greatest experiences life has to offer, whatever the movie.

I would have hung around and joined Lizzie for her print check, but Lizzie is one of the most difficult projectionists I work with. I kind of dread shifts where we cross over, and

I think Seb knows this, because it's rare we're scheduled together.

We used to get on. When she first started, we'd talk about TV and film all the time. She even made me a mix tape of all the TV shows she loved burnt onto a CDR. But I must have done something to really piss her off, because now we barely speak. Which is a shame, because Lizzie is one of the few people who won't talk all the way through a film or sit there feasting on the gross nachos we sell. She has fantastic post-movie observations too.

There are five projectionists in total. Me, Seb, Lizzie, Dave and Ronnie.

Dave's a great projectionist. His dad was a mechanic, which means Dave can strip a projector down to its bolts and put it back together. Blindfolded if needed. But he also has the worst taste in film imaginable. If Michael Bay made a film with Adam Sandler, Dave would be the first in line.

The fifth projectionist, Ronnie, is like a sub. If someone goes on holiday or phones in sick, we call on Ronnie. He's fifty-something and a bit of a burnout. He has hair like Neil from *The Young Ones* and was the first person to introduce me to Powell and Pressburger, two British film-makers who had a run of classic films from 1940 to 1951 that have not been matched in sixty years. He's also incredibly intuitive to moods. If you want to be left alone, Ronnie instinctively knows. Sometimes way before you know yourself. But if you're up for a deep, lengthy exploration of mind and soul, he puts the kettle on, sparks a fat one on the fire escape and nods along happily to every THC-induced life-altering

14

observation you make, observations that – while spectacularly profound in the evening air – shrivel and die in the cold, harsh reality of the morning.

The ability to sense someone's mood is crucial when working in a projection booth. The ceilings are low, the air conditioning rarely works, and with each room less than nine square metres – with the noisy, dirty projectors taking up six of those – the set-up can lead to a hostile environment, especially if you're in a bad mood or, I don't know, having relationship problems. It's sort of a blessing then that Lizzie is on shift, because I know I won't have to make much effort.

I'm determined not to check my phone incessantly for messages from Ellie, so I've limited myself to an 'on the hour' look.

Still nothing.

I've also agreed with myself that scans of her Facebook page are limited to every four hours, which means waiting until eight o'clock. Although, I reason, I'm halfway through my shift, so that milestone should sort of trump the four-hour one. And anyway, these are only guidelines, not rules.

Nothing. Nothing for five days, when she uploaded some very cool photos of our Scrabble match, including the make-shift tiles we'd had to improvise because we'd lost one K, both Js, one H and two Es.

That might end up being the last good night we have together. And even that included a pretty heated argument about the points' worth of the missing J.

She was right. It was worth eight.

She was always right.

Except about this.

4

5 November 2008 – 00.04 GMT
Obama 3
McCain 8
270 needed to win

The house erupted in a frenzy of boos when the senator for Arizona took the early lead.

Tom was livid, screaming at his guests, 'You charlatans don't even understand the electoral system. McCain was never going to lose Kentucky. Your idiocy appals me. Keep this up and I'll kick you all out before Iowa's announced.'

The audience's jeers turned from the TV to Tom, with several miscellaneous snacks sent as ballistic missiles towards their host.

I drank far too fast in the early part of that night and was already at the bottom of my third inexpensive, but not unpleasant, European lager from the local off-licence. Ellie had barely started on the drink I'd given her. I panicked my penny-pinching beer-buying had given her the impression I was cheap.

It would have been an accurate presumption. I worked as a projectionist. My parents were both in public service. I'd never had four figures in my bank account without a minus sign preceding them.

After a momentary lapse in conversation, my paranoia got the better of me.

'Is the beer okay?'

Ellie took a sniff and a sip and swirled it around her mouth.

'It's good.' This time she didn't lengthen the word. 'Beery with a hint of beer.'

I followed suit.

'I'm definitely getting a strong taste of sixth-form college.' I took another sip. 'A dash of unrequited love and . . . is that a soupçon of shame and regret?'

She laughed and said, 'You're funny.'

If she'd just said the latter without the involuntary former, I'm not sure I'd have continued my pursuit. People who don't laugh, in my humble opinion, are the worst people in the entire world.

With four years of hindsight, I know that if I'd voiced this insight Ellie would have said something like, 'So, a man could drive a busload of orphaned kids off a bridge, and as long as he was chuckling to himself as he went, you'd give him a tiny bit of credit for his *joie de vivre*.'

And I'd have said, 'Well, yeah.'

She'd have said this because she had – and still has – this magnificent way of downplaying hyperbole without making the other person feel like too much of an arsehole for over-hyping something.

Me not saying anything about a lack of a funny bone being worse than fascism was also another of those moments that made that night so special. There were so many points where I could have said or done the wrong thing and everything would have turned to shit and I would have gone home alone and put on some Joni Mitchell and drunk cheap gin mixed with whatever was in the fridge.

But I kept my inner monologue inner and instead said, 'I'm Nick.'

And she said, 'I'm Ellie.'

Then we shook hands. Like we were two normal people.

And then she asked, 'So what do you do, Nick?'

And I said, 'I'm a projectionist at The Royalty.' And I waited. I waited for one of four reactions.

Reaction number one would be to offer some form of recognition that this involved working in a cinema and was therefore 'cool'. It might be accompanied by an ask for free tickets. Which was always okay because I like people watching films.

Reaction number two would be to ask what the hell a projectionist was. This reaction was always disappointing.

Reaction number three was arguably worse than number two, if only for the number of times every projectionist has heard it. I was hoping with all my heart that she'd avoid this reaction, which was: 'Do you ever splice single frames of pornography into family films like in *Fight Club*?' If she had gone with reaction number three, again there may have been no coming back, even with the cool hair and the spectacular eyes, and you know what, I really liked the downplayed outfit, it's a thing in itself.

Then there was reaction number four. I'd only ever received reaction number four twice. Once from an old Italian man who played squash with my dad, and the other time from a super-geeky guy called Barry who worked as an usher and really wanted to be a projectionist, but all the projectionists had agreed we definitely don't want to be locked in a small room with Barry all day.

Miraculously, Ellie answered with reaction number four. 'Like in *Cinema Paradiso*.'

It was about then I fell in love.

5

The house feels empty without Ellie.

I find myself staring at her side of the bed, missing the way she sleeps.

Having not slept with my – or anyone else's – fair share of women, I can't say for certain, but I'm pretty confident no other person on the planet sleeps like Ellie does. She's always on her front, with her left palm pressed up against her forehead, like Homer J. Simpson in the middle of an annoyed grunt. Her right hand sits in the small of her back and her legs are bowed out, her crotch pushed up against the mattress.

I wonder if she's sleeping like that right now. Or if she's sleeping at all. Or if she's sleeping with someone else already.

I was never jealous with Ellie. Like most completely rational men, if someone else made her laugh, then sure, a small piece of me would die inside, but I've never so much as glanced at her phone, and the anonymity of her drawers and belongings are rightfully protected under European law. As they should be.

When I send her texts asking what she's up to, it's because I'm genuinely interested in what she's up to. Not because I think she's sleeping with Darren from Marketing.

Ellie, it's fair to say, was my first proper relationship. I'd had girlfriends before, but they didn't last long. My insecurities and the bullshit possessiveness that comes with crippling self-doubt soon put paid to them.

The relationship before Ellie was about four months long and ended because I was adamant she was sleeping around. I figured out later I'd convinced myself of her waywardness, purely in the hope that she would cheat on me and I could end things as the hero of the story, the heartbroken guy that everyone would set up on dates – 'Yeah, his ex, she fooled around behind his back, so he's a bit fragile. But he'd be great for you.'

I admit this not for redemption but because I need to understand if it's happening again.

Because now, alone in bed, I'm sure Ellie is sleeping with Darren from Marketing.

My phone buzzes. It's a text from Ellie.

How are you doing?

She never uses text speak or smileys and always uses correct punctuation. How could I have ever let her go? I pause for the briefest of moments to think whether replying instantly gives her relationship advantage and am immediately reminded of her mantra the night we met. To hell with games and mind-fuckery. Now and forever.

I'm okay. You? You want me to call? I type quickly and press send.

When waiting for a reply from a partner you've recently split from – where the reason for the split is still a foggy mess of confusion – time crawls. It's not like a conversation, where a pregnant pause can be uncomfortable. Silence over SMS is crippling. A watched phone never vibrates.

As if to prove the point, it's only when I glance up at the clock – 11.21 – that the message comes through.

I'd rather just text if that's okay? I hate speaking on the phone.

That she feels the need to write the last line sends my mind spiralling down a rabbit hole of questions. Does she think I'm unaware she hates talking on the phone? Does she think I've not been paying attention these past four years?

I can't prevent some apt Paul Simon lyrics written about Carrie Fisher flashing to mind.

I know, I reply. *What do you want to text about?*

Us.

Do you still feel what you said last week? Send.

There's barely a pause before:

I do.

I don't have anything else to say. I don't want to be with someone that doesn't . . .

I don't know how to type the rest. If we were face to face, I'd leave it hanging in the air, both of us knowing what I meant. But typing it out gives it a finality. It marks it down as evidence. I delete everything up to the first *I don't* and add *know what to say.*

I'm sorry, she types. *I wish I felt differently.*

The phone could have auto-completed the *That makes two*

of us message I send. I know that will be the last one for the night, but still I wait for a reassuring buzz to fill the air.

We're supposed to be going to my sister's house for Sunday lunch tomorrow. It's my mum's birthday. I can already predict the way everyone will stare at me, sitting alone.

Everyone will wait to see who will be the first to ask, 'Where's Ellie?'

One half of Simon and Garfunkel is singing about Princess Leia again.

6

5 November 2008 – 00.44 GMT
Obama 3
McCain 21
270 needed to win

Ellie and I were sitting outside, smoking by the back door, when another cascade of jeers met the results from South Carolina and West Virginia.

Again Tom was apoplectic that his guests were commiserating with each other over states he knew would be foregone conclusions, but his rage was falling on increasingly deaf ears as partygoers danced over the line of 'nicely sozzled' to 'utterly pissed'.

I was heading in the opposite direction.

With conversation flowing at a pleasant if not breathtaking pace, I'd slowed my drinking to a crawl. When my sobriety kicked in, so did my nerves, and I found myself suddenly jonesing for a cigarette. I knew the revelation of such a filthy, disgusting (see also: lovely, social) habit had the potential to put a swift end to any progress I'd made with Ellie thus far. But what sort of a relationship could be based on me hiding my vice, and after the *Cinema Paradiso* answer, a relationship was very much on my mind.

Luckily, Ellie was an occasional smoker and saw tonight as an occasion to smoke.

When we stepped into the garden, I used the only piece of arsenal in my *Wooing Women* handbook. Ask questions.

'Where did you grow up?', 'How are you finding London life?' and 'Where are you living now?' had been responded to in turn with 'Canterbury' – plus a run-down of the pros and cons of the cathedral city (pros: close to London and the coast; cons: poor music scene, nowhere to buy Converse) – 'Tiring but fun' and 'On Silver Street by the Chicken Cottage, but not too close to the Chicken Cottage.'

Silver Street was about a five-minute walk from the flat I was currently renting, so I was ecstatic at the close proximity of our houses and was daydreaming of how easily we'd be able to see each other in the early days of our absolutely-definitely-going-to-happen union.

Ellie's hair fell forward and she corrected it, presenting her ears again.

'So, what's your big, crazy, wave-a-magic-wand dream?' I asked, hoping she might come back with 'meet a cute guy at a party and get married and have his children'.

She didn't.

'Good question. I'm twenty-seven now and I always said that by the time I reach thirty I'll be living in New York

City.' She sang this last bit like it was the last line in the first verse of 'Mona Lisas and Mad Hatters'.

'And you?' she asked.

'Well, I'm only twenty-six, so I have much longer to work on my dream.'

'Let me guess. You wanna be a film-maker?'

I shook my head with a hint of overkill.

'Standing in front of a roomful of people telling them what to do? Nothing would fill me with more dread.'

It was then that she sized me up, squinted her eyes and had a eureka moment.

'You write!'

I nodded.

'Screenplays?'

I nodded again.

'I can see that, with your hoodie and your aversion to shaving and that look in your big blues.'

'What look?'

'Like you don't know.'

I was about to press her further when a drunk girl in a Metallica T-shirt came running through to the back door holding a trainer filled with vomit.

'Hey, someone just threw up into a shoe!' the reveller explained before hurling said footwear into the garden. Then she slumped down between me and Ellie and asked, 'Do either of you know where I can get some ketamine?'

It was then that I glanced down to see that the girl was only wearing one trainer and had almost definitely been sick in the other.

'Not on a Wednesday morning,' I said.

'There's a primary school about two miles south of here,' Ellie offered. 'You could try there.'

The drunk girl leant towards Ellie and stared at her menacingly. I was genuinely worried she was about to attack, and I'll admit there was part of me that wanted to see how handy Ellie would be in a scrap. Mainly because on the lover/fighter spectrum I was way down the opposite end from Muhammad Ali and thought it would be great if my someday wife would be able to protect our family with her brute strength.

Instead, Ellie kissed the girl on the nose.

In a move that was probably for the best for everyone involved, myself included, violence was averted as the girl blew a kiss back and smiled a wasted smile that had more in common with a sloth than an actual human being.

'Two miles south, you reckon?' she said hiccoughing three times in the space of the one short sentence.

Ellie nodded. 'Just ask for Mr Benson.'

Ms One Shoe stood up, saluted and made her way into the garden.

She'd gone about ten metres before she exclaimed, 'I found my shoe!' and promptly passed out.

'We should probably get her back inside,' I said, 'Or at least go find her a blanket.'

Ellie looked at me and said, with sincerity, 'You're one of the good ones, aren't you?'

The compliment made me feel both elated and anxious, so I attempted to cover it with self-deprecation hidden in an invitation to spend more time with me.

'It's way too early in the evening to jump to conclusions like that.'

'You're right,' she said, playing along. 'I'll give you until Texas to prove me wrong.'

7

For nearly four years I believed I had that thing I'd craved for so long. You have to understand that love is everything to me. It's Rick and Ilsa. It's Harry and Sally. It's Han and Leia. It's George and Mary. It's Peter and June. It's Wall-E and EVE.

At the end of our big break-up fight, I clammed up. It definitely wasn't the most mature option, but I genuinely didn't have a clue how to respond, and she kept offering new and increasingly unoriginal platitudes designed to make me feel better that had the exact opposite effect.

I stayed as silent as Buster Keaton and we sat like that for somewhere between ten and thirty minutes. Me staring at the carpet. Her staring at her interlocked hands as she chewed on both her thumbs at the same time.

Eventually she rose.

'I'm meeting my mum in an hour. We'll talk later.'

I said nothing and she left.

I was convinced from that moment on we – as we knew

us – would never be the same again. That was almost three weeks ago, and we haven't spoken – bar the occasional text message – since.

But I have a plan to change this.

★

Of all the possible places for a potential rendezvous, Ellie's dad's house is at the bottom of my list of ideal locations. Richard has never liked me, and the events of the past three weeks will have done very little to initiate a U-turn.

There's little I like about him either, except his daughter. And his flat, which is enormous and overlooks Battersea Park. Inside it has huge windows and ridiculous furniture; you'd only have to sell one piece of it and you could refit our entire one-bedroom home. Outside it has these oppressive double doors with security cameras poking out at you from every angle. I read somewhere that Elizabeth Taylor used to live around here in the fifties.

Did Ellie choose his place to stay knowing I wouldn't want to visit?

There are no names next to the buzzers, so I have to use a memory that's never served me particularly well. Armed with my peace offering, I press the top button. A voice I can't say for certain is Richard's says, 'Hello.'

'It's Nick,' I answer.

The short and testy 'And?' signals I've hit the right buzzer. I can picture him now, lounging about in his three-piece suit and his cut-throat shave, suave like Colin Firth.

At least I know I wasn't a father substitute.

'Can I come up?'

'Nope.'

A long pause is followed by 'She's not here.'

'Do you mind if I wait for her?' I ask in the least belligerent way I can muster.

'She isn't coming back tonight.'

My finger is getting sore from pressing the intercom button.

I carry on regardless, 'Do you know where she is?'

'You can text her, can't you?'

This is a reasonable question for which I have no reasonable reply other than that I was hoping the spontaneous, romantic nature of my visit might make her fall in love with me all over again.

'Look, she left her bike helmet at ours, and now the weather's getting better I thought—'

'You can leave it outside.'

More silence.

I consider one final 'Can you tell her I came around at least?' but figure that first, it'll sound a little desperate, and second, there's no way I can tell for sure he'll let her know. In fact, any desperation I show will pretty much guarantee he won't.

I press the buzzer anyway.

'That's really fucking helpful, Richard. Thanks. You know this isn't my fault?'

While he may or may not have heard, I think this might be the first time I've ever sworn in the presence of Ellie's dad.

It's certainly the first time I've lied to him.

31

8

5 November 2008 – 00.57 GMT
Obama 44
McCain 24
270 needed to win

Tom's house, much to his chagrin, was gloriously upbeat as the numbers started tipping towards Obama.

I remember wondering what he was hoping for as he stomped about telling anyone who'd listen – and plenty who wouldn't – 'Bob Barr is the man who would offer real change,' only to be met with the elegant refrain of 'Who the fuck is Bob Barr?' on every single occasion. Had he really hoped McCain would win in an early landslide and everyone at the party would be despondent and slink away home before 2 a.m.?

Tom has always struck me as the kind of person who would rather be right than happy.

As for me and Ellie, it felt good being the two least wasted people at the party, like we had a special bond. Us vs Them. The Sober vs the Drunk. Those who would throw up into shoes and we who would not.

Crucially, it meant we could actually talk and listen to each other, even with the increasing volume of the music. Somebody put The Shins on loud, and all the male attendees bopped their heads from side to side, myself included. I stopped when I saw the return of Ellie's wry smile.

'What?' I asked in a way that swayed heavily to the curious rather than the confrontational.

'You like The Shins?'

'Yeah,' I replied, edging towards confrontational.

'Okay.' She paused and looked me up and down. 'And the movie *Garden State*?' The wry smile was at peak wryness.

'It's all right,' I said, far more defensively than I'd intended to.

'I see.'

I know when I'm being teased, and this was some grade-A teasing.

'What? What does that mean?'

'Nothing.'

I turned fully to face her, and she turned to me.

'What does it mean?'

'Well, we've been chatting about an hour now?'

'We have.'

'I'm just trying to get a take on you.'

I resisted the urge to go full A-ha.

'And my admission to liking The Shins and *Garden State* has led you to a conclusion?'

'Not a definitive one, no.'

'So, what's this inconclusive conclusion that has you looking all smug and powerful?'

She faked offence.

'How much do you like *Garden State*?' Her eyes narrowed as if she knew I'd offer a lie.

'A bit.'

'Do you own the soundtrack?'

I grimaced. 'Maybe.'

'Did you see it more than once at the cinema?'

If anyone else had tried this line of questioning on me, I would have presented them with the definition of surly. But I already liked her and she knew it.

'I may have.'

'And I'm guessing, as you work in a cinema, you have a copy of the poster up in your house somewhere.'

'*Now* you're looking smug.'

'I'm right, though?' she asked, knowing the answer.

'You're right.'

She did a little victory leap, complete with a punch in the air and a twirl. I waited for her to land.

'So tell me, in your humble opinion, what does it say about me?'

'Nothing really. Just that you fit loosely into a type. Romantic, a little naive, super-daydreamy . . .'

I mock-fluttered my eyelashes and said in a teen southern California accent, 'You think I'm dreamy?'

'Laid-back. To a point. You tend to use humour when you feel uncomfortable, you're sort of self-involved . . .'

'Please go on.'

'And . . .' there was that one-second word turned into five, 'it tells me you think a woman's sole function is to swoop into your life and fix you, regardless of her own emotional needs, because you're the centre of the universe and she's just a supporting character.'

At this point I literally took a step back with shock at how effectively I'd been psychoanalysed on the basis of liking one film. I felt like I'd been hit by a beautiful and insanely observant truck.

'Well, that came out of nowhere.'

'Sorry. Was it a bit much? The good news is, in the grand scheme of things, these are essentially minor character flaws.'

I nod, still taking the assessment/assassination in.

'And anyway, whether I know you for just this night or for a million more nights, I'm sure I can be of some service.'

She informed me she'd get me a beer and walked away before I could respond.

I called after her.

'You do realise you just offered to swoop into my life and fix me!'

She turned, curtsied and disappeared into the kitchen.

9

My sister, Gabby, is super-cool and I love her with every fibre of my being.

Yes, she made me wear make-up more times than I'd have liked when we were younger. Yes, no matter my protesting, she still calls me the sister she always wanted. And yes, once – when she was taken over by the gods of teenagehood – she pushed me down half a flight of stairs. But she's also fiercely loyal and protective of me.

When I was sixteen, she took me to cool gigs, bought me beer and let me hang out with her really attractive friends. She'd never get too wasted when I was around, never let me wander off alone, and she'd always put me first, making sure the second I wanted to get home we were in a cab together, no matter how much fun she was having. And Gabby had a lot of fun when she was entering adulthood.

There was Anthony, Bill, Callum, Daniel, Dave, David, David 2 (listed alphabetically not chronologically). Geographically, there was Eric from America and Trey from

Australia. Dutch Butch, who was Dutch, and Butch Rich, who was from Switzerland. Then there was François, who was painfully, stereotypically French. He was her penultimate boyfriend and for a while I was worried he might be the final one. He came from a town in the south of France called Sisteron and would say creepy things to me like, 'I am from Sisteron and I am *on* your sister.'

Most of these guys were fun, some of them were mean. A couple of them were very fun for a while and then became very, very mean.

If – and it was always a big if – Gabby settled down, I always expected it would be with a celebrity or a surfer or some sort of surfing celebrity. I never thought she'd marry someone like Andrew.

Andrew is so boring he prefers to be called Andrew. Who does that? What normal person wouldn't shorten it to Andy?

He looks like, and very much is, an accountant. Andrew the Accountant. Oh Gabby, you could have done so much better. Andrew the Accountant, who, when you ask him what music he likes, responds with some bullshit like, 'Oh, I like a bit of everything.' Yet if you played him some mid-eighties Tom Waits or anything by The Paper Chase, his head would explode.

Don't get me wrong, he isn't a dick. He's super-polite and smart in both appearance and books. He's the kind of guy who pulls a chair out for you at dinner, while insisting that you have the last bread roll and he'll pay the bill. All before the starters are served. My parents love him. And my parents never love anyone.

Except Ellie. They also love Ellie.

And now I have to break their hearts by telling them that their dreams of both their children finding everlasting happiness are as dead as Sean Bean in every film Sean Bean has ever been in. But as I open my mouth, Gabby and Andrew stand up from their seats.

'We have an announcement to make,' Andrew says. Like he's reading the quarterly profits of a plumbing company that's really careful about overspending.

Gabby pulls out two little square white envelopes and passes one to our parents and one to me. We open them to see a tiny foetus in black and white.

'We're going to be a mum and a dad. You're going to be grandparents.'

She turns to me.

'And you'll be an uncle. Uncle Knick-Knack.'

And I just start bawling. Really disgustingly blubbing. And I know I shouldn't, because Gabby's never told our parents about the difficulty she's had trying to conceive. She didn't tell them because she knew they'd offer appalling advice and make it all about them. But she has confided in me and I know just how much this moment means to her. She wraps her arms around me and whispers in my ear, 'Are these tears for us, or for you, or because I quoted *The Addams Family*?'

And I sob, 'Both. All three. I don't know.' And she cups my head between her hands and we notice that everyone is crying. Except Andrew. Who I assume is incapable of tears, lest his circuitry become damp.

A group hug is administered, and I know now that there's

some good in the world and that maybe I'll be okay. These revelations after three weeks of misery mean I can't stop crying. And everyone laughs at their emotional response like British people do when they've let their guard down.

'Do you have a due date?' Mum asks.

There's an awkward pause as Gabby and I exchange a look to say we know what's coming. Mum and Dad exchange one that says they definitely don't.

'Mid November,' Gabby answers, with a faux grin that makes her look like she's seven again and has just admitted to stealing all the biscuits in the tin.

Mum does some quick calculations. 'Mid November? That would mean you're . . .'

'Four and a half months already.' She stands and shows off a well-concealed bump that none of us had noticed before.

'Four and a half months!' Dad finally joins in. 'That's halfway there.'

I resist the urge to sing Bon Jovi's greatest hit as I'm fully aware how difficult the ensuing conversation is going to be for Gabby. My parents are not bad people, but when it comes to being overly dramatic, even Nicolas Cage would advise them to rein it in.

'Why didn't you tell us sooner?' Mum asks in a shrill tone.

Gabby looks to me for support.

'We'd had some accidents.'

'Some accidents?' asks Dad in a wilfully stupid way.

'Miscarriages, Dad. Miscarriages. We didn't want to get too excited until things were . . .'

I pipe up with 'Cocked, locked and ready to rock!'

The line gets a laugh from Gabby, much to Andrew's chagrin, and our mother chastises me. 'Now's not the time for jokes, Nicholas.'

Using a full-name Nicholas means I'd better watch it.

'Why didn't you tell us about the . . . accidents?'

Even though she doesn't say the word 'miscarriage' and it's already been uttered – in front of the sprouts and carrots, no less – she still mumbles 'accidents' like she's dropping the N-bomb at a church fete.

I can see Gabby getting increasingly irate.

'Jesus. We didn't tell you because it's personal to us. We had each other and . . . some other help.'

Dad rises from his seat. 'You told Nick you were trying, didn't you? You told your brother and not us!'

'This is supposed to be happy news,' I offer in as flat a tone as I can.

'I just don't understand why you keep secrets from us,' Dad says, teeing Mum up for the perfect body slam of parental guilt.

'Are we not good parents?'

'For Christ's sake. We're grown-ups!' Gabby yells, her adolescent whine slightly undercutting her point. 'We decide who we tell and when! Next time I have a miscarriage I'll put it in the parish bloody magazine.'

A hush descends.

Andrew shuffles nervously in his seat. You can see he really wants to be the one to break the silence, to repair the family with his repartee.

He looks at me, and I pray to God that what's coming isn't what I know is coming.

'Nick, how's Ellie?'

I swallow.

'She's . . . erm . . . she's . . . yeah . . .'

Gabby clocks it immediately and gives me the same look Seb did.

Of course she knows something isn't right. She's been able to tell something isn't right since I was four and Richie next door stole my Thundercats trainers.

'Can I show you something in the car?' she lies, as I wipe away the tears still hanging off my face.

We excuse ourselves and creep out to her and Andrew's pristine white Mercedes. There's something to be said for Andrew's vocation, I think, as we walk the half a mile of driveway to the car from the front of their house. Gabby opens the door and I get in.

'This is a really nice car,' I say by way of distraction.

'What happened?' Gabby asks.

I stare at my shoes and kick them together.

'She said she doesn't love me any more.'

Gabby narrows her eyes in the way she's always done when she knows I'm being less than totally honest.

'Those were her exact words?'

I play with the glove box.

'Not exactly. But that was the general gist.'

The combination of her silence and her very hard stare makes me look at the floor as I reveal, 'It might have been more like "I don't love you like I should" or something.'

I look up to find Gabby waiting, like Oliver Twist, for more. After a lengthy pause, she realises that's it.

'That's it?'

'What do you mean, "that's it"? How would you feel if Andrew told you he didn't love you? How would Andrew feel if you told him you didn't love him?'

'One, I'm not sure I've ever told Andrew that I love him. He tells me every day and to be honest it's getting a little fucking irritating, after four and a half years. Two, saying you love someone differently isn't the same as saying you don't love them.'

That Gabby has never told Andrew she loves him is a big fat lie. During her wedding, at which I got monumentally pissed, Gabby made sure I wasn't drinking alone. This led to her banging down Jägerbombs and professing her love for her new husband more times than the lead singer of 2 Unlimited says the word 'no' in the song 'No Limit' by 2 Unlimited.

As for her second point, less love is still less love.

'So this is just the start,' I say, 'She loves me less and less over time and we become another one of those couples whose relationship gets increasingly weaker, until we either carry on in a loveless trance or break up. All she's done with this declaration is fire the starting gun on the end of us being us.'

I can't quite read Gabby's face, but I know she's not about to agree with me.

'You're having a tiff about something stupid. I'm sorry you're upset right now, but you'll get over it.'

'She's already moved out.'

'What?!'

The volume of Gabby's shout is loud enough to bring a rather concerned Andrew over to peer out of the window.

He offers her an 'Are you okay?' thumbs-up, and she shoos him away, like he's a pigeon after chips.

'Why has she moved out?'

I shake my head, exasperated.

'I just told you.'

'No, you said she doesn't love you the way she should . . . or something.'

'Yes, exactly.'

Gabby replicates my exasperation.

'So why has she moved out if that's all it is?'

I take a deep breath, assuming it must be the pregnancy hormones having an effect on my formerly intelligent sister.

'You don't get it, do you?'

'Evi-fucking-dently!' she yells, and I see Andrew making the curtain twitch again.

I place a hand on the car door and look Gabby in the eye.

'Can you tell Mum and Dad? Please?'

'Tell them what?'

'I have to leave.'

10

5 November 2008 – 01.08 GMT
Obama 83
McCain 34
270 needed to win

'We have to leave,' I implored Ellie.

My sudden need to abandon one of the best parties I'd been to in years stemmed from Ellie's revelation that she was a photographer. We'd been talking non-stop for over an hour, and even though I'd made good use of the woman-snaring queries, and even though she'd revealed her dream was to work in New York, I'd neglected to ask what she actually did for a living. The answer was that she worked as a photographer for the *Clapham Gazette*.

Once I'd stopped mentally listing all the cool photographers from the silver screen – Jimmy Stewart in *Rear Window*, David Hemmings in *Blow Up*, Alexandre Rodrigues in *City of God*, and I think you could get away with both Giovanni

Ribisi and Scarlett Johansson in *Lost in Translation*, even if the latter just took photos of her feet during 'a phase' – I decided that tonight had the potential of being such a momentous night that she'd be insane not to document it.

'The diagnosis of insanity,' Ellie answered, 'is a pretty steep leap for not wanting to do your job in your downtime.'

'That is insane,' I countered. 'If I didn't want to do my job in my downtime, I'd never get to watch any films.'

'Your job isn't actually to watch films, though, is it?'

'How do you know?'

'Because I've seen some films about it.'

'Touché. I saw the trailer for Tarantino's new one the other day. It's called *Inglourious Basterds* and has some French actress playing a projectionist who kills a load of Nazis.'

'That sounds awesome.'

'Doesn't it? Let's go get your camera.'

I offered her my hand and she took it. We were halfway to the door when a well-toned and ridiculously good-looking guy – who I would later learn was named Nathaniel – stepped into our path.

'You off already, are you?' he asked in as hostile a way as he could.

Ellie replied coldly and monosyllabically.

'Yep.'

She stepped around him and I followed suit, pausing only to hope that this new Adonis-like man in my life was anything but Ellie's former or, worse still, current beau.

I tried to imagine alternatives, especially to the idea that she might just be using me as a pawn in her present drama.

Perhaps he was her landlord and she played death metal really loudly at 3 a.m. and he had to go to work early. Maybe they were work rivals and he was her photography nemesis, the Eddie Brock to her Peter Parker. He could just have a chip on his shoulder because they met each New Year's Day at the January sales and she always made it to the best deals first.

These hypotheses could last the long, cold walk to Ellie's place, so as soon as we were out of the house and out of earshot of Hunky Bob, or whatever his name wasn't, I summoned up the courage to ask.

'Your ex?'

She shivered in her coat.

'Yeah.'

'How long have you guys been . . .'

'About a month.'

'And how long had you . . .'

'Two months, I think. In total.'

I may have audibly 'phewed' at that reveal.

I have a rule that a break-up requires at least ten per cent of the relationship's length to get over. So, if you've been dating a few months, leave it a week to get the person out of your system. If you've been together five years, you'll need a six-month recovery time.

'Did you just say "phew"?' she asked.

'I don't think so. I think I just exhaled a bit.'

She showed she didn't buy it by narrowing every part of her face. Her lovely ears included. 'He was a fixer,' she explained. 'Or an improver, at least. He'd try and get me

46

to eat better, or try out the latest fitness fad. I think people should be left to figure themselves out.'

This insight was the first moment I worried about our suitability. As someone who knows their own flaws and confronts their demons on a daily basis, I'd always believed that someone might come along who could make me a better version of me.

I let go of the thought and said, 'I suppose I thought he might be your boyfriend. As in present, as opposed to ex. And without putting too fine a point on it, I'm having a nice time and . . .'

'And?' She looked put out.

'I thought you might be hanging out with me to make him jealous.'

She stopped walking.

'Or something,' I added.

'Back up there, champ.'

The 'champ' was a wonderfully condescending choice of word.

'You thought I was trying to make my ex – who I didn't know was coming to this party until thirty seconds ago – jealous by hanging out and talking to you for a couple of hours? Even though *you* approached me?'

'It was just a thought that popped in there.'

'Well, pop it back out.'

We walked in silence for a minute, my mind racing with ways to take back my false step. Ellie stopped walking again. This time she broke the silence in spectacular fashion.

'Look. Listen. Look and listen. I hope – and think – the

previous comment had more to do with your insecurity than some assumption I'd be cold enough to just be messing about with you in order to mess about with someone else.' She took a deep breath in the icy air. 'But life is short and I don't believe there's time for games and mind-fuckery. So to hell with them. Now and forever.'

She started walking again.

I had the feeling she'd have kept going whether I followed or not.

11

'Should I buy a replica of the statue from *The Maltese Falcon*?'

'No.'

'It's only two grand.'

'Do you have two grand?'

I click off the eBay page and enter a different search. Seb looks up from his paperwork momentarily and shakes his head. It's 21.45 and he was supposed to finish an hour ago.

'I could buy a replica *Millennium Falcon* for just one grand.'

'Nick.' He clicks his pen. 'I'm trying to work.'

'Not stopping you.'

'You sort of are.'

He checks out the display screen listing all the films we're currently showing. The grand total of which is two. In an eight-screen multiplex, just two films vie for the audience's attention. *Avengers Assemble* vs *The Dark Knight Rises*. Marvel vs DC. Whoever wins, compelling and complex narrative cinema loses.

'The ads and trailers are just finishing on 7. Go sneak in the back, I don't mind.'

'Seen it. It was okay. I really can't be arsed with all this spandex lately. We don't get the new Wes Anderson, but we do get four copies each of Gruff Rhys Bale and Robert Downey Jr acting like he's back on the c-c-c-c-c-cocaine.'

A few weeks ago, Seb would have high-fived me for the excellent Queens of the Stone Age reference. Lately, he's just been work, work, work. To illustrate my point, he sighs heavily. 'Then go home. Have the night off. I really don't mind, but I have to finish this work.'

'Can't.' I enter 'Replica Dude's Rug' and hit search. 'I need the money.'

'For what?'

I turn the computer monitor to him.

'This sweet rug.'

He clicks his pen off again, this time setting it down on his notes.

'Nick. I know you're in a shitty place at the moment, but promise me you won't spend what little cash you have on anything stupid.'

He has a look of genuine concern on his face and I start to panic.

'Okay. I promise.'

'And go home. I'll clock you out on full pay. I can do the shutdown. I'll be here late with this anyway.'

Seb has always been good with favours, but never ones that are tantamount to defrauding our capitalist overlords.

'You sure?'

He nods, and while this is all most unlike Seb, I don't wait for a second. I grab my coat and bag.

'Cheers, brother. Double bill of Ashby tonight then. I ordered the fancy pants Criterion edition of *Harold and Maude* and *Being There* from my friend in the States.'

The look of concern is back.

'Worry not,' I say to soothe the beast. 'They were on discount.'

'Just don't forget the meeting at the end of July. The thirtieth. It's mandatory. Everyone has to be there.'

'I know what mandatory means. What's this meeting all about?'

'You'll find out in three weeks.'

'You're not going to let your longest-serving friend get the inside scoop, on the QT, very hush-hush?'

'Just be there.'

★

Bud Cort is swinging from a curtain rope and Cat Stevens is wailing in the background when my phone rings. I don't recognise the number, but it's local. I light a cigarette before answering. One perk of singledom is being able to run back to my nicotine harlot without feeling like I've reneged on my pact with Ellie to at least attempt to be cancer-free. As far as I'm concerned, no Ellie means no pact, and so I've been mainlining Marlboros for almost a month now.

'Hello.'

The voice replies the same.

'Can I help?'

I take a swig of my gin and Dr Pepper. It does a job.

'It's Terry.'

51

'Okay?'

'Your landlord.'

I immediately stub out the cigarette and waft the smoke away, momentarily forgetting that Terry's on the other end of the phone and technology hasn't yet got us to the place of sending smells over 3G. Stupid technology.

'Hey, Terry, how's it going?'

'I'm selling the house.'

'Which house? This house?' I jump to my feet, spilling ash into the carpet. I rub it in with my bare toes.

'No. I'm selling one of the other houses I own. I just thought you'd appreciate an update on my property portfolio.'

I wait for clarification of the sarcasm.

None comes.

'You're being sarcastic, right?'

'Clever boy.'

'Prick,' I say under my breath, this time forgetting that technology has got us to the point of sending sound from phone to phone.

'What was that?'

'Nothing. It was the TV. So how long have I got?'

'You and' – I can hear the paper rustling in front of him – 'Miss Ellie Brown have four weeks to move out.'

Because he seems to be taking a great deal of pleasure from the idea of turfing me out of my home, I think about revealing that ha ha, the joke's on him, as Ellie left a few weeks back. I only decide to keep quiet when I realise the reveal of this information would in no way constitute a win for me.

'Fine.'

'Good.'

'Right.' I pause. 'How quickly can I get the deposit back?'

'I wouldn't get too excited about that, Mr Marcet. After all, our contract clearly stipulates that this is a no-smoking house.'

'Which is why I've never smoked in it!'

'So the ashtray I saw this morning, brimming over with cigarette butts, you were just looking after it for a friend?'

'You can't come around unannounced and go through my stuff!'

Righteous indignation when I know I'm in the wrong is one of my strengths.

'I called Miss Brown about stopping by to check the smoke alarms. Did she not pass on the message?' The glee in his voice is too much.

'Prick.'

'See you in four weeks, Mr Marcet.'

Because this information is both extremely pertinent to my life as a whole and the sort of thing that will lead to me necking the rest of the gin in front of me, I figure it might be a good idea to write the conversation down. If I don't, there's a good chance I'll wake up thinking it's a dream and be unpleasantly surprised come 1 August.

When I can't find paper and a pen anywhere in the flat, I hollow-laugh at myself for ever considering the idea that I would one day be a writer. I told Ellie on that first night that I wanted to be a famous screenwriter, like my hero William Goldman. Not only did he write movies in every genre – *Butch Cassidy and the Sundance Kid*, *Misery*, *All the President's Men*, *The Princess Bride* – he also penned a couple of memoirs about Hollywood that made me dream of one day following in his footsteps.

Ellie encouraged me to pursue this dream on several occasions (sometimes nicely, the last time not so nicely), but I always found an excuse not to, despite wanting to so badly. My memoir would be titled *The Inconsistency of Mr Marcet*.

Now, literally without the necessary equipment to even write a shopping list, all I can do is curse my naive literary notions and drink gin.

*

The film ended half an hour ago. The gin and fizzy Benylin ended ten minutes before that.

I'm stuck in that drunk and lethargic state where I know all I need to do is get to the bedroom. But it feels light years away. I could fall asleep here and wake up with a cricked neck and a belly full of booze at 3 a.m. Or I could just get to my feet, take ten small steps and sleep soundly until noon.

*

I wake at 2.58 a.m., my neck feeling like André the Giant has had me in a sleeper hold for the past ninety minutes. I'm pretty confident I won't throw up – praise the Lord I kept to one type of intoxicant – but I certainly don't feel good, physically, emotionally or ecumenically. Aspirin and orange juice. That's what I need.

But like my earlier search for pen and paper, I come up

short, until a mild moment of epiphany tells me to check the bedside drawer on Ellie's side. Inside, I find everything I've been looking for: a box of Tesco own-brand dispersible aspirin, a packet of four blue biros, a not inexpensive bound notepad and a Post-it that reads: *For Nick, in case you need them. Ellie x*

Even now, when she's no longer here, she's still thinking of me. My heart now hurts more than my head.

I start to write a to-do list, beginning with *Find new house*. Then I cross it out and write something much more important. I give it the title *Why Ellie Left*, and at the top I write in large letters: *NUMBER ONE. WE PEAKED TOO EARLY.*

My intention with this document is twofold. One, I want to make sure I don't keep making the same mistakes over and over again. And two, I want to be ready. I want to be armed with actual hard evidence for the inevitable meeting between us. I want to have prepared statements and the truth on my side. I want to make her see the error of her ways, to make her see that I'm worthy of the best of her love.

I place the pad in the drawer beside my bed, because this is where I do the majority of my lamenting. And also because I don't want anyone to randomly come across a document so arse-achingly self-indulgent.

But I can't sleep.

So I take the pad out again.

And then I start to write something else.

First Intermission

The Girl and the Boy had been together just seven short weeks. For the first time in a long time, he felt confident in himself and his ability to be the equal half of a whole. While her happiness did not peak into giddiness as his did, she had discovered within herself and within their early coupling a peace she too hadn't felt for some time.

When the subject arose of where Nick and Ellie would spend their first Christmas as a couple, it was difficult for Nick to keep himself together. He dug deep to display a cool, carefree attitude to the entire event, but his mask was immediately seen through by Ellie. She sensed he'd need reining in from being completely overwhelmed by the season (and what it might signify), and so offered the compromise of 'family for the day' and 'together for the evening'.

In the former half of the bisected Christmas Day, Ellie opened another item of clothing from her mother. It was pretty, like many of the things her mother gave her, and therefore, without some major modifications, would never be worn. She smiled all the same, knowing that the thought very much counted.

It was just Ellie and her mother, Margaret, in the living room, tiny figures under the high ceiling. A gigantic, perfectly decorated tree, delicately positioned in the corner of the room, added to their lack of scale. Richard, her father, was in the kitchen and would remain there until the food was ready, save for the sporadic announcements that dinner would be served in x number of hours.

Ellie watched her mother opening the gifts she'd bought and looked for the same signs that might have given her away. Was her smile genuine enough? Was her response too quick? How much of her mother was in her?

They should have had the same dark hair, but neither had been happy with what nature had given them. Instead, they found comfort in a bottle, Ellie's a vibrant red, her mother's a platinum blonde. They both had dark eyes and perfect skin. So fair, it's not fair, one former classmate had told her.

Margaret opened a present. It was a scarf with foxes on it, alternating brown with white tails and white with brown tails. She wrapped it around her shoulders.

'Ellie, it's perfect,' she said. And Ellie smiled, thinking: if she really doesn't like it, she's an incredible actor.

'How are things going with Nick?'

'Really well,' Ellie replied, burying deep that uncomfortable feeling born out of never having really discussed dating with her mother.

'Oh, good.' Margaret left a pause before adding another

'good' for good measure. She motioned to the record player, a top-of-the-range, minimalist contraption that screamed, 'Yes, we live very comfortably, thank you very much.'

'Shall I?'

The silence before the music kicked in was tremendous. As soon as the choirs started singing, in came Richard.

'Dinner will be served in one hour.'

★

Three hours earlier and one hour and fifty-three minutes away, dependent on traffic (he had Google Mapped the distance on multiple occasions, accounting for everything from traffic jams to global catastrophes), Nick ticked down the moments until he could be with Ellie.

He'd accepted his parents' invitation and, along with his sister, Gabby, and her fiancé, Andrew, had spent the night of Christmas Eve in his family home as he had almost every year since he was a child. That all four of them would burst through his door at 7 a.m., a good four hours earlier than he would usually wake, was as annoying as it was predictable.

'Come on, come on. It's present time,' his dad bellowed.

Nick struggled to open his eyes and comprehend the avalanche of good feelings and happy faces. Even Gabby, who prided herself on her indifference to most moments of joy, marked 25 December as a day to purge all misanthropy. Twenty-four hours in which to revel in pleasure and play.

He clocked the clock, moaned and buried his head under the pillow.

'Just five more minutes.'

61

'Just five more minutes,' the quartet chorused back.

'Tradition is tradition,' his mum said, and nudged her daughter, who thrust a carefully wrapped gift into his hands.

Curiosity won out over fatigue and Nick sat up, the enthusiasm of the group as infectious as a zombie plague.

'It's a book,' he deadpanned.

'Well, duh,' Gabby replied, and he peeled back the wrapping paper with glee, like a puppy trying to open a chew toy he can hear but can't see. After seconds of paper-ripping rage, he revealed a compendium of the films judged most essential to any cineaste, its title the rather ominous-sounding *1001 Movies to See Before You Die*.

'Thanks, sis.'

'Don't be dying before you've seen them all!' she said, a manic grin on her face.

'Time to get up!' His dad's voice getting increasingly louder.

'No!' Nick protested strongly as the others tugged at his covers.

'Come on!' they yelled back, starting a to-and-fro pulling of the duvet.

Finally Nick shouted, 'I'm billy bollock naked, all right?'

One by one they jumped off the bed, their faces turned to mild disgust. All except Andrew, who didn't know where to look, finding some solace in his feet.

His mother was shaking her head as they filed out.

'I know what to get him for next Christmas,' added Gabby.

*

For Ellie and her parents, Christmas Day was a day to get through rather than look forward to. The spectre of the past was amplified by the season. Sitting at the table, she had noticed more and more that her mother and father barely acknowledged each other.

Ellie was selected for both cracker pullings and asked to pass all food items, from sprouts (complete with bacon and sweet chestnuts) to gravy (never granules, always home-made). All conversation was directed through her and this soon became exhausting. She wondered if this observation – that their intimacy was flatlining – was due to her having finally found someone she could be intimate with. Or whether there was something on the horizon between them. A grand finale to a union defined by its mantra of keeping calm and carrying on. She waved away the thought, reminding herself that the occasion – fake tree, fake snow, fake smiles – always brought with it melancholy and temporary sadness. Always only temporary.

Focusing on the positives, her thoughts turned to Nick. Knowing him as she did in such a short space of time, she was already well aware what this evening would mean to him. He would be planning and thinking and worrying and aiming for perfection, so she had put in the same level of commitment that she predicted he would.

Presents had been chosen in direct response to what she guessed he would get her. He would, she surmised, not be one to spend vast sums of money on 'things'. Events, possibly. Gestures, almost certainly. But not things. And so she had pre-empted any extravagance by placing a £10 limit on their gifts. This, she countered, would mean that time spent would be the true test of the gift's worth.

Her thought train was derailed when the family cat, a tabby by the name of Ophelia, leapt onto the table. Without raising his voice or swiping at the animal, her father calmly pushed his chair out, put his large hands around Ophelia's waist and placed the cat back on the floor.

'While I'm up,' he said, 'would anyone like anything else from the kitchen?'

Margaret shook her head, and so Ellie invented a request simply to make him feel useful.

'Some water with my wine would be great, thanks, Dad.'

She studied her mother's face, long enough to elicit an enquiry as to whether anything was wrong. Ellie shook her head no and offered a quiet 'It's nothing.'

Richard came back in, placed the water in front of Ellie's plate and sat back down. Ellie looked away from her mother and over to her father. Then she stared directly ahead. To where his chair should have been.

Without knowing it, she was soon hypothesising what he would look like now. Would his cute button 'dinosaur nose' have been the same? Would he have had acne scars from his teenage years? Would he have kept his hair long or buzzed it off like every other boy in town?

Just how unique would he have been?

This Christmas daydream triggered a memory from his first day of school. With Ellie having been through it all two years ahead of him, he looked to her for her worldly wisdom and came through the momentous occasion with flying colours. He glowed with pride as he returned triumphant and placed his school bag on the kitchen table. His proud parents waiting.

'What did you learn on your first day?' Richard asked.

'Erm' – at that age he always started his sentences with erm – 'I learnt the boat song and that Billy Simpson likes turtles.'

Ellie remembered Richard smiling at Margaret with devotion and pride, the woman who had brought this little boy into the world for him. In this memory her dad took his son's bag and prepared it for the next day. He was surprised to discover the sandwich he'd made seven hours earlier still intact, if a little flat.

'Why didn't you eat your sandwich?' he asked patiently.

'It's yucky,' came the swift reply.

To show the boy the error of his ways, Richard took a huge bite and rubbed his tummy. 'No. See. It's yummy.'

The four-year-old looked to his mother and to his big sister.

'No, it's yucky. I dropped it in the mud and Billy Simpson stood on it by accident.'

Margaret clasped her hands over her mouth. Six-year-old Ellie's mouth fell wide open. And then the laughter started. It was a laughter like she'd never known and had never been able to replicate since. Their bodies convulsed. There was genuine pain in it. But a perfect joy of pain. Her father, who was in many ways the butt of the joke, laughed hardest. Her brother was now rapturous at having brought this fun into their home.

Back at the table, Ellie studied her mother's face again, this time looking for laughter lines. She found none, but became fascinated by the lines above her nose. Two horizontal, two vertical. Join them up and you'd have a square the size of a locket. Ellie knew the picture that would fit perfectly between those lines.

★

Nick's mum was singing frantically in the kitchen. There was a direct correlation between the pitch of her voice and her stress levels, and right now, if dolphins lived next door, they'd be banging on the walls. It didn't help that, even though food was yet to be served, his father, Harry, was already asleep.

'Sorry it's taking so long,' Karen called through. Before adding with a peevish discontent, 'Obviously, if I had another pair of hands . . .'

'We did offer,' Gabby reminded her.

'I wasn't talking about you. You are our guests.' And with that, she drained her glass of red, shot her sleeping husband another set of daggers and disappeared back behind the beads that separated the kitchen from the living room.

Because they rarely had guests, there weren't enough chairs to go around. Nick was sitting on the floor while his sister and Andrew claimed the sofa. Between them was a coffee table upon which sat a half-finished game of Trivial Pursuit. To their left, in his tatty brown recliner, was their napping father.

Nick was taking on the two of them, who had decided to work as a team. As Gabby and Andrew were soon to be married, they felt it necessary to do everything as a team. They had been engaged just a few short months.

Because Andrew had picked Paris for the proposal, Nick had this weird feeling of having the upper hand in the relationship with his soon-to-be brother-in-law. As if this one clichéd action would always make Andrew predictable.

Another playing wedge was placed in Nick's wheel as a torrent of profanities came from the kitchen. The final 'shit' was accompanied by a clattering of pots and pans. Nick and Gabby gave each other the familiar look of 'here we go again' as Harry finally stirred.

'It's all ruined. The spuds are spoiled and the bird's burnt. You might as well order a pizza!' Karen cried out, making for the stairs.

Leaping from his seat and taking off after her was par for the course. It was a familiar dance, but no less painful for their offspring to watch. If Gabby was worried how this snapshot of their family life would seem to her partner, she didn't show it. Perhaps, Nick thought, because Gabby was so far out of Andrew's league, it would take cold-blooded murder for him to ever think her unworthy of his love.

Even in such an event, he would probably help dig the grave and take the blame.

Brother and sister entered the kitchen to see a very mild state of disarray. The bird that was labelled burnt had a slight charring, the potatoes were certainly edible and the clattered saucepans were tidied in minutes. It was an overreaction they'd encountered a thousand times before and so they set about making it just so.

67

As quickly as the parental hysterics had begun, they were over and forgotten. It must have seemed strange to an outsider like Andrew, thought Nick, but melodramas like this were part of the Marcet tradition. It was who they were. If Andrew was to be part of this family, he'd best get on board.

★

Ellie arrived just after seven armed with two presents. One small and one so monstrously large it caused Nick's jaw to meet the floor.

'Happy Christmas!' she exclaimed, brandishing her gifts.

Nick took the parcels from her and kissed her passionately before adopting a broad northern accent of origin unknown. 'By 'eck, love, step inside. I'm not paying to heat the street.'

Ellie looked at him like he was insane, and laughed. It was a one-two he was familiar with and one he adored.

Navigating her enormous gift up the stairs proved not without its difficulties. His shared accommodation was big enough for two people to live comfortably, or for four to live awkwardly. His landlord had opted for the latter. The lengthy expedition to the third floor did allow Nick time to wonder what the hell Ellie had got him, and if she'd broken the present budget rule that she had herself insisted upon.

Once inside his tiny room, a room that shared more in common with student digs than the home of a man in his mid to late twenties, they were caught wondering whether they should tear into the presents or tear off their clothes.

Half an hour later, they opened their gifts.

'We agreed on a ten-quid limit, right?' Nick asked, nervous of the answer.

Ellie nodded as he ripped away what might have been more than £10 worth of wrapping paper from a promotional DVD standee of one of his favourite recent films.

'Technically,' she said, 'I didn't pay anything for it. I fluttered my eyelashes at a very nice checkout girl in Sainsbury's and she said I could have it for a small donation to charity.'

Chuffed by the gift and the thought behind it, Nick made the obligatory remarks to temper expectation – 'This smashes my present out of the park', 'What I got you doesn't compete', etc., etc., – and handed her a carefully wrapped package that he'd asked his sister to carefully wrap for him the week before.

'It's a book . . .' she said, in that way people do when you've obviously bought them a book. A panic set in that it wasn't good enough and he began speaking at the speed of light.

'Because you were telling me how much you liked the band when you were younger.'

She lit up as she saw the front cover, a pensive picture of her favourite singer. She managed to squeeze in 'It's great' before he came back with the usual refrain of 'You have it already, don't you? I can take it back.'

To put a stop to it, Ellie grabbed his face and told him, 'No, I don't, and you can't. It's very thoughtful, and in a weird coincidence . . .'

She presented him with the smaller second gift. A mix

CD labelled *My Phonic Youth*. She explained, 'These are a few of the bands I loved when I was younger. It has loads of this guy,' she held up the book as a cue card, 'and loads of bands that inspired him. The Vaselines in particular are awesome and weird and weirdly awesome.'

'I also made you a present,' Nick said, locating a second package he'd hidden away just in case he'd got the mood of the gift-giving wrong.

'If anybody saw us they'd puke, right?' she asked, not without reason.

She opened up the little shoebox to discover trinkets from their first few months together. She went through them one by one.

'Our first cinema trip . . . A map from the museum . . . It's got everything. This is so nice.' She paused. 'You didn't keep the condom wrapper from our first night, did you?'

'Even I'm not that sentimental,' he lied.

Ellie sat up straight in his bed and started flipping through her new present, occasionally holding up random pictures of her childhood hero looking young and full of life.

'How are your folks?' Nick asked.

'They're okay. Christmas is always tough. Things are always a little . . . staged? Yeah, a little staged.'

It was quite early in their relationship to form such an ability, but Nick was already pretty skilled at figuring out when Ellie wanted to open up about something and when she was just looking for him to skip over a moment. He felt this might be the latter and was instantly validated when she breezily intoned, 'Soooo, what's the plan?'

70

He jumped out of bed and grabbed his props.

'Food.' He held up a bag of fancy crisps and a box of Maltesers. 'Drink.' A bottle of red and one of white. 'And for our entertainment, my favourite Christmas movie.'

'Sounds perfect.'

'Although I should say it's not really a Christmas movie as such, it just has some Christmassy moments.'

Ellie screwed up her face. 'Please don't say *Die Hard*. I hate it when people – and by "people" I specifically mean men – say *Die Hard* is their favourite Christmas film.'

Nick put her mind at rest quickly. 'It's not *Die Hard*. Although would you hate me if I said I watch it every Christmas?'

'No. I get it. It's a good excuse to watch a great movie. I just hate that smug look people have when they say it. Like it actually sums up the time of year better than say *Elf* or *Gremlins* or *It's a Wonderful Life*. Is it *It's a Wonderful Life*?'

'I'm not sure you need to see me crying that much so early in our relationship.'

'It's a bit late for that, remember? The cinema? That ad for cornflakes?'

Nick blushed.

'It was the present he always wanted! And anyway, the plight of George Bailey is a different affair. I cry at the opening. I cry when Mr Gower hits his bad ear . . .'

A sorrow took over Ellie's face as Nick recited the bleaker moments of everyone's favourite feel-good festive flick.

'It is an astonishingly sad film,' she said. 'Like, if it was actually real and not a film and so there was no angel to help him, George Bailey would have jumped to his death. On Christmas Eve. Leaving behind a wife and four kids.'

Nick's eyes grew cartoonishly wide at this devastating observation. If he was being completely honest, it was the line "if it was actually real and not a film" that disturbed him the most.

'Anyway . . .' He pulled a DVD of *The Apartment* out from behind his back. 'Here's my pick.'

Ellie read the name on the cover out loud and informed him she'd never seen it. 'What's it about?'

'This sad sack who works for an insurance firm. He's in love with this woman who's having an affair with his boss, and because he doesn't want to step on anyone's toes, he lets them use his apartment for their trysts.'

'Good use of the word "trysts" there.'

He thanked her for the compliment and put the film on. Out of the corner of his eye, he watched Ellie watching on as the story unfurled.

★

Seconds after Shirley MacLaine delivered one of the greatest closing lines in cinematic history, Ellie declared that she liked the movie very much indeed. Then, with a glint in her eye, she said, 'Right, I'd best be off.'

Nick called her bluff and they danced back and forth for a while, each playing it cool that she was definitely leaving until he couldn't take it any more.

'Okay, okay, okay,' he repeated. 'I forbid you to leave.'

'That's more like it. Although if you say, "I haven't given you your real present yet," I may kill you in your sleep.'

'Seems more than fair.'

That rare mixture of excitement and nervousness suddenly filled the room. That feeling of having been intimate with someone, that you knew them, and in a second realising that the person you were staring at was suddenly unfamiliar. For a moment they were lost in each other and he could hear himself mouthing the words, 'I love . . .'

He stopped himself.

'You can say it,' Ellie said, before she kissed him and finished his dialogue for him.

'I love you too.'

That Christmas, the Girl smiled as the Boy lay there sleeping. She smiled for the memories of the day. She smiled for where she was at that exact moment. But mostly, the smile was for herself. For all she had done to make this evening special. Her greatest gift, making him think it was mostly his doing.

End of First Intermission

12

5 November 2008 – 01.21 GMT
Obama 103
McCain 45
270 needed to win

Ellie had a real pace on to get back to hers.

I couldn't tell whether her quick adjustment of speed was due to the weather (hovering around zero degrees), the fact that we were missing the party, or worse, the sudden realisation that she was walking in the dark at night with a relative stranger.

I attacked the latter option head-on.

'I'm definitely not a serial killer, by the way. I faint at the sight of blood.'

'It's okay. I made it very clear to a friend where I was going and who I was leaving with. Plus, Tom vouches for your character. You can relax. I feel at ease.'

She looked me up and down.

'And quite frankly, if push came to shove, I know I could take you. You have very weedy arms.'

She was right. I did and still do.

She continued, 'Here's an analogy you'll like. I feel like there's more of a Nora Ephron vibe about tonight than a John Carpenter one. And I'm usually good with vibes. Even if you did say that women are just supporting characters in the film of your life.'

I stopped walking.

'No!' I corrected her. '*You* said that about me.'

She stopped too, looking up and to the right.

'Oh yeah.' Another extended word, followed by a quick rat-a-tat-tat. 'I take it back.'

Then she started walking again.

I thought there was something spectacularly great about how quickly she admitted to the mistake, instead of petulantly arguing about it. Just accept it and get on with life. A minor fault has been made, it's been addressed, please move along.

She didn't even feel the need to start a new subject straight away, the two of us just walking in a fairly comfortable silence for a few more minutes. But the comfort of silence only lasts as long as you don't think about it. Once it rooted in my brain, I had to end it.

'What are we, about ten minutes away?'

'Five.'

I knew I needed questions that couldn't be answered monosyllabically.

'I'm hungry.'

'There's always the Chicken Cottage?' she suggested.

'That's a disgustingly good idea.'

She smiled.

'Do you eat there all the time?' I goaded, trying to give as good as I got after the weedy-arms thing. 'Like breakfast, lunch and dinner?'

She smiled again. My smile quota was high.

'They call me Chicken Lady and have my picture on the wall.'

'Really?'

'No, Nick. Not really.'

Silence again for a few hundred more metres.

'Will your housemates be up?'

'Housemate, singular. And no, Jamie's away.'

'Jamie, he's—'

'She's . . .'

I held in another phew.

'. . . gone to visit her grandparents this week.'

I also held in another reference to us being alone in her house and instead blurted out:

'You look really nice.'

She blushed and glanced away.

'Sorry, that was weird. I said that like we were an old married couple and you'd just come down the stairs after getting dressed up for a night out. "You look really nice." I mean, you do, but I don't know why I said that.'

'It's okay. Thank you. It's nice to be told that you look nice.'

I nodded and looked at her again. Just to check.

'Well. You do.'

The bright lights of the Chicken Cottage were in view.

13

Breaking up with someone is expensive.

I'd like, just once, for a married pair of lottery winners to hold court at their press conference and state firmly for the record, 'What will we do with the money? We're getting a divorce, of course.'

The husband will stare happily at his soon-to-be-ex-wife and say, 'We've been wanting to for years, but we could never afford it.'

The wife will beam. 'Without this win we'd have ground out our last years together for sure. But now. Now we can buy separate houses, go on separate holidays. What's the point of staying together when we're not financially dependent on one another?'

They'll laugh, callous, cynical laughter at the members of the open-jawed press, eager for a happy dreams-come-true fairy tale, now having to put up with this slice of real-life Lars von Trier bleakness.

An idea so misanthropic wouldn't have crossed my mind

three weeks ago, but now it's my one coping mechanism. Love has turned its back on me, so all love must die.

Knowing I have to find a new place to live could not have come at a worse time. A week ago, two more digital projectors were installed, putting Humphrey and Katharine on the scrapheap of life, alongside Ingrid and Cary. Only James and Donna (named after the *It's a Wonderful Life* pairing of Stewart and Reed) and Billy and Meg (for Crystal and Ryan) remain now.

More digital projectors means fewer staff needed, and no one has seen Ronnie for weeks. As manager, Seb still does full-time hours, while Lizzie, Dave and I are left fighting for the scraps.

July is almost over and the mandatory meeting is in a week's time, when I'm sure Seb will keep on insisting that I 'diversify', which is management speak for him wanting me to take some shifts downstairs, selling popcorn, ripping tickets, etc. The very idea of facing customers after a decade of hiding in the shadows fills me with unease. I envision old teachers and girls I liked from high school coming in with their families and seeing me wearing an apron covered in Ben and Jerry's. They'll smile and say 'hey', but inside they'll be thinking, 'Fuck, poor Nick. I always thought he might make something of his life, but here's the proof that that prediction was complete horseshit.'

The alternative to taking on downstairs shifts means losing a roof above my head. I can't decide if the apron humiliation is worse than moving back in with my parents a week shy of my thirtieth birthday. I rationalise that friends and enemies are less likely to knock on my parents' door than they are to want to watch the latest *Harry Potter*, meaning my shame will be much better hidden behind closed doors.

★

I haven't spoken to my parents since the day of Gabby's announcement, successfully dodging the multiple calls from them, presumably wanting to ask how I am in the absence of Ellie.

I've chosen a nice busy pub to meet them in. One with tables close to each other so they can't make too much of a scene. Knowing the next-door diners might hear our conversation should keep them in line.

They arrive ten minutes late and Mum starts in with the apologies.

'Sorry. Sorry. Sorry.'

'Apologies lose their meaning with repetition,' I tell her, recycling a line she would often throw at me in my childhood.

Dad huffs as he takes off his jacket.

'Glad to see you're in a good mood. Have you ordered?'

'Not yet. I was politely waiting for you,' I say.

'Pay as you order, is it?'

I would have asked him what that was supposed to mean, but I know exactly what it was supposed to mean and calling him on it might mean having to open my wallet for my meal.

He huffs again. 'So, what do you want?'

'The beef.'

'Karen?'

Mum always takes an inordinate amount of time to decide

and then picks the healthiest option. It's the same every single time. Take an age to order. Order the salad. Complain that she wishes she'd chosen whatever I'm eating, thus making every mouthful ridden with guilt.

I sometimes think my parents feast off guilt. It gives them power.

'Erm . . .'

Here it comes.

'I'll have . . .'

I roll my eyes and she sees it.

'The cheeseburger, please, love, extra bacon. And a Coke.'

Dad smiles and winks at her, then offers me a drink.

'What's that one you like, Blue Moon?'

I nod, and he starts humming his version of Elvis's version of the song, much to my irritation. Mum looks smug as she sees me visibly taken aback by her order, like she's George Clooney and she's just robbed a bunch of casinos. As opposed to being a middle-aged woman who's finally ordered something she wants.

Still, there's something unnerving about both of them today. The sass from Dad about not paying, the pride in Mum's eyes at the ordering of a burger. I keep quiet, hoping their evil scheme will reveal itself in time.

We sit in silence as Dad makes his way to the bar to order.

Mum smiles again and I retort with another roll of my eyes.

'So,' I say, finally, 'aren't you going to ask me how I am?'

'How are you, petal?'

'Awful.'

'Oh, I'm sorry to hear that. What's the matter?'

Then it dawns on me.

Fucking Gabby. She hasn't told them.

'Gabby didn't tell you?'

Dad returns from the bar with the drinks.

'Tell us what?'

'Nothing. It doesn't matter.'

He puts the glasses down in front of us and waits, looking at me for something I'm sure he'll make clear any minute now.

'I have a favour to ask,' I say.

'Bloody typical,' he huffs.

'What?!' I offer in what I will admit is a very testy way, but they're totally at fault, bringing it out in me with his weird humming and her weird happiness.

Mum chimes in. 'Let's hear him out.'

'Please, proceed.' Dad says magnanimously.

'I need a place to stay for a bit.'

They offer each other a conspiratorial glance.

'Shall I?' Mum asks Dad.

He extends his hand to say 'by all means'.

'We were going to tell you the other day at Gabby's, but, well, first she made her announcement and then you ran off without saying goodbye. We've tried calling you, but—'

Dad butts in. 'We're going to New Zealand.'

First the burger. Now this. What is with them?

'Cool. I'm sure I'll have found somewhere to live by the time you get back.'

The conspiratorial glance returns.

'We're moving there,' Dad says.

'To live,' Mum says.

I put down my pint.

'No, you're not,' I say.

Their smug grins are overbearing.

'I think you'll find we are,' Dad offers.

'When? Why? You can't. What about the baby? Your grandchild? You're just going to leave it?'

'Well, we'll have more than enough from selling the house to return whenever we want,' Mum counters.

'You're selling the house?!'

'Already have a buyer.'

I am in shock, but with a surprising amount of awe. My parents rarely surprise me, and in this moment, I think I might be genuinely proud of them.

'Why New Zealand?'

'Well, we quite liked those films you used to watch, the ones with the little fellas and the men with the pointy ears. It looked really nice.'

The pride evaporates.

'Mum, New Zealand doesn't actually look like *Lord of the Rings*. They use an amazing amount of digital effects. You can't make life-altering plans to move to a country just because Peter Jackson and Weta made it look "really nice".'

She shakes her head, unsure of what either a Weta or a Peter Jackson is.

My questions keep coming.

'Why now?'

Dad takes a big deep breath, illustrating that he'll answer this one.

'I hope one day you'll discover this, but raising children is exceptionally hard. To begin with, they cry. A lot. And sleep much less than they should. Then they cause you worry, every single day. This worry continues into prepuberty and gets ramped up when they become teenagers and they sleep much more than they should. Probably catching up on the sleep they decided they didn't want when they were babies. It used to be that when your youngest got to eighteen, they were out on their own and you finally got to do what you liked as parents. Some silly sod seems to have upped that age to thirty. Well, now it's our time. You've got an okay job, a lovely girl and I'm sure the house thing will sort itself out soon enough. You're thirty next week and that seems time enough to get your shit together. And you're welcome for the drink and the meal.'

'Speaking of . . .' Mum pulls a present from her bag. 'Happy birthday, love.'

It's clearly a book, and my money's on *A Tourist's Guide to New Zealand*.

'I hope you're not too disappointed, petal. The house may be sold, but we have until the end of the month. You and Ellie are more than welcome to stay there next week. We'll be off on a farewell UK tour seeing old—'

'Mum.'

She stops talking.

'Me and Ellie broke up.'

There isn't enough time to say anything else before the food arrives.

14

5 November 2008 – 01.33 GMT
Obama 103
McCain 45
270 needed to win

While I was never a stranger to ordering food at half one in the morning, there was something about devouring a bucket of fried chicken in front of a girl I didn't know but was sure I liked that made me suddenly feel super-self-conscious.

I scanned the menu for something that wouldn't leave me dripping in chicken grease and salt, but found the option to be lacking. For some reason a nice fresh salad was not on the list of alternatives.

Perhaps that was why the place was deserted. The lack of healthy options.

'What are you getting?' Ellie asked as a dozen mangy-looking bird carcasses were thrown under a flickering heat lamp.

'I'm not sure,' I whispered back. 'I don't feel that hungry any more.'

She nodded, adopting a hushed tone of her own.

'Me neither. I'm usually a lot more drunk when I come in here.'

'What do we do now?' I asked.

'Have you made eye contact yet?'

I shook my head.

'Then follow my lead.'

She started backing out of the shop slowly, her eyes on the menu all the while. I followed suit, knowing how stupid we both looked and not caring in the slightest.

It was then that for the first time I thought: this girl likes me. I mean, she must do, right? To be being this silly? And surely she was thinking the same as me about the smelly, greasy food. Surely? Maybe she thought something was going to happen. Maybe she thought it was going to happen tonight.

I was beaming.

But as we turned to run, something, or more specifically someone, made this little fantasy come crashing to a halt.

*

I'd met Vicky Johnson two months before I met Ellie, in a notorious meat market of a club north of the river.

It was the kind of place I'd never choose to go in my wildest nightmares, but we were celebrating Seb's engagement and his friends had poor taste and even poorer judgement. Although the honour for poorest judgement that night firmly belonged to me. How I wished I'd stayed in and watched a Michael Haneke marathon. The ending would have been much happier.

Having never been a strong drinker, and being one hundred per cent the victim of peer pressure, I was on my arse before eleven o'clock. I remembered very little of the night, but Seb – who should have been comatose after what his friends made him neck – reliably informed me that I had turned the charm to overload. He said he overheard me laying on the compliments to Vicky, feigning interest in topics I despised and generally agreeing with things I didn't believe, in a way he later described as 'bewitching'. His exact words were: 'You were so damn captivating, I would have slept with you that night.'

It wasn't the first time I'd used alcohol to inebriate the awkward me, to lull him to sleep so those feeling of nervousness and self-loathing couldn't second-guess my each and every move. But it was the first time my Mr Hyde had taken over to such an extent I ended up having sex with someone I'd only just met.

And although there was nothing inherently wrong about that – I was single, she was single, we were two consenting adults – the idea that I'd become someone I wasn't just to get laid made me feel cheap and wrong and, moments after it was over, incredibly unfulfilled. Most people could brush off the simple regret of a one-night stand, but I wore it like a noose for weeks afterwards.

As for the following morning, I had every opportunity to make an escape. An honourable one. She gave me the window.

'If this is just a one-nighter, that's fine,' she said as I got dressed. 'But if you want to see me again, I'll give you my number.'

She wrote it down, then offered me the pen and a piece of paper. When I didn't take either of them straight away, the air in the room disappeared. The silent pause I contributed didn't help.

She tentatively withdrew the stationery.

'It's just we seemed to have a lot in common last night.'

'We did?'

The inclusion of the question mark was a poor choice.

'Yeah, the fun runs, the dance festivals, the holidays in the sun.'

I hated all those things.

'Oh yeah,' I lied. 'Totally.'

'You weren't just lying to get in my pants then?' She nudged me in a way that I was sure was meant to be playful but was really quite painful. I thought at the time that her strength probably came from all the running and dancing.

'No. Of course not.'

'So . . .'

She waved the pen again. Not wanting to be impolite and not being devious enough to do something simple like miswriting one digit, I gave her my number.

In total, over the span of twelve days, I received eleven missed calls and twenty-one text messages. She sent the first before I'd left her stairwell.

★

To say that Vicky was not pleased to see me and Ellie, giggling like children, leaving a Chicken Cottage empty-handed at 1.30 in the morning was an *Avatar*-box-office-sized understatement. That she was half cut was evident immediately. Her make-up was slightly smudged and her eyes were heavy-lidded. Her two girlfriends hovering behind her were sober by comparison but reeked of Jäger and beer.

'If it isn't Nick the Dick,' Vicky yelled, slurring the 'the'.

Ellie blinked twice, waiting for me to explain how I knew this semi-dressed, semi-conscious whirlwind who was spitting insults at me.

'Hellooooo,' I said, stretching the word to breaking point to help me find the right name.

'It's V—'

'Vicky,' I said, hedging my bets that there weren't many Vivians or Veronicas under the age of thirty.

'Oh, you remember my name then?'

'I do.'

Ellie had remained at my side but wisely chosen to adopt the role of casual bystander. Now Vicky turned to her, sneering.

'And who the fuck are you? His latest fuck and chuck?'

Casual bystander no more, Ellie opened her mouth to speak, but I wanted very much for this to be my fire to extinguish.

'This is my friend Ellie.'

Vicky looked us both up and down. It seemed to take hours.

'So.'

She burped.

'How's the band coming along? Haven't seen your album hit the charts yet.'

Ellie's eyes grew wide. So wide that even though I wanted the ground to swallow me up, I wanted a few more seconds on earth to look at them.

'I did a Google on you, and it turns out that half of what you told me was a massive pack of lies. Here's a hint – make your Facebook profile secret if you want to run around tricking your way into girls' pants.'

I knew I needed to stem the tide of vitriol, but I also knew I needed to be extra careful with both members of my audience.

'I'm sorry. I should have called.'

'Oh, here's where you say you lost my number—'

The immediacy and brutality of my 'no' was designed to let both her and Ellie know that I didn't have – and never had had – any intention of seeing her again. In hindsight it was pretty cold, and I felt Ellie shift awkwardly.

'Vicky. I'm sorry. I was thoroughly drunk that night – not that that's any excuse, but if I'd been sober I wouldn't have—'

'Oh, thanks!'

'No, I didn't mean that. You seem like a really nice—'

'You know what? Fuck you, Nick. I thought you were a nice guy, but you're not, you're a fucking liar and a sleaze-bag. So if you don't mind, I'm gonna eat me some fucking chicken.' And with that, she shoulder-barged me out of the way and made for the counter.

I held the door open for Ellie, as some paltry apology for the last few minutes of her time. She accepted it and we walked past Vicky's friends and back out into the crisp night, my cheeks now red not just from the cold air.

'Ellie . . .' I started as we left the Chicken Cottage a distant, demeaning memory.

'Nick, don't worry about it.'

'Really?' The rising intonation of the question hit a very unmasculine high note.

'Yeah. Anyway, it's you I feel sorry for.'

'Me?' Even higher this time.

'Yeah. I mean, about five minutes ago, all was going pretty well for you. Now, pfff, your chances of having sex tonight are sitting at around zero per cent.'

I smiled broadly, and a butterfly-inducing thought crossed my mind.

There was a chance.

15

If these walls could talk.

They'd tell me I'm an idiot.

Twenty-four months we lived in this flat. And until recently I would have described the majority of those months as phenomenal. The same could not be said for the inner workings of our accommodation.

A bog-standard one-bedroom flat half a mile from the Tube, no one broke the mould when they built this house. But the chronic mould nearly broke us.

It was in the bedroom, the kitchen, the living room and the bathroom. It took just four weeks to seep through the quick paint job the landlord had carried out in order to sucker unsuspecting tenants. I was adamant we would find somewhere else to live, but Ellie, being Ellie, set about on a mould mission to rival Alexander Fleming's.

When our landlord said he'd never had a problem with it before, she determinedly decided she would see to it herself. She spoke to the neighbours first, to pinpoint the worst areas, then started scouring the internet for long-term solutions. She was tireless and unwavering in her action. But never obsessed. If it was me – and it wouldn't ever have been me, because my plan was always to just move out and move on – I would have gone cuckoo ripping up walls and hammering holes where no holes needed to be hammered.

Ellie, on the other hand, was just single-minded. Clear in her goal. Find the source. Eradicate the problem. By the end of the first summer, there wasn't a fungus to be found.

The rest of the place still had niggles. The taps were a law unto themselves, dripping like chlamydia one day, breaking your digits with their force the next. The fuses tripped if you switched on more than two lights at a time. The windows and doors all had draughts.

But it was our home. And we loved it.

We loved our batshit-crazy neighbours and their batshit-crazy pets. We loved how close it was to both work and our favourite pub and the best damn Chinese takeaway a man and woman could ask for.

We had a five-year plan for this place. Yet here I am, in year two, putting our – but mostly my – belongings in boxes, ready to say goodbye.

*

The only time I go through these little memorabilia chests is when I move home. They live under the bed, gathering dust, opened occasionally to throw some new things on top of the old, but the things themselves are never touched.

Except on the day before moving day, when the bed gets dismantled and the boxes reveal themselves.

There's one full of cinema tickets, from *Back to the Future 2* (I was seven) to *Attack of the Clones* (the last film I actually paid to see). Leafing through the stubs, I find it a little depressing that I don't have any physical evidence of the hundreds, possibly thousands, of films I've seen since I started working at the cinema. I know there are a few stubs in assorted other boxes, mainly from holidays and special occasions, and I'll find them soon enough in the inevitable deep dive down memory lane.

I put the lid on the box and open another, labelled *School Dayz*.

This one is mostly photos, a few ties and a shirt with various warm wishes and insults scrawled over it in biro. The warm wishes are mainly from the girls in my year and the insults are mainly drawings of penises or variations on the word 'penis' from the boys. This was standard practice and in no way reflected any draw I might have had with the girls in my school or any animosity from the boys.

Nothing in this box really interests me, and I know I'm only looking in it to delay the inevitable. I sigh and pick up the box labelled *Ellie and Nick*.

The lack of actual photos is even more depressing than the lack of cinema stubs.

With Ellie being the photographer, she automatically got custody of the physical memories we made together, but there are a few special pictures taken at various points in our relationship. The ones around the flat that she left behind. Still in their frames.

My favourite is a selfie she took of us, way before selfies

were actually referred to as selfies. We're sitting in the back of our car midway through a weekend trip to see her parents in Sheffield. We'd been together two years then and we were still as nuts about each other as we were in our first few months. I honestly thought that would never stop.

In the photo, she's laughing and biting my ear and taking the photo, all in one.

It could have easily ended up a blurry picture of the ceiling of a VW Polo and the tops of our heads. But it didn't. It's perfect. It's happiness captured.

Of course, I could pack these boxes away and go on Facebook and pore through folder after folder labelled *Trip to Scotland* and *Beer Festival '09*, but that's not the point. That, to me, feels weird and stalkerish and I've already done it for the last two weeks. I pick up the next item, underneath the framed photos of happier times.

It's a diary I started after being brought to a wobbly mess of tears by *The Diving Bell and the Butterfly* – a film about a guy with 'locked-in syndrome', which leaves him only able to communicate by blinking one eye.

He wrote a book about living with the condition, which I own but haven't read.

The film, however, made me feel like the biggest shit in the world for having the tools to write but choosing not to. I thought: if he can write a paragraph in a day, I can devote ten minutes of the day to document what I do.

I bought the diary in January 2010.

I stopped writing in it in March 2010.

I go through phases like this now and again. They never

last long. Much to Ellie's chagrin. She always wanted me to find a goal outside of 'being a projectionist forever'.

*

A couple of months before we broke up, we were having a lazy Sunday afternoon drink in Borough Market. It was a cold day for April and the wind was whipping up the Thames.

'Don't you want to do something else?' she asked.

'Like what? Like the manager position?'

'Well, it would be a step up.'

'Seb's already said he's going for the role and he can have it. I don't want the stress.'

'Because your life is so stressful,' she said, the words dripping with sarcasm.

'It would be,' I retorted, 'if I took the manager job.'

She sipped on her pint. There was something far away about her that day; she had that faintly despondent look as we walked over London Bridge. I recognised it as the look in which you're so deep in thought, landmarks you've seen a million times before are presented in a completely different light.

'I dunno. Don't you have stories to tell?'

'Not really.'

'What about writing movies?'

'I have more chance of making it in the NFL than as a screenwriter,' I said, confidently regurgitating a line I'd read in the *Guardian* that week.

'What's the NFL?'

'American football.'

'Oh.' She paused. 'Why not say you have more chance of making it in English football?'

She had a point.

'I don't know, it's just a thing I read. You want me to play American football? 'Cos I will.' I sang to lift her mood. 'For yooooouuuu.'

'Why would I want you to play American football?'

'It was a joke.'

The act of explaining that my jokes are jokes always riles me, and we sat in the same uncomfortable silence that had become uncomfortably common of late.

'Okay, so you don't want to be a famous Oscar-winning screenwriter?'

'Well, I do, but the odds—'

'What about making a short film?'

'About what?'

'About anything!' She was getting more and more frustrated, so I tried turning it round on her.

'What about you? Don't you want to do something with your life?'

'Yes. That's the point.'

'So what are you doing about it?'

Another gust blew in from the river and added an extra level of frostiness to the chat.

'I've started looking for a new job, actually. Something life-changing.'

I remember worrying.

'Does your life need changing?'

She put her hand on mine to comfort me and I pulled it

away like a stroppy, petulant fool, seeking the comfort of my pint glass instead.

'Evolving,' she offered as a compromise. 'My life needs evolving. You forget I'm older than you. I have less time before I meet my maker.'

'If your maker ever tries to take you away from me, I'll kill him. Or her.'

I offered her my hand to take again and she did.

'It'd just be nice if you evolved with me.'

'Then I will Darwin the shit out of my life. I'll compile a list of attainable and satisfactory jobs and do whatever it takes to get one of them. After all, when you grow tired of looking for jobs in London, you grow tired of life.'

She moved round the table and sat next to me, nuzzling up to me in the haze of a weekend wasted. Confident again that her decision all those years ago was the right one. That human heat made the day suddenly feel warmer.

'What do you want to do tonight?' she asked.

I shrugged.

'Watch a movie?'

She offered the smallest of nods and I completely missed that her assurance had vanished again.

'Okay, Nick. Sounds good.'

*

Looking back on it now, awash with melancholia and looking for an answer, I decide to add this to the *Why Ellie Left* list. She saw me as stuck in a rut and lacking motivation, just a brick that if she clung to she'd drown.

Who wants to be a brick?

I take out the notepad, already looking a little battered, and write the second reason, *I'M A BRICK*, directly underneath *WE PEAKED TOO EARLY*. It's a tale as old as time. Boy meets girl. Girl wants to do something with her life. Boy doesn't. Girl leaves boy.

I'm getting closer to knowing why she went. Or at least I think I am. The clarity of 20/20. I put down the diary and pick up a Christmas card from December 2008. Our first Christmas together.

She'd signed it: *You'll always be 'Nick the Dick' to me.*

16

5 November 2008 – 01.47 GMT
Obama 103
McCain 49
270 needed to win

'You know, Nick the Dick isn't that bad a nickname,' Ellie said as we left Vicky and her cohort to their post-club feast.

'I am so sorry about that,' I offered hopelessly.

'It sort of makes you sound like a virile motherfunster. Also,' she put on a silly radio-presenter-style voice, 'when's the album drop?'

I stopped to bury my head in my hands, partly to cover up my bright red cheeks and partly to see if doing so would make the entire world go away.

It didn't.

'What are the fucking odds?'

'You tell me, lover boy. Might we bump into more of your conquests on the way to mine?'

I was beginning to get testy, which I knew wouldn't help the situation, but there we are.

'Can we not? I do genuinely feel really bad about it all.'

She looked at me with a mix of puzzlement and pity.

'Then why didn't you just call her?'

'This will sound really up my own arsehole, but . . . I just didn't want to disappoint her.'

'Yeah, she would have been crushed, I'm sure.' Ellie stopped and put her hand on my arm. 'Sorry, that was mean.'

I didn't want to say anything in case she removed her hand.

'It's okay. I think I'm learning that sarcasm is your default setting?'

She removed her hand and said in a stupid helium-filled voice – think a mix between Christopher Lloyd at the climax of *Who Framed Roger Rabbit* and Mickey Rooney in *Breakfast at Tiffany's*, but quite a bit less racist – 'Oh right. Sarcasm is for losers, yeah?!'

I smiled and giggled and smiled some more and forgot all about Vicky and guilt and everything else in the world. Ellie simply looked proud that she'd made me laugh. Happy in my happiness. She glanced up at the house we were standing outside.

'This is me.'

*

Moments later, I was in her room, and it was a glorious splurge of personality laid out on the walls and floor and furniture and bed. It gave me that comforting feeling, like I'd been there a hundred times before.

I could have been placed in this room without ever having

laid eyes on Ellie and still fallen in love with her. Everything in it was modest and makeshift and messy and her. I sat on the edge of the bed and took it all in as she excused herself for 'bathroom reasons'.

I contemplated sitting on my hands to make sure I didn't touch anything I shouldn't. The idea that she might walk back in and find me inadvertently fingering something forbidden brought me out in a cold sweat.

Look with your eyes, not with your hands.

It was safe to say that the room was notable for what it lacked as much as what it contained. There was no TV, no curtains and no wardrobe. In place of the latter there were two rails of clothes – mainly hoodies and jeans – at the foot of the bed. The layout reminded me of a charity shop, and the floor – such as it was, with the rest of her outfits strewn all over it – a charity shop changing room.

As for plenty of people born after 1980, a large Mac monitor had replaced the standard telly. The screen saver cycled through shot after shot of amazing photography. I remembered thinking I'd happily stare at any of those images on rotation for hours, and that if they were hers she was insanely talented. I also remembered that a wave of doubt washed over me as to whether what I wanted to happen could actually happen. I was sure I could make myself an attractive proposition to someone who was good-looking or to someone who was talented, but not to someone who was both.

I moved on.

One wall was a Pollockesque mural of photos of different sizes and shapes and abilities. Ellie herself was in a small number of these pictures so I deduced this was not a portfolio of her work.

The wall to the left of the gallery housed two shelves above the aforementioned Mac, which sat on an equally untidy desk. One shelf was loaded with books on Adams, Arbus and Avedon. The other was something I could initially only describe as a shrine. On it were four photos of a young girl, who I assumed to be Ellie based solely on her cuteness and eye colour. I hazarded a guess that her dyed red hair came after she was seven. In each photo there was a little blonde-haired boy. Two years old in one, maybe four or five in the others. Again, completely estimating, I guessed the girl in the photo was a couple of years older and that they were sister and brother. I would have also said that Ellie was happier in these photos than in any of the others.

Alongside the frames, hence the shrine description, were two candles and a teddy bear. It was also the only part of the room that seemed to be cleaned on a regular basis. I reached out to touch the bear, forgetting the rule I'd laid down to myself, just as Ellie re-entered. I drew my hand back and faux-scratched the back of my head.

I expected a line excusing the mess, but it never came.

'I won't be long, just need to grab some lenses and a flash. Do you really think this is a good idea?'

'This is history. I think you'll regret it forever if you don't.'

She shook her head at the exaggeration.

'Yep. I can see that now. Ellie Brown. Born 1980. Died 2102. Lived a full life but really regretted never taking pictures at that party she went to that one time.'

'Just pack your bloody camera, will you. They'll have declared Georgia by the time we get back.'

She lobbed a cushion at my head.

'Where's your music?'

'On that.' She pointed to the Mac.

'No CDs? No vinyl?'

'No cassettes or MiniDiscs either. You can root through my playlists instead if you like. If, y'know, you're trying to assess me as a human being or potential mate.'

'I did that hours ago,' I said as I made my way from the bed to the chair next to the computer.

I still didn't know if the things I did to make sure I attracted the right partner were the same things other people did. Like wearing T-shirts with bands that I liked on them, or obscure film references. I knew the hope for me was that one day a girl would come up to me and say, 'Cool band,' and I'd say, 'Yeah,' and follow it up with 'I saw them play Union Chapel a few years ago,' and she'd say, 'Me too,' and we'd fall in love forever. But when I saw someone else wearing a T-shirt with a band I liked or displaying an obscure film reference, I had no idea if they'd picked it out with the sole purpose of ensnaring a partner or whether they just thought it was a cool T-shirt.

Which brings me to Ellie's playlists.

They were a thing of wonder. Funny, well structured, cool but very uncool in the space of a few tracks. And as I studied them – with titles such as *You forgot to buy coffee, you damn fool* and *Songage for a snoggage* – I realised they were meticulously crafted, linked by themes and wordplay. Had she done all this just for the moment when some tall(ish), handsome(ish) stranger came to visit? And did it matter?

'These are some amazing playlist names,' I said.

'Thanks,' she replied in a way that was breezy enough for me to still not understand the intention behind said compilations. 'They all have a story.'

I read a few more. '"You dumped me. No, I dumped you. Ad infinitum"?'

'The perfect mix of depressing break-up songs and victory break-up songs.'

'Some of these are a little hard to figure out, though.'

She stopped packing and made her way to the back of my chair, leaning over me to read the screen. Our proximity made my belly flip. Her breath on my neck almost ended me.

'What's this one? Stevie Wonder, Ben Folds, Divine Comedy. They're really nice songs for such an in-your-face title.'

'"I'm sorry your genitalia had to go through that".' That was for my friend who gave birth. All the songs are baby-making songs. But y'know, not "baby-making" songs.'

'You have a friend who gave birth? How old did you say you were?'

She picked up the recently thrown cushion and struck me with it again.

'Twenty-seven.'

'Pervert,' I replied. 'Ensnaring a younger man in your lair of iniquity.'

'I'm beginning to think you're an idiot.'

'It has been said.'

107

I was getting giddy again, so I turned back to the screen to keep my cool.

'And this one, "Sex noise"?'

'That's a playlist where a singer makes a sex noise at some point.'

'Hence all the James Brown.'

She went back to her packing.

'Play "The Apocalypse Song" by St Vincent.'

I did as I was instructed and was glad I did. A punky female singer with a throaty voice sang of 'time' and 'light' and 'carbon' over a clangy guitar.

'She's good.'

'She's my latest hero. I saw her play the Roundhouse last month. She's not just a great singer, she wails on the guitar.'

I made a mental note to listen to every song this St Vincent had ever recorded and get email notifications of any upcoming gigs. And there it was, following a line about 'a little death', an orgasmic tic.

'Sexy, huh?' Ellie asked with just the right level of ridiculousness. 'So, do I pass your music test?'

'Tenfold,' I offered, perhaps a little too breathlessly. I cleared my throat. 'I was hoping there'd be a DVD collection somewhere so I could judge you correctly.'

'Nah. I don't really like films.' Her smile grew broader as my face fell further. After a moment she put me out of my misery with a simple 'You're too easy!'

I sat back down on the bed dramatically.

'I was going to say, who doesn't like films? Everyone likes films.'

She studied me again, like an antique clockmaker figuring out the cause of the ticking.

'Is that why *you* like films?'

'What do you mean?'

Cue the seventeenth broad, knowing smile of the evening.

'Nothing. Don't worry about it.'

I studied her back. But she wasn't half as easy to read.

I wonder where we'd be right now if she was.

17

I have rather successfully completely unpacked the basket of memories.

In front of me lie hundreds of trinkets collected throughout our four-year relationship. From receipts from fancy restaurants to assorted Valentine's gifts and all the sentimental souvenirs in between.

Procrastination on this scale, to the point of fully doing the opposite of the task in hand, would not stand under the reign of Ellie. But now, as I rule my kingdom alone, I can do as much self-harm as I wish.

This ill-timed poring through our treasure trove of keepsakes has, however, unearthed a trilogy of documents that add weight to my hypothesis that Ellie hightailed it because of my lack of drive.

The documents in question are three lists of things we wanted to do before we died. We compiled them during a winter weekend binge of *Grand Designs* around two and a half years ago. Because of some silly off-the-cuff comment about how I'd like to build my own house one day, Ellie had questioned how I'd get to this lofty rich man's folly when I was, at present, poorer than a church mouse awaiting pay day.

She passed me a piece of paper and a pen and took one herself.

We compiled our individual lists and then merged them together for one entitled *10 Things to Do Before We're Ashes and Dust.*

Top of mine was *Build a house.*

Top of hers was *Own a house.*

I wanted to travel the world.

She wanted to visit San Francisco, São Paulo and Tokyo.

I said, *I'd raise the next Coen brothers (or Wachowski sisters).*

She said, *I'd have kids.*

At the time we thought it was great how our dreams and goals and ambitions synched up. Looking at it now, it's just hard evidence – if hard evidence were needed – of how grounded she was and how . . . well, whatever I am.

I scribble number 3 on the list of reasons why she left – *PRAGMATISM (her) vs IDEALISM (me)* – and pick up a diary from 2010. It holds even more proof of my worst fears, but my pilgrimage down memory lane is interrupted by a phone call from an extremely pissed-off Seb, who reminds me of the absolutely mandatory and not-to-be-missed-under-any-circumstances meeting I'm currently missing.

I gather my things and run out of the back door, wishing I hadn't started smoking again as I start wheezing within seconds.

I decide to walk – rationalising that Seb can't get any more mardy with me – and reflect on the contents of the diary I was reading moments earlier. It documented a very uneventful February in which Ellie and I did nothing because we were broke from a very eventful Christmas and New Year.

It strikes me how little time we give to the normal and everyday. Entries mainly consisted of what shows we were bingeing in 2010 – *Spooks, Mad Men*, etc. – and which pubs did the best Sunday roasts. I know I'd wanted to include wry observations about our life together, but the intention had only manifested in some choice dialogue of hers. Namely, 'Do you think Morrissey secretly likes watching *Man v. Food*?' and 'If there is a God, why did she make ants?'

As much as none of the above is an insightful deep dive into where our relationship was after two years together, the banality of it actually speaks volumes. There were no entries complaining about things she'd done or said, no examples of me pouring out my heart and soul due to anxieties about where we were heading.

Life was simple and simple was good.

Maybe we should have fought more. Seb and his wife, Tracy, fight like Persians and poodles, and not just since they spawned mini-thems. There was many a time I'd hear him either calming her down or riling her up over the phone down by the bin yard.

And now they're a family. Kids, cars and a mortgage. That volatility has to be good for something, right? Me and Ellie, we were an even keel, a straight road, a monorail. Look where that got us.

I arrive at the front of the cinema at 10.14, and Lucy, one

of the team leaders (see: lackey given a title and an extra quid an hour to do the manager's work for them), tells me they're all in Screen 6 waiting for me.

'Did Seb seem pissed off?' I enquire.

She nods enthusiastically, with a smug half-smile.

I enter Screen 6 to find Lizzie, Dave and Ronnie sitting in silence in the front row, with Seb pacing up and down in front of the screen.

'Sorry. Sorry. I'm being kicked out of my house. I forgot about the meeting, okay, can we forgive me and move on?'

I throw my bag down next to Ronnie and give him the international 'I'm scared I'm in trouble' face of open-mouthed gritted teeth.

'Right,' says Seb, 'now that we're all here . . .'

I raise my hand as if I'm in primary school.

'Do I have time to get a quick coffee?'

Seb's look suggests I can find out the answer to that question at the same time I'm finding out the answer to the question of how much pain he can inflict on me with a wooden spoon.

'Oooookay,' I say.

He tries again.

'Now that we're all here, I have some news. Some hard-to-say news and some hard-to-hear news. But news that, if we're all honest, we've known has been coming for some time.'

He swallows hard and we all follow suit. My stomach does front flips and back flips in equal rhythm.

'As of next month, we will be an all-digital cinema, with

113

a fully automated system. The last of the projectors will be stripped out by the first of September, and we will no longer be showing thirty-five-millimetre film.'

He continues, 'To coincide with this date, we have been asked to see if anyone wants to put their name forward for voluntary redundancy.'

He looks sick from the guilt of being the one who has to ask.

'The decision has been made that redundancies will be issued to all projectionists before the end of the year, but I've had assurances from Mandy and the managers downstairs that anyone who wants a job on the floor has one waiting for them. You'll go straight in as team leaders . . .'

Lizzie and Dave groan at the suggestion, but Seb ploughs forward.

'. . . and your previous experience of helping run the projection booth will stand you in good stead for any management positions that may follow.'

More groans.

'Does anyone have any questions?'

Ronnie's hand goes up.

'Who will run the digis?'

'Until the end of the year, myself and whoever remains, but ultimately the intention is that the shows will be one hundred per cent automated. The downstairs managers will be trained to make up playlists, upload files, et cetera.'

Dave's hand is next.

'And what about maintenance? Lamp changes, line-ups? The managers going to do that?'

'Eventually, all technical maintenance will be carried out by off-site engineers. I've sourced some details of the companies we'll be working with. Dave, I know you'd be just as good as any of them and would happily pass on your details with a glowing reference.'

While I don't doubt that Dave completely deserves this job opportunity, I'm more than a little jealous that my friend isn't paying me the same compliment.

Lizzie doesn't put her hand up, just asks, 'And you?'

'As the floor managers will be trained to manage the digital projectors, I'll be trained to do the floor manager's position.'

Seb does not appear thrilled at the prospect, but his sympathy and attention is firmly on the rest of us.

'Nick, do you have any questions?'

'What's the redundancy package like?'

He can't hide his pity.

'A month's wage for every year you've worked here. Plus ten per cent for those who take the voluntary package.'

The immediate financial benefits go some way to making us all feel slightly better and are met with murmurs of approval.

'Everyone can take as long as they want to think this through. We don't need answers today.'

'I'll take it.'

I don't realise I've said it until I've said it and everyone looks at me.

Seb repeats his earlier call for us to take some time.

'I don't need to. I'll take it. We'll all be out of jobs by the end of the year. No point running down the clock.'

My voice isn't exactly quivering, but there's an uncertainty to it that makes everyone a little uncomfortable.

Seb seizes the moment to end the meeting, and I'm the first to make my way to the exit, thinking: if I can just get home and sort out the other cornucopia of shit in my life, I'll work this latest setback out later.

★

I've barely made it a hundred yards from the cinema entrance and am as surprised as anyone by the identity of the person chasing after me, calling for me to wait.

My money would have been on Seb, ready to give me another lecture on maturity and responsibility, closely followed by Ronnie, spewing pearls of wisdom courtesy of Mary Jane. But no, it's Lizzie, running and yelling across the street at me, insisting I stop and give pause to a decision that almost immediately calls time on the best job I ever had.

When she catches up with me, she's a little out of breath and the summer sun has already caused beads of sweat to form around her sandy blonde pixie cut. She steadies herself with her hands on her knees, hunched over.

'You should cut down on the smokes, Lizzie.'

She takes one out and lights it, as if to tell me to do myself in mime.

'Fuck me, you walk fast.'

I must be looking longingly at the smoke rising, because she offers me a cigarette of my very own.

'Only when I'm trying to get away from somewhere before I do or say something idiotic,' I say, before I take one.

116

She regains her composure, the nicotine working like Popeye's spinach.

'How are you doing?' she asks.

I shrug and inhale.

She nods. 'It's a bullshit state of affairs. I'm as progressive and forward-thinking as the next woman, but why do they have to take our fucking projectors?'

'If it ain't broke . . .' I offer.

'Leave it the fuck alone.'

It's been a while since I've spoken more than half sentences to Lizzie. Nearly four years, in fact. And this is definitely the longest we've chatted about something other than what needs maintaining on a Kinoton FP 40 projector.

I'd forgotten how much she swears.

'I'm sorry to hear about you and Ellie too.'

I consider reminding her that when Ellie and I first started going out, and I was telling Lizzie how happy I was with my new girlfriend, Lizzie snapped and said something along the lines of 'and I'm sure her pedestal is the greatest pedestal ever'.

But then I remember that she'll be hurting from the cinema news too, and another shrug is all I have right now.

She continues, 'I'd like to be able to call her a bitch, but I know she wasn't and I know what she meant to you, so . . .'

'It was inevitable,' I say.

Lizzie looks at me, puzzled.

'How so?'

'What's the line from *Cinema Paradiso*? "Even the greatest love eventually fizzles out."'

'You really believe that?'

117

'I believe in all the wisdom of Alfredo.'

We simultaneously lean against the wall behind us, take a drag and look as wistfully as we've ever looked in our lives back at the building across the road. The building that has felt like a second home to us for years.

Lizzie turns and asks, 'You fancy catching a film next week? Me and you? The Coens have a new one out. It's just written by them, but y'know, a film written by the Coen brothers has to be better than half the fucking excrement out there.'

She's babbling a little and I'm pretty sure it's because her offer is a pity invite.

'I'll let you know,' I say. 'I've got to find a job, a home and a new girlfriend, so . . .'

'Give me your phone.'

I do as I'm instructed.

She presses a number of keys and hands it back.

'That's my new number. Maybe I can be of service.'

★

Seb rang about half an hour after I'd said goodbye to Lizzie. I'm convinced he didn't mean for it to come across as a lecture, but it sure sounded like one, full of life lessons and tutoring titbits such as 'You need to do this' and 'You need to do that'.

His main beef seemed to be the speed at which I had made my decision and the financial insecurity my impending joblessness would bring. I tried to reason with him that the redundancy package would be more money than I'd ever seen in all my life and that I'd find a new 'career' way earlier if I had more time on my hands.

He countered by suggesting that I'd be allowed to look for work while still working here and that working on the floor as a team leader would bring in almost as much as I was making before. I ended the conversation with some regretful words about being a 'lifer in a McJob' and that I had fuck all tying me down, unlike some people, and that now seemed as good a time as any to split.

Understandably, he had little left to say to that, and I felt for a moment like I'd won a small victory by being the last to say anything. The feeling of success didn't even last half the walk home.

Now, back at the house that I'm being evicted from, that I lived in with the partner who dumped me, about to temporarily move back in with my parents, who have seen fit to leave the country, I think about my new status of being redundant and I feel, for the first time in quite some time, really sorry for myself.

I hate this feeling. It's self-indulgent and pointless and so I counter it in the only way I know how. I think about the saddest films I know. I think about Björk's Selma in *Dancer in the Dark* and the line 'Say goodbye to Frankie' from *In America*. I think about the young George Bailey being hit by Mr Gower in *It's a Wonderful Life*. I think about the couple in the opening five minutes of *Up* and I think about the dog in that episode of *Futurama*.

And then I think about Ellie, at seven years old.

And I think, Nick, whatever your sorry tale, someone always has it worse than you.

18

5 November 2008 – 01.55 GMT
Obama 103
McCain 55
270 needed to win

You're late! You're late! You're so, so late! – a playlist Ellie described as 'one to get you going first thing in the morning' – was kicking out PJ Harvey's 'This Wicked Tongue'.

I would usually have found it unacceptable to play music this loud at 2 a.m., but Ellie had no neighbours (the house next door had been for sale forever) and her flatmate was away visiting her grandparents.

The volume of music was also very necessary as we were both flagging, having lost track of the mission – get to Ellie's, grab camera, get back to party – and opted instead to spend twenty minutes discussing the benefits of adding bad songs to good playlists simply because they fitted.

She thought you could. I protested otherwise.

I put forward the closed-minded case that 'A terrible song is a terrible song.' She argued that songs you abhorred, put in the right context, could become songs you loved, and cited the example of 'Hip to Be Square' by Huey Lewis and the News in the adaptation of *American Psycho*.

She was damn fucking right.

As Polly Jean reached a crescendo, and Ellie poured me another whisky from her 'Scottish selection', I realised I really didn't want to go back to the party.

What if she bumped into an old friend? What if she saw some guy she'd fancied for forever and he finally said hello? What if one of my friends started joining in on our conversation?

Here in the sanctity of Ellie's bedroom there were no people-sized distractions. Her attention was all mine and mine was all hers.

Here I could make a lame joke about 'having a PJ day', and when it wasn't picked up on, there was no one there to say, 'What do you mean, a day in your PJs?' and I wouldn't then have to explain I meant a day listening to PJ Harvey, followed by the awkward silence that ensued after the explanation of a joke that wasn't that good in the first place.

'Ha, I just got that,' she said, when the song finished. She pointed to the Mac. 'A PJ day, like, a day listening to PJ.'

I shrugged, making sure she could see my nonchalance, and then mouthed, 'Marry me,' making sure she couldn't see my total and utter creepy devotion.

To remain here alone together, I reasoned, I needed to distract her some more with questions, preferably utilising objects within the room. I decided that photos were the way forward.

'Is that your mum and dad?'

She affected a prim, posh voice. 'Indeed, that is Moobum and Poobum.'

I followed suit. 'Moobum and Poobum, how delightful.'

'They're good people. Yours?'

'Yep, I have a moo and a poo still. Still together. They're okay, I guess. Bit dull.'

Despite her having zero evidence to prove or disprove my assertion, she seemed offended on their behalf.

'Everyone always thinks their parents are boring, but I bet they get up to all sorts of secret stuff that would blow your tiny mind.'

'Well, I doubt they're secret assassins or have their own pirate radio station, but I could be wrong.'

'You could be. And are. They are both those things and that's why I've lured you here. To put an end to Mr and Mrs . . . name . . .'

'Marcet.'

'To put an end to Mr and Mrs Marcet's reign of contract killings and unlicensed MOR broadcasts.'

I took a step towards her and looked into her eyes.

'How dare you suggest my parents listen to middle of the road music!' I exclaimed dramatically, fighting for volume over Modest Mouse telling Charles Bukowski he was an asshole. 'And since when is John Denver considered middle of the road anyhow.'

It was her turn to step forward, and when she did, our

noses were inches from touching. She dropped the facade to pick up another.

'I love John Denver.'

'Me too.'

And then, instead of actually kissing her, I simply thought, 'I'm going to kiss her, I'm definitely going to kiss her. Right now,' for long enough that the actual possibility of me kissing her was non-existent.

There was a window for this type of thing and I was way over it. I stepped back, cleared my throat and turned to the shelf behind me.

'And this.'

I picked up one of the four photos I'd assumed were of Ellie as a child, on the same shelf as the teddy bear and the candles.

'This is you?'

The photo was of a young girl, maybe six, and a boy, maybe four, smiling and making sandcastles at the beach.

She turned her back on me and answered with a quick 'Yep.'

'Very cute,' I observed, taking care not to a) be overly effusive about the appearance of a six-year-old, or b) make a weird and embarrassing comment about how good-looking our kids would be.

'And this guy?' I said, pointing to the boy crouched down holding the bucket. 'Should I be worried about him?'

I didn't notice her voice had gone into a near whisper.

'That's my brother, Lucas.'

'Ellie and Lucas. Your parents chose nice names. What's he do?'

And as I turned to see her face, I knew the answer before she said it, the reason for the candles and the teddy bear and the pride of place on a shelf away from the other photos. The reason why she was suddenly talking in a hushed, reverential tone.

'He died.'

'Oh Ellie, I'm sorry, I—'

'It's okay,' she said as she perched herself on the edge of the bed, her legs all of a sudden unable to do the job they'd been tasked with.

'What was he like?' I asked.

She looked up at me and shook her head, wearing the most peculiar expression. It was part bemusement, part total gratitude. I found out why in the following seconds.

'Do you know, I've had long-term relationships with guys, maybe six, seven months, guys who've stayed over here countless times, and they've never asked. Not once.'

Unsure what motion to make, I nodded.

'I'd like to tell you about him, if that's okay? And what happened?'

I made my way over and sat down next to her.

'It was a year after that photo was taken. I was seven. He was five. Our annual family holiday. We always went to Oban in Scotland, every year, because my dad went there with his parents. Or so he'd say. Mum would say it was because he wanted to stash up on whisky and they made the good stuff. Not that he was a boozer or anything. I only remember him having the occasional glass on holiday or on a special occasion. You ever been? To Oban?'

I shook my head, no, and considered letting her know that it was the shooting location for a superb romantic comedy called *I Know Where I'm Going!* but realised that this wasn't the time to interject with pointless film trivia.

She continued.

'We'd been in the car driving all day, and so when we arrived Mum and Dad said we could go out for ice cream. Lucas wanted to order this mammoth thing with a stupid name, Chocopalypse Now or something. It was a holiday, so Mum and Dad said yes. While he only managed about half of it, it still seemed like an extraordinary amount of food for a boy his size. As you can see, he was pretty scrawny. So when he started to complain about a stomach ache, we just assumed it was the ice cream. Lots of "eyes are bigger than your belly" mickey-taking.'

She took a deep breath for the hardest part.

'His appendix ruptured, they think, on the way back to the cottage. It shouldn't happen so fast, and even when it does, you have time. If he'd made it to the hospital sooner . . .'

She trailed off before finding something to ground her footing.

'This was before mobiles and fucking Wi-Fi and all those great new things that could have saved a life.'

It was the first time I'd heard Ellie swear since she told me her ethos on 'mind-fuckery'. She made swearing count. Used it when it was needed. I sort of felt pissed off with myself for chucking curses out with little or no thought.

One day I might need them.

She stroked the side of the picture frame.

'The older I get, the more I feel for my parents. All the "why didn't we's" they must have obsessed about. "Why didn't we take him to the hospital sooner?" "Why didn't we listen when he first started to complain?"'

She shook her head at the questions, as if she was actively shaking them out of her mind.

'I read somewhere that the brain is designed to remember bad memories better than good ones. Some sort of fight-or-flight, Darwin, evolution thing. You're wired to recall bad stuff so you can deal with it better next time.'

She was sitting next to me, but she was years ago.

'I can't. I can't remember a single bad moment with him. All he ever wanted to do was sit next to me and cuddle.'

A heavy sigh signified she was done thinking about it, and so she wrapped it up thus: 'You can go two ways with it. Hate the world and its random acts of unkindness, or decide that you only have one life and you'd best live it because it won't last. I chose the former for as a long as I could. I prefer the latter.'

Throughout her telling of this tale I felt all the muscles in my face sagging and the familiar sting of tear ducts awakening in the corners of my eyes. She was staring at the picture of her and Lucas and so hadn't noticed, but eventually she looked up to see the mess of snot and tears on the bed next to her.

She let out a surprised little laugh at my woeful appearance, but one with zero malice.

'Nick.'

'I'm sorry, I . . .'

'It's okay.'

'I'm sorry.'

'You don't need to say sorry.'

She looked at me with compassion. This person telling me of her loss was comforting me, making sure I was okay as she remembered and recounted the most difficult time in her entire life.

And then she kissed me.

19

I declined Lizzie's invitation to the new – written but not directed by – Coen brothers movie, concluding it was definitely a 'nice person feeling sorry for a loser' invite. Instead I decided to go alone.

I turned up early so I could apologise to Seb first. He was so disgustingly magnanimous about the whole thing I could feel myself getting enraged again, ready to throw insults and a hissy fit. I know he has my best interests at heart. He wants me to keep working here until I find another job, to have the protection that he thinks I need. But while I phrased it wrong, I meant what I said about not being tied down.

This is an opportunity.

A unique opportunity.

The trailers are almost over and I'm still the only one in the screen. Usually I'd be praying that no latecomers arrive and sit right in front of me, babbling incessantly while grazing on popcorn. I'd never let them get away with it, of course. On several occasions I've either called on a fellow projectionist for backup or stopped the show myself. This approach has, in the past, almost led to violence, but the end result – a respectful, non-talking cinema audience – is, to me, entirely worth it.

Today, though . . . today it sort of feels lonely to be the single audience member.

Today I want the confrontation.

Reviews for the film have been sniffy at best. Not that I care what the reviews say. Sure, I still read movie magazines, subscribe to a few actually. I even sent in a few articles once, to some of the big magazines, but I never heard back. Maybe that could be my next job. Maybe I could try harder.

I wish Ellie was here.

It has been almost seven weeks since she left, offering me 'space' and 'time'. I'm not sure what I've achieved with either of them.

I could call her. We're still friends, after all. We talked about being friends, didn't we? It's already a bit blurry. Maybe she'd want to hang out with her old pal Nick and watch a film. I could walk out now and buy us two tickets to the 17.30 show instead.

I don't mind watching the first ten minutes again. I have no idea what's going on. Colin Firth is pissed off with Alan Rickman because he's being a dick and now he's hitting on Cameron Diaz. Is that age gap obscene? A quick IMDb check on my phone. It's okay, there's no one else here. Twelve years. Not grotesque by Hollywood standards. Shit. Cameron Diaz is forty. God, I'm old. I still remember that entrance in *The*

Mask. A star was born in a moment. How often does that happen nowadays?

Nowadays. What a depressing adverb. Directly compare now with the past.

Nowadays, Nick goes to the cinema alone.

Nick goes home alone nowadays.

Nick, nowadays, wanks himself to sleep at night.

This film is appalling. Or I'm just in a terrible mood. I wonder how many films have been unfairly judged because a critic or studio head was having a shit day. Would *Citizen Kane* have been recut if George J. Schaefer had had a hangover on the first screening? Would George Lucas have had to bin *Star Wars* if Alan Ladd Jr had had a strop on when he pitched it to him?

I just want to be distracted. I should have chosen something with explosions and car chases and endless fist fights. Something loud and brash and colourful and sparkly. Something to take my mind off her.

But instead I'm reliving time we spent together on a daily basis now. Holidays always seem to take hold of the temporal lobe more than other days, and right now I'm fixated on the second night of our trip to Istanbul.

It was, without doubt, one of the best days of my life.

It was our third Christmas together, and instead of doing the usual round of 'Whose parents do we visit?', 'Didn't we do yours last year?', 'Can we please do yours again?', we decided to get the hell out of England.

The destination was Ellie's choice, prompted by a visit to a photography exhibition at the Tate. She'd returned talking excitedly of the angles of buildings and the magnificence of the old quarter, and I'd decided to surprise her with winter tickets, knowing that the heat of Turkey at any other time of year would destroy me.

Spending most of your waking hours in a dimly lit, windowless projection booth has a detrimental effect on how you deal with the outside elements. For me, too much sunshine is like kryptonite. My job has transformed me into a Lost Boy, a Nosferatu, a Dracula: Dead and Loving It.

The journey was the typically hellish combination of crowded train to Stansted and 'compact' flight on EasyJet. We kept the snark to a minimum and promised that we'd hit the ground running after an early night.

And hit the ground running we did.

More than ever in my recollections of Ellie, this memory finds itself by way of montage. Two young lovers in lands unknown.

A: Our couple are awake in bed, wrapped around each other. They start the day playfully rolling around under the sheets.

B: Room service arrives and the half-naked girl hides behind the door as the boy wheels in the breakfast and signs the bill. (Even though the 'extras' are paid for by her, her treat, as they always are.)

C. They eat great-tasting foreign food with the morning sun beaming through the window.

D. Out on the streets they walk arm in arm. A mass of two thick coats; you can't see where one ends and the other begins.

E. They watch another couple fighting, passionately. They smile at each other. Never us. That'll never be us.

F. A meal out at a fancy restaurant. The waiter tries to communicate something to the boy, trying to make sure he's ordering what he thinks he's ordering. The boy dismisses him with a nod of the head and a slightly patronising smile. The waiter arrives with the food and waits to see the boy take a mouthful. The boy gasps for air at the heat of the food. He grabs for his glass. Finding it empty, he grabs the girl's. The girl is laughing so hard she falls off her chair.

G. More drinks. More laughter. More hand-holding. More kissing. More intimacy.

H. And the montage ends as it started. The couple in bed. Wrapped in the soft cotton sheets and each other.

This always used to be soundtracked by – let me see – something upbeat and bouncy and cinematic and free.

Something by Feist.

Or 'Impossibly Beautiful' by Julie Feeney.

Or any of the first four tracks off *Begin to Hope* by Regina Spektor.

Now, it's maudlin music. Instrumentals only. One note, played over and over again. A soundtrack of impending dread.

*

I've only ever walked out of three movies in my whole entire life.

The first was *Vertigo*. I know, I know. But in my defence, I was thirteen and believed *Terminator 2: Judgement Day* to be the greatest movie of all time. I just didn't get it. I grew up, revisited it and have forever chastised myself for my youthful indiscretion.

The second was the 2003 remake of *The Texas Chain Saw Massacre*, which was annoyingly corrected to *The Texas Chainsaw Massacre*. I'm not someone who thinks that all remakes are inherently wrong. Without them we wouldn't have *The Maltese Falcon* (1941), there'd be no *Scarface* (1983), and Tim Burton would only ever have made one film.

The third was *The Sisterhood of the Traveling Pants*. Nothing against the film. It was simply not made for me and I was not made for it. We parted amicably half an hour in.

This will be my fourth.

There may be ten minutes left, there may be another hour. I have no idea. I have paid no attention to what's going on. I was somewhere else.

Somewhere good.

As I grab my things and stand to leave, my notepad slips out of my bag. I glance around the cinema and see I have solitude. I switch the light on my phone on, and in the partial darkness, I begin to write again.

Second Intermission

Second Incursion

The Girl didn't measure happiness the way he did. She'd coped well enough without it for some time, and therefore it wasn't something she fixated upon. The Boy, raised on happy endings and perfect conclusions, felt it was something he could give her.

It was Nick's twenty-seventh birthday. The rock-star death age. Joplin, Jim and Jimi.

He'd tried explaining this to Ellie, how this year might be his last on earth due to the proclivity of the Grim Reaper to take the best of humanity at one score and seven years.

After a useful reminder that you had to actually do something with your life to earn a place in the 27 Club, Ellie relented and told him, 'If this is the case, it's my duty to make sure you have a final birthday you'll never forget.'

With gusto she tackled the putting-together of his present. Booking the flights, finding the right place to stay. But it was the invitation she was most pleased with. Dusting off an old box full of arts and crafts materials, she spent the entirety of a Sunday afternoon designing the perfect vehicle for an RSVP. The card itself was made up of little pictures of film reels and projectors, and in the centre in elegant calligraphy were the words *YOU ARE CORDIALLY INVITED TO THE 2009 CANNES FILM FESTIVAL.*

'This is . . . I just . . . I literally have no words,' Nick blabbered as he opened the card.

'The hotel's a hole,' Ellie countered. 'I just want you to know that up front. I don't even think it has one star, but this time of year everyone puts their prices up and . . .'

He was on top of her, kissing her neck while at the same time still incanting his appreciation as she continued to attempt to temper his expectations.

'. . . it's only for two days, it's all I could afford. But we can always try and stay longer. Camp on the beach maybe? And the flights are super-basic.'

Nick moved his mouth up to hers to let her know she didn't have to add any caveats.

'You.'

He kissed her.

'Are.'

She started to unbutton his shirt.

'Amazing.'

★

Ellie tried her best to play down the date. In two days they'd be in the south of France, but she knew her mind would be in Scotland. She'd made every effort to convince herself that a change of scenery would do her good. That the usual

138

rituals of remembrance only made her blue. This was her chance, she truly believed, to replace a sad anniversary with a happy one. Our first trip together, she thought. What could possibly go wrong?

As they stood on the platform, the rain pouring down, the announcement stated for the umpteenth time – in a voice too carefree for the occasion – 'This is a safety announcement. Due to today's wet weather, please take extra care whilst on the station. Surfaces may be slippery.'

They'd been at Clapham Junction station for forty-five minutes and hadn't seen a single train. Nick was reciting a mantra to himself to fend off the demons: 'This time tonight we'll be in the south of France.' Ellie rubbed his arm.

After the fifty-seventh announcement that 'Closed-circuit television and remote video monitoring is in use at this station for your personal safety and security,' they overheard an attendant speaking about 'one under' and put two and two together.

He was reminded of a moment in the rather obvious – but not without its moments – deity comedy *Bruce Almighty*, where the titular Bruce, stuck in traffic behind what looks like a nasty car accident, laments how bad things always happen to him. He had previously considered it on the nose as far as character development went, but as he waited on an ever-more-populated train platform in the best example of the British climate, he was starting to feel very, very Bruce.

Ellie, as pragmatic as ever, looked for solutions.

'I'm not going to tell you not to worry about time, because I know that won't work, but we do still have an hour before the flight.'

'It's okay,' Nick replied, trying to copy the announcement's breezy intonation but doing little to hide the foot-tapping nervousness that was pulsing through his every muscle.

The display updated from '15 minutes' to '30 minutes', and a collective groan made its way up to the heavens as the heavens kept coming down.

'Let's grab a taxi,' Ellie offered. 'It'll only be about thirty quid. We can just make ourselves a meal instead of eating out tonight.'

Nick looked down the track, as if his looking might encourage the train to show up. It didn't, so he nodded and lifted up their bags.

As they struggled down the stairs, which seemed to be designed to accentuate slippage rather than reduce it, a hive mind grabbed the other passengers and they too started heading for the taxi rank. Nick and Ellie joined the back of a queue and spent the next twenty minutes praying their train wouldn't come.

It did, of course, the second their bags were in the boot.

*

'I suppose,' Nick wondered aloud, 'missing a flight by two hours is dramatically less infuriating than missing one by thirty seconds.'

It was the type of comment that didn't require a response. But when none came, he felt hurt and began to catastrophise as to why she was ignoring him.

It wasn't one thing, she would have told him if he'd asked. She was tired, her period was due soon, she was fixating on some negative comments at work. And most importantly, she'd just had to pay for a new flight, meaning the next month would be on even more of a budget. What she wouldn't have mentioned was the real truth: that she couldn't stop thinking about Lucas.

The day before had featured a perfect moment to tell Nick of the unfortunate timing, to get it off her chest and out in the open. To let her thought out where it could run freely, as opposed to growling angrily in the cramped corner of her mind and heart. But the moment came and went and here they were.

They settled into their seats, offered each other a wordless 'it's okay' and took out their in-flight entertainment. His was low-brow, a well-worn copy of *Jurassic Park* he'd had since he was ten. Hers was a much more intellectual but equally thumbed *Love in the Time of Cholera*. They'd tried book-swapping once but barely made it through the opening chapter of the other's novel. Ellie rationalised it was because these were nostalgic tomes and didn't really represent who they were now. Nick became anxious it was because his taste was too dorky.

That their new flight was subsequently delayed by exactly the length of time they'd missed the first flight by was a delicious slice of unnecessary irony.

After take-off, Nick's ears clogged up and he couldn't hear a thing, especially not Ellie asking if he could pass the bottle of water he was drinking from. When he finished the remaining millilitres of precious liquid, she looked at him with a level of disdain he'd never witnessed before. He saw her mouth, 'Thanks a bunch,' and his ears popped just in time to discover his crime.

They were both beginning to get angry-hungry at a time before they understood that anger-hunger was the cause of 96 per cent of all fights between loved ones, but were reluctant to pay £2.90 for a Twix. The hostility between them transported itself off the plane and into the rental car.

★

Due to the train and flight delays – plus an incident at baggage collection that remains unresolved to this very day – they had lost six hours of their forty-eight-hour holiday. There was a small but unignorable part of Ellie that viewed the complications of the trip as a blessing. They were a further distraction when distraction was exactly what she needed.

If Nick knew the process of her thoughts, if he knew that to cope with the negativity of one subject she would focus on another even more negative topic, he would try to figure out a better, less problematic solution.

Because she knew his need to do this, she kept her thoughts to herself.

After emptying the vending machines of their glucosey goodness at Saint-Geoirs airport, they staved off their joint crabbiness and were starting to resemble their normal, happy selves again.

The sun had begun to set when they first picked up the rental car. Now, a little over two hours from their destination, the sky was pitch black. Ellie had never been a fan of driving at night, but had offered on this occasion, as an extra distraction to her whirring mind. This left Nick to play with the iPod and curate the in-car entertainment.

'Is it weird that I still know every line of every song even though I haven't heard this album in about ten years?' he asked.

'Is it weird that I think it's weird that you listened to *Jagged Little Pill* with the same level of devotion I – as a fourteen-year-old girl – once did?' she answered.

He gave a sigh of relief at this, knowing then that the tensions of the trip thus far had been relegated to the level of irksome. Ellie started singing along again to the opening track.

As Alanis invited the car's occupants to see if they could cope with a couple of seconds of silence, Nick and Ellie turned to each other with perfect synchronicity to the beat in the pause of the song. As they did, a shudderingly awful sound took over as the car thumped over something unknown.

Ellie screeched on the brakes.

'What the fuck was that?' she said, using a rare but appropriate curse word.

They stepped out of the vehicle and gingerly approached the front of it.

Splattered over the number plate and broken left headlight was a crimson solution they were both unused to seeing in such a large quantity.

'What do you think it was?' she asked.

'Probably a rabbit,' he replied, aiming for casual.

'There goes the excess then.'

They climbed back into the car and made it approximately fifty metres before an obscene clunking began to radiate from underneath them. With every thud, Nick winced and Ellie screwed up her eyes.

'What are we going to do, Nick?'

He didn't have a clue, but felt a genuine buzz that she was looking to him for answers.

Still two hours from Cannes and the comfort and warmth of their one-star hotel, and with the time approaching nine in the evening, there wasn't much to hope for in terms of shops being open, and they hadn't passed a village for miles.

Up ahead a sign read: *Sisteron 1km*.

'I could walk it?' Nick said, hoping beyond hope that she wouldn't take him up on his generous offer.

'Not to play damsel in distress, but I don't really fancy being left in the dark by the side of the road in a place I don't know, where I could definitely be attacked by wolves.'

'Do they have wolves in France? I could Google it, I've got data roaming.'

She looked at him in silence, exaggerating her blinking, a little disappointed in herself for having entrusted her safety to him.

Finally she coughed and said, 'Do you think you could use your roaming to search for a French recovery service? Le AA, perhaps?'

Bashfully he typed in *Le AA*.

The first results were all for a law-enforcement agency in the US.

He tried *French recovery service*.

The results were less than comforting.

'I'm just getting hit after hit for "Make sure you get roadside recovery before you travel. And keep their number close at hand."'

'This is how I die,' Ellie said. 'Eaten by wolves next to my boyfriend who doesn't plan ahead.'

She didn't mean for her words to sting as much as they did, and yet at the same time, her frustration was boiling over.

'Let's just drive slowly to this,' he pointed at the sign, 'Sisteron place. It's less than a mile.'

Ellie agreed and started the car. As they took off, something about the name Sisteron kept playing in Nick's head. He began reciting it in time with the clunking, which soon became a crunching, which soon became unbearable until Ellie pulled the car over again and erupted.

'Stop saying Sisteron!'

And that was when it hit him.

'Gabby!'

Ellie climbed out of the car for the second time and yelled across the bonnet, 'You know it isn't your family's job to rescue you?'

'What's that supposed to mean?' Nick replied, before quickly reclaiming his current thought. 'Gabby used to date a guy, a real prick, called, what was it? Franco? Francis? François! That was it. He lived in Sisteron. I remember it because he made terrible jokes about being from Sisteron and on my sister. I fucking hated that guy.'

Ellie was still nonplussed by his unexplained plan. 'How exactly does this help us?'

'Guys would do anything for Gabby. Especially ex-boyfriends. I'll message her and see if he still lives nearby. He might come and pick us up. Or at least know someone who can.'

Ellie started blinking again.

'Let me get this straight. You want to message your sister to see if she can message an a-hole ex-boyfriend to see if he can message his random mates to pick us up?'

Nick was getting increasingly irate at how this was becoming all his fault, thinking to himself – and only to himself – how if he'd been driving they wouldn't be in this mess.

'What's your master plan then?' he snapped.

Ellie threw her arms up and started scratching both sides of her head. She didn't need to seek out the negative thoughts now; they were all-encompassing.

Look at how badly he copes when things don't go his way. When it's not all sunshine and lollipops. How long will I have to wait for him to grow up? And finally, the one she'd kept pushed way, way down, *Can't I do better than this?*

She took a deep breath. 'Just give me five minutes, Nick.'

After half a minute, she'd made up her mind.

'Fine. Whatever. Do it.'

*

When François arrived, leaning out of the window of his sports car, looking a million euros, Nick remembered everything he'd forgotten. How François used to ridicule him at every available opportunity. How he came on to anything that moved. How fucking gorgeous he was.

He climbed out of the car and kissed Nick on both cheeks.

'*Merci*, François. I really appreciate this.'

François playfully slapped him where he'd just kissed and

said, '*Mon petit frère*, I always loved how you used to try and speak French for me. Not many of you English bothered.'

He looked at the car.

'So, what happened?'

'*Un grand lapin?*' Nick offered.

Without laughing François said, 'You were always very funny, Nick. Very funny man.'

And then he slid up to Ellie in a way that was both effortless and creepy, invading her personal space and taking her hand in his.

'You and this guy, eh?'

Ellie smiled politely and said, 'Very much actually.'

She said it as a favour to Nick. She knew he'd be feeling insecure, and now that her blood had calmed, her thoughts turned to making him feel okay again. Still, she couldn't help shake her head at his decision to make a point of standing between her and François. A decision she was sure François got a kick out of.

'How's Gabriella?' François asked with a nauseating wink.

Ellie quickly interjected. 'Who's Gabriella?'

'He means Gabby,' Nick said, unsure as to whether he was projecting a hint of jealousy onto Ellie in the millisecond she thought there was a secret woman in his life. 'She's very good, thank you for asking. Getting married next month.'

François sighed heavily, and Nick knew what was coming next.

'Ah, the things we used to do. Come on, you can tell me all about her on the way back to mine.'

★

'What's the French for incredible?' Ellie asked.

It was more of a test than an actual question. If Nick laughed, or even smiled, she would know they were on terra firma. If he missed the joke completely and tried to correct her, she'd know the evening would be a write-off. She wasn't entirely sure what his silence meant.

There was, like in every joke, a large degree of truth in what she'd said. One side of the apartment was almost completely glass and it overlooked a lit pool that might or might not have belonged just to François. The open-plan kitchen had an island and the sort of slimline built-in appliances that you just had to look at to turn on. Every piece of art on the wall was either strongly phallic or yonic or both. This place and its contents were hand-picked to drop both jaws and drawers.

Ellie was trying not to be too blown away by it for Nick's sake, but her eyes were wide like a four-year-old seeing their birthday cake.

'Red or white?' François offered. 'Or something stronger?'

'Actually, we'd best be turning in if you don't mind,' Nick replied.

He tried to avoid eye contact with Ellie, as he knew she'd be giving him a look that said 'You're being insanely rude.' Because she couldn't meet his eye, she elbowed him in the ribs to get his attention and whispered it, swapping 'insanely' for 'inordinately'.

'Red, please, François,' she added.

'Yes, red,' Nick parroted, hoping his host wouldn't take him up on his first answer and send him off to bed, while snuggling up to his beloved with a bottle of Shiraz on the most expensive-looking couch he'd ever seen.

'But just one,' he whispered to Ellie.

'Fine,' she whispered back.

'Doesn't seem like my master plan was too bad after all.'

She rolled her eyes in reply, as François returned handing over two wine-filled glasses that had more in common with mixing bowls than drinking vessels.

'How many bottles are in this?' asked Nick.

As they sat on the couch sipping their delicious wine, a sense of calm seeped into their bones. The conversation was light and jovial and François stopped being François just enough for Nick to begin to relax.

He spoke fondly of his time in England and was very humble about his wealth. The three of them chatted about what Nick and Ellie hoped to do when they arrived in Cannes tomorrow, and François offered them a free meal at a fancy restaurant where he knew the head chef.

The wine started to go to Nick's head, and he didn't even mind when François dropped in the occasional double entendre, going so far as to laugh at a couple of them.

Conversation turned to various foods they'd sampled. Nick mentioned how he and his former classmates had tried horse on a school trip, and Ellie said she'd eaten both alligator and ostrich at a music festival in Wales.

Nick, with a slur in his voice, rounded up the topic with the line, 'I'll try anything once.'

At this, François smiled and excused himself. Once he'd

left the room, Nick put his hand on Ellie's knee and said, 'Let's go to bed. I'm done in.'

The tiredness in his eyes reminded her of the length of the day, and she acquiesced, putting the rest of her wine to one side.

'Sure. Let's.'

Just as they stood up, François reappeared in the doorway, stark bollock naked, wearing nothing but a megawatt smile.

Nick looked at his penis.

Ellie looked at his penis.

Nick looked at Ellie.

Ellie looked at Nick.

Ellie put her hand over her mouth to stop herself bursting out laughing.

François raised his eyebrows suggestively.

He pointed to himself. 'Me.' He pointed to Ellie. 'You.' Then he pointed to Nick. 'And you.'

Not knowing what to do or say, Nick found himself looking at François's penis again. It had become as hypnotic as the snake in *The Jungle Book*. Only a confident 'So!' from the naked man snapped Nick out of his trance.

'No. No. No,' he said, shaking his head from side to side.

And that was when Ellie uttered four unforgettable words.

'You're so conservative, Nick.'

She knew the damage she'd done the second the words were out of her mouth. He was crushed, and when she saw his expression, her face fell and she immediately put a reassuring hand over his.

'I'm so sorry, Nick, that was a joke. A really bad joke.'

She pointed at François's penis. 'François, no, we would very much not like to have sex with you.'

Her immediate retraction of the words did little to steady Nick's nerves, as François shrugged a shrug that redefined 'you win some, you lose some'.

'If you're sure?' He reached back behind the door he was standing in front of and returned with a dressing gown. 'You are sure?'

'We are very sure. And I think we'd like to go to bed now. Just the two of us.' Ellie was now speaking for Nick. Because Nick could no longer form sentences.

'Nick?' François tried, one more time.

Nick shook his head silently as François finally covered up his cock and balls.

'Your room is down the corridor on the left. I'll call you in the morning. Is seven too early?'

'Seven would be great, thanks.'

Ellie led Nick away from the scene of the crime, a suppressed giggle in her mouth.

When they reached their room and shut the door behind them, she fell onto the bed laughing. She was laughing so hard she could barely breathe. She laughed herself to sleep that night, but Nick lay awake, staring at the door, François's genitals seared onto his mind.

Ellie's 'joke' playing on repeat.

*

A preoccupation with their hangovers replaced Ellie's jollity and Nick's fear-induced paranoia when they stirred the next day. News from the mechanics only exacerbated the self-loathing that accompanied most mornings after.

Having the information relayed by a painfully free and easy François – who had seemingly brushed off last night's indecent proposal without a second thought – was the foul-tasting cherry on top.

The rental car was a write-off. Arrangements had been made to return it to the hire company, but no alternative vehicle was available until well after their flight home. The choice was now carry on to Cannes by bus for less than half a day, or admit defeat and try again another year.

Reluctantly they both agreed on the latter.

Once the decision had been made, and seeing them so despondent, François offered them the place to themselves for the rest of the morning. They thanked him for his hospitality and never mentioned 'the incident'. He departed with a cheap shot about Gabby giving him a call when her marriage got boring.

*

Lazing by the pool in the mid-morning sunshine, sipping at cocktails created with expensive alcohol neither of them had heard of before, conversation was thin on the ground.

Eventually Nick said, 'I can wait. Cannes isn't going any-where. When I'm a famous film-maker we'll come back here and tell everyone all about our misadventures.'

Ellie's smile barely registered as one. It was then that it dawned on Nick that this sadness, this absence, had little to do with current events. That they'd been living with it since before the train, plane and automobile.

Panic set in at his quandary. Say something and open up a conversation he might regret. Or remain silent and let his imagination guide him to the deepest levels of hell.

'Ellie, is there . . .' He'd barely started when she began to cry.

'I'm so sorry.' Her face matched her words. She was genuinely, unequivocally sorry, but for what he still had no idea. He needed patience, to let her compose herself, to give her time, but all he wanted to do was scream, 'Tell me! Tell me what it is!' He held it together and was rewarded for doing so.

'Today is Lucas's birthday.'

He wrapped his arms around her and pulled her close as she started to let out days of pent-up emotion.

'I really tried my best. I didn't want to let it get in the way. I thought I could . . .'

'It's okay.' He rubbed both her arms at once. 'It's okay.'

They stayed that way for several minutes, him holding her, her leaving fresh tear stains on his T-shirt. When she finally broke away, he met her eyes and asked, 'Why didn't you tell me?'

Ellie matched his eyeline. 'Honestly?'

He nodded.

'I was worried you wouldn't be able to cope with it. That you'd want to . . .'

'Try and fix you?'

She nodded.

'And there isn't any fixing for this. Sometimes I'll be blue about it, on days like today especially.' She paused. 'But I should have told you. I should have. I am sorry.'

Nick finished his drink and looked out at the shimmering water.

'I can see why you didn't. You're right. I would have tried to fix you.'

'Maybe instead of fixing me you could just, I don't know, help me.'

At that moment she wasn't sure if he knew the difference. She wasn't sure if she'd made it clear enough that finality wasn't the thing she was searching for.

Back in England, one week later, she got her answer.

*

'Look,' Nick said, looking more serious than she'd ever seen him, 'I know this is a risk and I don't want to, I don't know, step on toes or trivialise or—'

'What is it?' Ellie said, as supportively as she could, knowing full well he could babble for England if allowed.

He passed her a video camera.

She eyed it with suspicion.

'Is this about the François thing, when I said you were so conservative? I've explained a million times that was just a joke.'

'God, no! But it is Cannes related, I suppose.'

He proceeded to tell her his idea. He wanted her to record a message for Lucas. He explained that there was never any reason for anyone to see her recordings except her. She could say anything she wanted. Treat it like a diary or a confessional or just a chance to reminisce.

She knew as well as he did that it wasn't for her little brother, it wasn't really a message to him. It was just a way for her to bring him back. Even if it was only for as long as she was talking.

'I love it. I really, really love it.'

'You do? It's not me trying to fix you or anything, or—'

She kissed him to silence him, to stop him overexplaining a simple, caring gesture for which she understood his every intention.

'I love it.'

'Then I promise that every year, every April, I'll get the camera out from wherever it's gathering dust and you can record a new one. Because if I know you just for this day or for a million more, I'll always try and help you feel okay.'

The Boy's ability to turn sadness into joy was unarguable. When he wanted to, he could prove himself to be exceptionally caring. But the Girl understood the importance of consistency better than he did. She knew that when someone spends all their time making noise, when silence comes, the contrast is deafening.

End of Second Intermission

20

5 November 2008 – 01.59 GMT
Obama 117
McCain 73
270 needed to win

The kiss was just a kiss.

While the setting – our bodies in close proximity to the bed, the ungodly late hour, a fair amount of booze in the system – could certainly have led to more, less was definitely the better option in this instance.

Wiping a tear away from my cheek with her thumb, she thanked me for listening about Lucas. I said it was okay and we continued with short, sharp questions about how the other was doing until we both felt okay. The word okay was used a lot.

She was the first to stand.

'So,' she said, 'do you want to go back to the party or—'

I jumped up and answered too quickly, thinking I was giving the correct answer.

'Yeah, erm, definitely, sure, sounds good, I mean, if you want to go back . . .'

'Oh yeah, I mean we didn't come all this way to not buy chicken, be yelled at by your ex-girlfriend, have a good cry and then have a snog.'

'She wasn't my girlfr—'

I stopped myself this time.

'You're teasing me again. We're back to teasing.'

'Oh, the teasing will never stop, Nick the Dick.'

'I'm okay with that,' I admitted. And I very much was.

'And *I* am okay and all is okay. Except I am' – listen out for the elongated middle 'or' – 'extraordinarily hungry. Should I fix us a quick sandwich?'

*

The kitchen was a state.

While even the most proper of people should just get over the mess of a bedroom, an untidy kitchen is intolerable. For starters, there are the health ramifications. This was London, you were never more than six feet from a rat. Why incite them?

Then there's the annoyance of not having anything to use. If your sink is overflowing with crap, you'll have to rummage around for the thing you need, in and under and around the rest of the crap. No. This simply would not do.

'Where are your rubber gloves?' I asked in a rather matronly tone.

Ellie was at first shocked and then intrigued as to where this was going.

'There may be a pair under the sink,' she replied.

I opened the cupboard expecting to be greeted by a kraken, or at the very least a family of vexed mice, put out by my intrusion this early in the morning. Instead I found only the gloves – never used – and a few cobwebs.

I moved everything out of the sink and filled it with non-branded washing-up liquid and lukewarm water, while Ellie fished a questionable loaf of bread from the cupboard above my head.

'That's in date, right?' I asked with unbridled scepticism.

She answered with a face that said 'relax', and the non-reassuring words 'I'm sure it's fine', which worried me even more.

'You really don't have to do my washing-up. I was going to do it tomorrow.'

I raised a single eyebrow.

'I was!' she contested. 'Now put your eyebrow down and tell me what you want in your sandwich.' She opened the fridge. 'Cheese or ham?'

'What's the date on the ham?' I asked for the sake of my weak constitution.

I saw her read it and grimace. She tossed it on the top of the overflowing bin and turned with a smile.

'Cheese it is.'

I quickly washed the things I knew she'd need, for fear she might just grab any old dirty plate to put my magnificent feast upon. She held the loaf up to the light and crinkled her nose, deeming the bread fit for human consumption. I was suddenly not hungry but knew I'd eat the sandwich anyway as a gesture of goodwill.

'I hear Bill Murray sometimes turns up to parties on college campuses and does their washing-up,' Ellie said.

'I hear he goes up to people on the tube, taps them on the shoulder and says, "No one will ever believe you," before disappearing into the night,' I offered back.

'Like Batman.'

'He would have made a great Batman. I curse you, Tim Burton.'

'Hey, I love Tim Burton films.'

I dramatically took off my gloves and threw them into the bubbly water.

'Well, that tears it. I thought we had a future together, but I can never love a woman who loves the films of one Timothy Burton.'

She blushed and I realised I'd taken the role play too far with my ill-thought-through and far-too-soon inclusion of the L word. I put the gloves back on, carried on with the task in hand and pretended I hadn't said it, hoping she'd go along with this alternative timeline.

'That said, I really liked *Big Fish*. How's the sandwich coming?'

I turned around to be presented with – 'Ta-da!' – a sandwich cut out in the shape of a little man. Not wanting to wait for me to clean the utensils, she'd simply grabbed a tool from the back of the cupboard – in this instance a gingerbread man cutter – and made do. On top of everything else, I was now in awe of her spontaneous survival instinct.

'That's one of the greatest things I've ever seen,' I said,

before reaching forward and decapitating the little bread man with my teeth.

I took a punt. 'Do you want to go to the cinema with me?'

She blinked twice. 'You're a fast mover, aren't you? Shall we see how the rest of the night goes?'

'No, I mean tonight, now. Do you want to go to the cinema with me?'

She looked at her watch to present me with the evidence.

'It's three minutes past two in the morning. And we have a party to go to.'

I took the keys to the cinema from my pocket.

'I have keys.'

She didn't pause before replying.

'I'm in.'

21

Ellie sent me a message two days ago, saying she had some important news she wanted to share. For reasons known only to the gods of irony, we have decided to meet in a Camden pub called The World's End.

It'll be two months to the day since I last saw her. That particular piece of trivia is as heartbreaking as it is baffling. How we've managed to avoid each other for that long seems like an Olympic feat, but here we are.

Since she texted, her big news has been whirling around my brain constantly. I see it on spinning newspapers in black and white, landing with a thud, her coloured surname the basis for Fleet Street's terrible puns.

QUICK FOX BROWN JUMPS INTO ANOTHER'S BED – this is how they'll announce her new boyfriend.

BUN IN THE ELLIE? – Well, that one's self-explanatory.

Could she be, though? What bigger news is there? Could it be mine? Yep, only been a grand total of eight weeks, three days and fourteen hours since our fight.

At least I'd get to see her at Christmases again.

As this last thought rambles through my head, I realise I've accidentally got quite drunk. She's not even late. I just arrived early and, having been wasted last night, the two double gins in the space of thirty minutes have coalesced with the previous evening's winery to put me at one hell of a disadvantage for this upcoming grudge match. Maybe it's not a disadvantage. Maybe some lubrication will get me speaking my mind on a few things.

As she walks through the door looking incredible, any advantage I may have had evaporates like . . . like, like crisps in tea? Christ, I am pissed.

I stand to hug her and stumble a little. She leans in and puts her arms around me. We both go to kiss the wrong cheek and abort. I wonder what others in the pub think of this awkward exchange. Do they imagine we're on a first date? That we're related? If I were an innocent bystander, my best guess after witnessing an embrace as cringeworthy as this would be 'she's the girlfriend of his best friend who recently died and they've agreed to sort out the funeral together despite having never really seen eye to eye'. That is until I realise that's an elevator pitch for a pretty shitty romcom.

'You want a drink?' she offers. 'Same again?'

I nervously push my empties to one side.

'Please. Gin and tonic.'

'Nice summer drink. I'll join you.'

She puts her jacket down on the chair opposite me and I scurry back to my side of the table. She opens her handbag and takes out her purse.

'Back in a sec.'

I take out my crumpled little notepad and specifically the well-thumbed list titled *Why Ellie Left*. Reflecting on our abandoned Cannes trip had inspired me to add the – admittedly maudlin – *BECAUSE THINGS NEVER WORK OUT THE WAY YOU WANT THEM TO*. I think I wrote that after a few. It was in at the number 4 position, below *WE PEAKED TOO EARLY, I'M A BRICK* and *PRAGMATISM (her) vs IDEALISM (me)*.

I wish I'd written more and wonder if I'll ever steer the conversation on to these bullet points as I notice her phone is on the table in front of me. I try to work out if I have enough time to grab it and ascertain crucial information about who she's been talking to, what's she's been up to.

I'm probably drunk enough – and low enough – to actually do something so unbelievably stupid and counterproductive to my happiness, but thankfully the bar is almost empty and she's back before I can betray any trust that may be left between us.

'Your beverage,' she says, handing me my third drink in thirty minutes.

'Thanks,' I say to her. Go slow, I say to myself.

'How have you been?' she asks, trying to inject a breezy intonation to her words. 'I've been Facebook-stalking you but haven't seen any updates.'

'I don't use it any more,' I lie, having just checked her page moments before she arrived. 'And to answer your previous question, I've been better. You?'

'Ups and downs.'

'And this big news of yours? An "up", I assume?'

Even without the worry I see etched on her face that I'm in 'one of those moods', I have enough presence of mind to realise I'm being a belligerent shitbag. What I don't have is enough presence of mind to stop it.

'I have some news too, actually,' I offer, steering the conversation towards me and how I'm feeling.

'Okay. What's yours?'

'My parents are going to New Zealand?'

Her expression suggests this isn't front-page material and I realise I've buried the lead.

'That'll be nice for them. I didn't think they were the long holiday type. Have they even been out of their postcode before?'

'No. To stay. I mean they're going to New Zealand to stay. To live. Forever probably. I mean, what have they got left? Twenty years tops. It'll probably be forever.'

Her face is awash with pity and I haven't even got to the good part yet.

'There's more.'

'Nick, are you okay?'

'I have more news . . . well, you know about the house. I've also been made redundant.'

'Oh Nick! I'm so sorry.'

Her sympathy is genuine and it crushes me. She looks at me the way she used to and I want to scream how sorry I am and how much I want to make it right. How I want to find out all about what she did today and the day before and every day since she walked out. But I don't. Because she asks this:

'Why didn't you tell me?'

And like that, my blood's pumping again.

'Because you dumped me,' I tell her.

Her eyes flick from soft to wild rage in an instant, a sight seldom seen.

'No I fucking didn't.'

Yes she did.

'You were the one who wanted to spend some time apart,' she says, her voice trembling a little.

Is she insane?

'Are you insane?' Our voices are rising in volume with each exchange.

She steadies herself. 'We had a big fight. I said some things, things that I still stand by, but things I know must have been hard for you to hear. And then after a day of ignoring me, I asked what you wanted and you said, "Not this. So we might as well be apart." I said I'd give you some space and go stay with my dad for a few days and for you to call me when you were ready.'

She leans across the table for the big reveal.

'You never called.'

We sit in anger for a few minutes, me trying to think of anything and everything rather than face up to the idea that she's right about what she just said. I find the perfect diversion from accepting any responsibility, the thing that has been keeping me up at night. The big news.

'So, what's your news? New boyfriend?' I spit out, the vitriol at its most vitriolic.

This, more than anything else, raises a smile from her.

'I believe in the ten per cent rule. Some idiot once told

168

me that you should spend at least ten per cent of the time you've been in a relationship trying to figure out where the hell that relationship went wrong before you move on.'

A callback such as this is almost enough to break me, but I keep it together, not showing a flicker of acknowledgement for the intimacy we used to share.

'I've been offered a job.'

'Good for you.'

If I could jump out of myself for a second, I'd kick seven shades of shit out of me. Who I'm pretending to be is killing me. I hope and pray she knows I would never be this indifferent to her. That all I want to do is wrap myself around her and find out every detail of what she's been doing since we last talked. To hear about her news. To hear about her day.

But something is pulling me to the depths.

She stands. 'Maybe this isn't the right time.'

'Sit, come on. We're friends, right? I want to hear about my friend's new job.'

The completely wanky way in which I say 'friends' is more than enough ammunition for her to justifiably leave. But instead she sits back down and I instinctively know there's more than just a job announcement coming.

'So who's the job with?'

'It's with AP.'

I can see she knows I have no idea what this is.

'The Associated Press. They're a non-profit news company. They collect news from around the world and distribute it to others.'

I shrug.

She grits her teeth and continues.

'Anyway. They have offices all around the world. Although their main office is in New York.' She pauses and lowers her voice. 'Which is where I'll be working.' Another pause. 'If I take it.'

My eyes are wider than they've ever been and my eyebrows are trying to escape off the top of my head.

I am Bambi versus the full beams of an articulated lorry.

I just about manage to emit some noises that could be mistaken for the words 'oh', 'okay' and 'so'. I also squeak out a 'that's' but fail to complete the sentence, instead circling back to the 'so' a few more times.

I gain a form of consciousness for long enough to down my drink, hoping the gin will provide an alcoholic slap in the face. Ellie, tentatively, almost embarrassed, sips on hers. The slap works and I sit forward with renewed vigour. I even clap my hands together for some reason known only to my nervous system.

'Ellie,' I say with a weird use of her first name. 'I'm really, really pleased for you. This is your dream.'

She edges forward in her seat. 'I have you to thank for it. When I sent my portfolio to them, I included a few shots from the Obama thing.'

She didn't say 'our night', which I must admit I'm hugely grateful for. If she had, my gin would be two parts tears.

'The feedback was that I'd "captured a moment of history from a unique perspective". I'm not sure what was so unique about a group of white, liberal twenty-somethings in England watching an election, but I took the compliment.'

This should be the happiest moment for her, the realisation of a lifelong dream, but she still looks so defeated. And that's on me. If my list has done anything, it's crystallised why she's better off without me.

#2 I'M A BRICK. I'M A BRICK. I'M A BRICK.

'When did you apply for it?'

'You remember that night my mum came around?'

Margaret's drunken visit. Until the day I die.

I nod.

'It was the next day. I was in a pretty bad place and applied the hell out of it.'

'When does it start?'

'October the fifth.'

'A month!' My exclamation gets looks from the barman and our fellow drinkers.

'And a week,' Ellie offers, as if seven days will change everything.

Anything more I can think of to say sounds bitter and sulky and so I keep my mouth firmly shut and let her do the talking.

'So, the redundancy? When does it . . .?' she asks.

'Next week.'

'That's quick.'

'I took voluntary redundancy. No use putting off the inevitable.'

The pity look is back. The same one offered by Seb and Lizzie and pretty much every person I come into contact with lately. I'm done with it. I'd rather be hated than pitied right now.

'Did you get a decent pay-off?'

'Close to five grand.'

I can still recognise when she's having an idea: she squints slightly and bites her bottom lip, her teeth almost in the corner of her mouth.

'Well. You could come with me?'

'Where?'

'To Outer Mongolia, Nick. Where do you think? America.'

I won't allow myself to drag her under.

'Why? We don't have a future together?'

'Says you.'

'Don't I get a say?' I blurt out, realising as I'm saying it that this makes no sense.

'Of course you do. If that's what you want. Just don't go around telling people – or yourself – that I dumped you, feeling sorry for yourself and blaming me for your life falling apart.'

Another sharp intake of breath. From both sides now.

The second such silence in two months.

Neither of us budging.

Her with gritted teeth.

Me with pouty lips.

We wait each other out and the waiting lasts another lifetime.

22

5 November 2008 – 02.21 GMT
Obama 175
McCain 97
270 needed to win

I can't for the life of me remember why, but Ellie was wetting herself laughing. All I do remember is being particularly proud of myself for being the cause of the laughter. We had left her house and were making our way to the cinema together, the cold night turning even colder.

Before we left, I'd asked to borrow a book from her shelf. It was titled *Sex, Drugs and Cocoa Puffs* and was written by an author I liked. He wrote mainly about pop culture, but peppered his books with weird hypotheticals about swapping your vocal cords with alt-rock singers, or how much extra you'd have to be paid to go to your regular job in evening wear.

I'd read the book a couple of times before and was pretty sure I knew where my copy was, but I reasoned I needed something of hers so I could make an excuse to see her again.

I sort of felt bad that I'd a) lied about having never read the book, and b) chosen such a lame, clichéd trick to try and see her again. Was she laughing because she'd uncovered my ruse? No, because I wouldn't have been happy about that. And I definitely was happy. Had I told a joke? Nope. Can't remember. Whatever it was, she was doubled over and I was beaming like I'd won a BAFTA.

'Christ, that's good,' she finally said, wiping away tears of berserk joy and regaining her breath.

She had a great laugh and she laughed often. Making her laugh was one of my favourite things in the entire world.

'Will you get into trouble for taking someone to the cinema in the middle of the night?' she asked in a way that I could only describe as deeply flirtatious, purposely making a meal of the word 'trouble'.

'Nah, I take girls there all the time.'

I managed to keep the straightest of faces in my delivery and this time it was her turn to appear genuinely put out.

I quickly confessed to my joke, 'That was a good one, right?'

She nodded with the corners of her mouth turned down in a way that looked very Robert De Niro like, and I got a little confused as to why that turned me on.

'Well played, sir. But have you?'

'Have I what?' I said, realising what the question was before I'd finished the sentence. 'Brought girls to the cinema in the middle of the night?'

I was sort of gobsmacked at the realisation that I hadn't. It totally seemed like something I would have done.

But then nobody had ever given the *Cinema Paradiso* answer before. So, technically, nobody was worthy.

★

When we arrived at the back entrance to the cinema, we both independently decided we were now the world's greatest bank robbers on the heist of the century. Think Newman and Redford in *The Sting*, George Clooney and friends in the *Ocean's* films or the cat burglar in *The Simpsons* going after the world's largest cubic zirconia.

We kept to the shadows, running between lamp posts. We checked over both our shoulders incessantly – and then once over each other's shoulders. We froze when we heard a cat screech down an alley and both dropped to the floor when we heard police sirens.

Once the coppers had cheesed it, we got to our feet and I pointed for her – SWAT team style – to meet me at the back door.

'That was awesomely timed, what with the sirens and everything,' she said.

'Not really,' I replied bluntly. 'There's always police cars going full pelt because this is an insanely dangerous part of town. Especially at this time of night.'

She punched me on the arm, hard enough for me to need to give it a little rub.

I took out my keys and opened the door to the immediate and abrasive sound of the security alarm.

'Shit,' Ellie shrieked. 'I thought you said it was okay!'

I couldn't help but take a little pleasure in her unnecessarily over-the-top reaction after the teasing I'd endured from the second we'd met. Then, for fear that she might leg it into the night and get lost, I quickly put her mind at ease.

'It's fine, I know the code.'

I turned on the tiny flashlight on my keys – the one I used for taking notes during print checks – and located the alarm panel.

'2001,' I said, pressing four buttons, 'for Mr Kubrick. 333 for Kieslowski.' Three more. 'And 7 for Mr Fincher.' The shrill beep stopped.

I turned to see Ellie rolling her eyes.

'You're such a geek.'

'You ain't seen nothing yet!'

We ran through a pair of double doors and into the cinema corridor.

It was hard to see with the lights on their lowest setting, just purple strip lighting lining the floor and buzzing neon above each of the eight screen entrances. Years of stumbling about in the dark here, after hours, gave me a great opportunity to take Ellie by the hand.

'Pick a number from one to eight.'

'Four.'

'No, I don't like four, it's too close to the screen and there's a small mark in the upper right-hand corner.'

'Okay.' A slight frustration was present in her voice, a warning to be careful, Nick. 'How about six?'

'A fine choice.'

We entered the auditorium and I flicked a switch, bringing the lights up over the silver screen, illuminating the curtains on either side. I think it's a glorious sight, a blank white screen, home to a shit-ton of possibility.

I went to a Q&A to see one of my favourite film critics once, and she was asked if she looked forward to watching bad films as much as good ones, because then she'd get to write a funny, scathing review.

She said, 'Every time I sit in a cinema, waiting for the film to start, every inch of me hopes that over the course of the next two hours I will be shown something incredible. Something that makes me fall in love with movies like I did when I was a child. No matter how many times I may be disappointed, I never lose that hope.'

I looked at Ellie and smiled.

'Good, isn't it?'

She stared at the blank white screen and squinted.

'Needs a little something, don't you think?'

'Fine. Follow me.'

I led her up the stairs. When we reached the top, her eyes found the back row and she stopped and stepped backwards.

'Hey hey hey, I told you before, you are not getting laid tonight.'

Rather than reply, I simply pushed on the exit door that she clearly hadn't noticed and motioned for her to follow me.

'This way to where the magic happens.'

'You're really loving this, aren't you?'

I beamed as she followed me up the stairs to the booth.

'You have no idea.'

Inside the booth, Ellie was presented with a tiny snapshot of my inner self. Film posters lined the walls, film magazines were piled in one corner next to a tatty, beat-up chair, and CDs – mostly soundtracks – littered the bench where we made up the films.

It felt like I was showing her the intimacy of my home, rather than my workplace.

'Welcome to Projection Park. All in all, we have eight projectors in residence – James and Donna, Ingrid and Cary, Humphrey and Katharine, over there is Billy, and this, this is Meg. Meg meet Ellie, Ellie meet Meg. We're getting a "digital projector" next year, but that's just a fad.'

'A robot projector? You'll have to call her Brigitte after the Maschinenmensch in *Metropolis*.'

'God, that's good. I'm stealing that.'

'By all means.'

I leant with ironic seductiveness against Meg and whispered, 'You want me to fire her up?'

Ellie nodded and we took a few small steps towards a very big cupboard.

Inside was a shelf labelled (rather embarrassingly) *Nick's Flicks*. On the shelf were ten mini reels holding my favourite trailers from films released between 2002 and 2008. The films were, in no particular order: *Adaptation*, *Shaun of the Dead*, *Before Sunset*, *The Station Agent*, *Oldboy*, *Children of Men*, *Eternal Sunshine of the Spotless Mind*, a thirty-year reissue of *Chinatown* and the most recent addition, *WALL-E*. The tenth trailer I quickly grabbed and hid behind my back.

I was too slow.

Ellie saw and asked, 'What was that?'

'Nothing?'

The knowing grin returned.

'*Garden State*?'

I nodded, ashamed, and placed it back on the shelf.

'What would the lady like to watch this evening?' I corrected myself. 'This morning?'

She studied the selection with great care before picking one up and asking the assistant (me) for help, effecting a well-crafted posh voice.

'*Children of Men* would be a fine pick, but a little morose for the current circumstances, no?'

I nodded sagely, enjoying my role as butler, as she picked up another.

'*The Station Agent*? I have not heard of this.'

'American, ma'am. 2003. An independent film written and directed by a Mr Thomas McCarthy about a young man with dwarfism who lives a life of solitude before . . .'

'. . . he observes that life is better spent in company?'

'Very astute of you, ma'am.'

She dropped the pantomime as quickly as she'd picked it up.

'Oooh, *Oldboy*. I love that film.'

'Nothing says first date like a pissed-off Korean guy with a hammer.'

She turned to correct me.

'This isn't a first date.'

I cocked my head to one side.

'I invited you to the cinema and you said yes.'

She cocked her head the other way.

'This isn't a first date. And I have decided,' she said as she passed me a reel, 'while seeing Jake Gittes on the big screen would be a special treat, I can't say no to Joel and Clem.'

179

I took the trailer from her with a bow and grabbed a leader from the cupboard, narrating as I went.

'As you'll see, Meg, Megan, Meggie here has what we call a "platter system". To play our little feature we need to make a "loop" on this "ring" using a "leader".'

'Are you going to do bunny ears every time you mention something faintly technical?'

I turned and raised the ears again.

'"Yes."'

I placed the mylar onto a spool and made up the leader on the ring, the sharp edges of the film bouncing between my forefinger and thumb until all that was left was a spinning bobbin.

Removing the rubber band and the trailer's little cardboard label, I spliced the film to the end of the leader and began winding again. Noticing my audience wasn't exactly enraptured by the process, I invited her to have a go.

'Me?' she asked in a faux-ditzy way, putting her hand to her chest and checking the empty room to make sure she wasn't mistaken.

I nodded.

I stepped back and she took my place at the bench.

She held the frame to the light; her photography skills meant no warning against touching the image was needed. She gripped it with just the right level of care and attention.

'Look, it's a mini Mark Ruffalo and he's dancing in his pants!' Her mouth was wide with joy. 'What's the wavy bit?' she asked, pointing to the soundtrack.

'The sound.'

'Aw, mini Mark Ruffalo voice.'

'You like Mark Ruffalo, yeah?'

'Who doesn't?'

It was a fair question.

She wound the film on and almost immediately snapped her left hand back, yelping in pain. I could see the thin, almost paper-cut-like incision in her finger.

'Sorry,' I offered, cringing as I said it, 'I should have warned you, if you grip it too tight, it can burn a little.'

I held up two calloused digits.

'Do you want me to take over?'

She stepped to one side and motioned for me to finish the job, which I did, transferring the ring to the platter.

There's something balletic about lacing up a projector, the twisting and turning and spiralling of the film as it hooks onto rollers and threads through sound drums. At the halfway point of the exercise things slow down as the film reaches the gate. It's fiddly to line up the frames and the sprockets and usually takes a couple of tries and the odd frustrated 'oh shit', 'ah piss' and 'fuck it'. But then the graceful motion commences as the film rejoins itself on the next platter.

A perfect loop of beginning, middle and end.

I stood back, proudly admiring my finished work. Ellie looked on, suitably impressed.

'Now, we have thirty seconds after I push this button to get out of the booth and back down the stairs to our seats. You ready?'

She offered me two thumbs-ups. 'I'm ready.'

I pushed the button.

23

Ellie's pub revelation has led to some much-needed amendments to my opus, *Why Ellie Left*. I know it needs a new heading. An honest one. One that doesn't give a false account of where the blame lies. I think for a moment, doodling on my notepad, as the bus veers around a corner.

I write, *The Reasons We're No Longer Together.*

I am as much a part of the break-up as she, and admitting this is akin to standing up at an AA meeting. What I still don't know is why. I have the suspect. Me. The room. A flat in Clapham. I just need to work out the murder weapon.

The list still stands at four, and the reasons are solid. I think about what's happened in the last few months. There are certainly factors I've been choosing to forget. Whether or not those factors are really my fault, I'm still not ready to say. I'm still not ready for the truth. But the truth is out there.

Just as I'm close to something near a revelation, the passenger next to me sneezes onto my pad. He raises a hand by way of apology and I put the pad into my bag and stare out of the window.

The cosmic forces have aligned to make my last day of work the day after my parents abandon me. I moved from the flat to theirs at the start of September, but in six days' time they leave, and I will be both homeless and jobless. I'm yet to find a remedy for either ailment.

As melancholic as all this might seem, I'm still on my way to the cinema. And so I have hope and happiness. Because there's no such thing as a bad day when that day contains at least one trip to the cinema.

This trip, however, will be tough.

I'm not even supposed to be here today, but Seb gave me the heads-up and added a mini shift to the rota. He knew that as hard as it would be for me, I'd want to be here for this.

★

The massacre – for want of a better word – is already in progress.

Seb has picked Dave for the task, which makes sense as he is easily the best at wielding an Allen key. Billy is already in pieces, splayed out on the floor.

Meg is next.

I enter silently and stand to one side. Dave looks up and nods with reverence. He has the Kevlar out ready, the boxes for the lamp and all the other bits and pieces, to be packaged up and sent to wherever.

'Do you mind if I . . .?' I ask, holding up a CDR.

I've come prepared.

'Usually I'd invoke first starter's privilege with the music, but yeah, seeing as it's you, go on.'

I put the CD in the player and press play on the most suitable song I can think of – the stripped-back AOL sessions' live version of 'Yoshimi Battles the Pink Robots, Pt 1' by The Flaming Lips. Seb enters and stands beside me. He pats me on the back as Dave puts on the protective mask and Kevlar suit. The plastic face shield and bright yellow outfit makes him look like Marty McFly stepping out of the DeLorean in 1955.

'Would you both take a step back? You know, health and safety?'

He's right to issue the warning. The lamps are 7000 watts and filled with xenon. If one went off in your face, you'd be like Mel Gibson in that movie about the guy who didn't have a face.

There's always a heavy thunk when the lamp is released. It feels like Dave is removing Meg's heart. He places it safely in its case and takes off his safety equipment.

Next the lens is taken out and wrapped in foam. Those are her eyes.

The amplifiers and sound system are staying put, her ears harvested for the new digital overlord.

Sorry, Yoshimi. Those evil robots won.

*

Seb and I are down by the fire escape, smoking. All I can think about is the good times we had here, shivering in the winter, hiding from the heat in the summer. Early-morning coffees and light-night beers. Sharing stories of our weekends, seeking advice on our relationships.

I hope we stay friends, but you never can tell. He has kids, a wife, a home, a job. I am zero for four in comparison.

'That was pretty brutal,' I eventually say.

'Made infinitely worse by you naming them,' he points out.

It's a fair cop. I'm not sure the *Toy Story* films would have reduced quite so many children – and grown-ups – to quivering messes if our anthropomorphised heroes were simply known as the spaceman and the cowboy.

'You went for a drink with Ellie, right? Seb asks. 'How did that go?'

The question makes me think of the day after the evening me and Ellie first met. I was so happy telling Seb all about our stupid fun night and he was so happy to hear it.

'Drinks with Ellie? It was bad. *Matrix Revolutions* bad.'

He winces at the utter horror of the thought of it.

I continue, 'She's got a new job. In New York.'

He replies with a single and quite appropriate 'Fuck.'

I use this compassionate cussing as the green light to let it all out.

'Seb, I was such a dick. She was patient and kind and it's a damn miracle she didn't walk out after about thirty seconds of my petty bollocks.'

Seb's nodding does nothing for my confidence. It's far too easy for him to picture what I was like in that pub with Ellie, having seen the stroppier side of me after certain films that shall not be named failed to live up to expectations.

'As she was trying to share this great news, trying to open

185

up to me about stuff, all I could think was "you dumped me, you dumped me, you dumped me".'

'You were together four years. It's perfectly natural for you to feel a little bitter. Her choosing to leave must have been devastating.'

I know deep inside I cannot continue the lie, and so . . .

'But she didn't.'

'What?'

'Choose to leave.'

Seb blinks and his eyes dart about like he's trying to work out the plot of a David Lynch film.

I put him out of his misery.

'She didn't dump me. I mean, she didn't fight for me, but that's not the same.'

'So what happened?'

'I still don't know.'

There's only an element of truth to this.

I think about mentioning how Ellie asked me to go with her to New York, but it was so obviously just a pity ask I decide not to. And then, as if he's poking around my brain . . .

'You could always go with her. A last-minute romantic race to the airport seems pretty Nick Marcet. Maybe a jukebox above your head playing Take That's "Back For Good".'

A reference of a reference. Seb gets me.

'Is there really no way back for you two?'

'I hate myself enough without standing in the way of some amazing job in America. If I'd had this quasi-revelation

186

a week ago, who knows. But now, as Meatloaf famously sang . . .'

'If I do that, I'm an arse-hat.'

I take a deep breath.

'Seeing her did remind me of one thing, though. One bad thing I've ignored for a while. When we were sitting in the pub, I remembered how much I preferred being alone with her behind closed doors, rather than out in public. I could feel people looking at us, even though we're not together. Strangers have always been suspicious of us being a couple. Like, I must be super-wealthy or famous for someone as bog-standard as me to be with someone of her calibre.'

Seb has a look on his face I've seen him give his kids. It's paternal concern but with a hint of 'you-really-should-know-better'.

Without saying a word, he pulls me in for a hug.

He gives good hugs.

I'm gonna miss him when the inevitable death of our friendship rolls around.

24

5 November 2008 – 02.41 GMT
Obama 200
McCain 115
270 needed to win

'Go, go, go!'

We ran, giggling like children, out of the door and down the stairs, trying not to trip over each other's feet. She took the lead but overshot the back entrance to the screen.

'This way! Seven seconds.'

I considered singing Neneh Cherry. I wisely resisted.

Down the screen stairs we ran, taking our seats just as the fake Lacuna Incorporated title card hit the screen.

Eternal Sunshine of the Spotless Mind is one of those rare examples of a good trailer to a great film. Even though it's not used in the film itself, I'll never be able to hear ELO's 'Mr Blue Sky' without thinking of the original promo.

The cast has never been better. It's Carrey's best role,

Winslet's best role, Wilkinson's best role, Dunst's best role. Okay, maybe Ruffalo is better in *Zodiac*, but that's the only one that's even open to debate, and it's hard to subjectively qualify Mr Mark Ruffalo. He's just great in everything.

To back this point up, Ellie did a little *squeee* noise when he appeared on screen in the aforementioned underpants-dancing scene.

And as quickly as it started, the trailer was over, white light shining on the screen once more. I looked up to the port, the dust dancing in the beam from the projector.

'I know we have to go, but there's just one more thing I have to show you.'

★

'It's spectacular,' she said breathlessly.

To be fair, the breathlessness probably had as much to do with climbing the fire escape as it did with the view. But she was right. It was spectacular.

Keep your eyes away from the usual attention-grabbing landmarks – the Gherkin, Canary Wharf, St Paul's – and London will appear differently every time you look at it. I used to come up to the roof every night when I first started in projection, but like the sanctity of the booth, I'd never shared it with someone who wasn't a colleague.

I looked over to Ellie and saw that she seemed less happy, a little pensive and reflective.

'You okay?'

'Yeah, it's just the film. Makes me a little sad, y'know.'

I didn't know.

'But it's a happy film . . . well, a happy ending.'

She looked at me quizzically.

'How so?'

I explained. 'Well, they end up together. They "meet in Montauk". They learn from their mistakes and—'

'But they don't.'

'Don't what?'

'Learn from their mistakes. That's the point. They don't get the chance to. They'll end up making the same mistakes next time, the only difference being they have the knowledge of the memory-erasing procedure, so you'd hope they wouldn't use it again. But Clem is presented as deeply impulsive, so it's possible she could walk back into Lacuna in a few months' time and do it all over again. That's why the ending isn't fist-in-the-air happy. It's cautious. It's bittersweet. At best.'

I pondered her point of view for a moment or two.

'That's a little pessimistic, Ellie.'

'That's kind of the point of the film, Nick.'

I felt this last statement was somewhat patronising, and the mood shifted.

I should have asked her then. I should have asked her, 'Do you believe in true love?' I should have found out if our ethos was aligned, if our philosophy was simpatico. But I didn't. I just waited for the awkward moment to end.

And when it didn't, I forced it to with a diplomatic 'That's what makes a great movie, though, when you can see different things from the person sitting next to you. When you can interpret the same scene a hundred different ways.'

190

'I semi-agree,' she semi-acquiesced.

After a calming pause, she followed it up with a wink and the extremely irritating utterance, 'But on this one, you know I'm right!'

It had been a little over three hours since I first laid eyes on Ellie Brown and I was already emotionally invested in the idea of us, way beyond where any normal person would be. I knew I wanted to be with her and so I knew I had to let little things go. Little things like varying interpretations of cinema's modern classics.

On this first night, at this moment, I persuaded myself there'd be a later date where I could show her how wrong she was and how right I was. I could hold out until we watched the film in its entirety together on our first anniversary. I could happily wait a lifetime to show her that Joel Barish and Clementine Kruczynski were soulmates, that they were destined to be together, that they were meant to be.

I had all the time in the world.

25

It takes me until my final shift to Google Ellie's new job. It's an amazing opportunity and I feel another wave of self-hatred that I prevented her from enjoying it fully. I think about calling her to say sorry, to wish her well and let her know how excited I am for her.

I can't ask her to stay for me. I knew that before, but it's made concrete now, seeing the offices, the reputation the company has, the huge break this is.

Because the digital switchover has been so seamless and everything's now automated, there's nothing for me to do. I pick up where I left the last shift, searching for jobs, typing the word 'film' into Indeed.com and being mortified by the results.

A receptionist role at a small UK independent film company raises my hopes before dashing them on the rocks with the deadly phrase 'must have similar experience'. If Ellie were by my side, she'd be imploring me to go for the internships and runners' jobs, telling me I have to start somewhere and that she'll support me. She'd be telling me to start writing again. To send off short screenplays to local directors. To send features to screenwriting competitions. Get something out there. Even if it's just to get feedback.

But I hate feedback. Unless it's positive affirmation, and I've been in short supply of that for some time now.

The monitor tells me there's thirty minutes left on the last film.

Thirty minutes left on my life as a projectionist.

I'm still battling with my decision to jump before I was pushed.

★

Seventeen minutes left.

We never used to have a constant countdown. Sure, we knew the film's running time and knew when it started, so it was simple maths to work out when it would end, but we never had this ticking clock counting down to the apocalypse.

Before, we'd simply take a look at the platter and estimate how much of the film was left by, well, how much film was left.

The other projectionists are in the pub already for the leaving drinks. Ronnie hasn't worked a shift since the announcement, and Lizzie and Dave have both been informed there's a good chance that by Christmas the full redundancy will be in effect. Seb saw this as the best last chance for us all to get together. I've considered not going, but I fear he would hunt me down like a T-1000 if I didn't.

Sixteen minutes to go.

★

It feels just like any other shift, and yet completely and utterly unique.

Today is the first day of the rest of my life.

Every day was the first day of the rest of my time working in this cinema.

Until today.

Four minutes remaining.

I look at the control panel for the digital automated system, and I look at the hammer lying next to it. It's hundreds of thousands of pounds' worth of equipment and I could destroy it in seconds.

What would my crime be anyway? Criminal damage? What's the sentence for that? A quick online search says six months. I could learn a skill inside. Be the next Andy Dufresne. Minus the non-consensual bum sex.

Dream big, Nick.

One minute.

So, this is it.

There will be no fanfare. No round of applause as I exit the building. I don't even have a box of items to carry as I go. I will get to hand in my name badge and walkie-talkie, though. There's something symbolic in that.

Speaking of. I pick up the walkie-talkie and make my final announcement.

'Mark, it's Nick. Final film is on the credits. I'll be down in five.'

A fuzzy voice responds with a simple 'Yep,' and so I power down for the last time and go to join the others in the pub.

'This is Nick Marcet, last survivor of the *Nostromo*, signing off.'

I steal a film splicer on the way out.

★

My four former colleagues and friends are holed up in the darkest corner of the pub by the back door. You can take the projectionists out of projection, but . . .

When they clock me, the three guys hoot and bang the table, but in a reserved way that doesn't draw too much attention. I can see immediately that Dave and Seb are pretty squiffy. Ronnie is on the soft drinks, because when you smoke as much weed as Ronnie, alcohol is the last thing you need.

Lizzie is dressed up. Which is weird for her. Or maybe it isn't. It's been a while since I saw her in anything other than the cinema uniform of black polo shirt, black trousers and black shoes. I think I decided she was a goth, but I don't think she is. Anyway, she looks nice and like she's made an effort.

As I approach the table, I adopt my best north London accent and say, 'Can I get any of you cun . . .'

Before I can finish the line, a broad smile crosses Seb's face as Dave, Lizzie and Ronnie curse me out. They each hand him a five-pound note as he holds up a pre-scrawled-upon piece of paper saying *Shaun of the Dead*.

I applaud his prognostication. 'Well, can I?'

Seb stands and bear-hugs me.

'Sit yourself down. I'll get these with my Predictable Nick winnings. You have some catching up to do. What'll it be?'

'Quadruple gin?'

He smiles and slaps me round the face, just hard enough to sting.

'That's my boy.'

I take a seat between Lizzie and Ronnie, who places his hand on my shoulder and looks deep into my eyes giving me his best 'I know the secret to the universe' look.

'I know right now things are bad,' he says, 'but this too shall pass. This too shall pass.'

I have no intention of harshing Ronnie's buzz.

'I know, man, thanks.'

'The Chinese use the same word for crisis as they do for opportunity.'

I nod silently for fear that verbal agreement might provoke more sage offerings, and pick up Lizzie's slip of paper with *There Will Be Blood* written on it.

She shakes her head. 'I thought you'd come in and say, "I'm finished." Her Daniel Plainview impression could rival Adam Buxton's, and I find myself laughing for the first time in a while.

Lizzie shuffles her chair closer. 'Seb said you might be looking for somewhere to stay?'

I glance to the bar to see Seb play-fighting with one of the staff, and I wonder when I'll get my drink. I'm not sure I really want to be here sober.

'Yeah, I'm sort of homeless in a few days' time,' I reply.

Ronnie jumps back in. 'You can stay with me, dude, just say the word.'

'Thanks, Ronnie, I'll get back to you. I have a few options

to consider.' The idea of waking up in Ronnie's hotboxed living room for the next twenty years fills me with various kinds of angst.

Lizzie leans forward and whispers, 'If you don't fancy that, one of my housemates moved out last week and we've yet to find a replacement. You're welcome to come and take a look before you decide.'

The proposal doesn't immediately make me think no, so I offer a sincere thank you as Seb returns with my drinks.

'Fucker said I couldn't have a quadruple in the one glass, so I bought you three doubles. That'll learn him.'

I can't see what the lesson is – or how there's any way Seb could be doing the teaching in his condition – but I take the drinks happily. He raises his glass and we all join him.

'A toast! To Meg, Billy, Ingrid, Cary, Jimmy, Donna, Humphrey and Katharine. You fine metal bastards. So long, and thanks for all the film.'

We cheer, and I knock back my first drink.

*

I'm having a really good time. The drinks help, of course, but I often forget how great everyone is.

We've spent the past hour sharing our memories of the best and worst days the projection booth gave us. Dave wins the 'worst day trophy' with his tale of a dropped copy of *Lord of the Rings: Return of the King* on opening night. I still remember running up the stairs to see him flailing around in the spaghetti-like mess of it all.

His MacGyver job to fix it, however, was a work of

architectural genius that would have made Frank Lloyd Wright piss himself. He interlaced the other copy of the film to play across two projectors simultaneously. A fairly standard practice in some cinemas, but not ours, which was ill-equipped for anything so complex. The only downside being he had to physically hold the film for the entire running time.

'Three and a half fucking hours on your back holding that roller,' Seb hollers, to Dave's pride.

I get second place for the day I accidentally added the trailer to *Kill Bill: Volume 2* to a *Finding Nemo* Kids' Club performance. I still have nightmares about putting children off cinema for life.

Lizzie spits up her beer when Dave remembers we referred to the incident as 'Killing Nemo'.

I forget how much fun Lizzie is and how much we have in common. We love the same movies and music, we hate the same politicians and celebrities. And she looks good tonight. Really good. She's got this Diane Keaton in *Annie Hall* thing going on with her outfit. I really want to get her to say 'Well, lah-di-dah.'

Seb's currently in full story mode about the time our former boss, a real creep of a guy, was caught doing something he shouldn't in Screen 3.

'I swear to God, this little usher, she must have been straight out of school, came running up to me screaming' – he adopts a young-girl run and shrill voice – '"There's a man alone in the screen and I think he's"' – he puts the back of his hand to his forehead like a Southern debutante inches from fainting – '"touching himself!"'

The table erupts.

'Christ, what was the film?' Seb ponders, shaking his head, unable to recollect due to his blood alcohol content currently sitting at the level of Richard Burton.

Lizzie smiles. 'You dirty, filthy boys. I bet you've all done it. Alone in a booth after dark.'

A chorus of unconvincing protests is fired back.

'Liars,' she says, shaking her head. 'Well, I have.'

She downs her drink and follows it up with a declaration that she'll be getting the next round, as we collectively pick our jaws up from off the floor. As she makes her way to the bar, the remaining boys – and we are boys in this moment – try to come to terms with the not unpleasant image Lizzie has just left in our minds.

The silence is deafening and only broken by Seb loudly exclaiming:

'It was *Shrek 2*! He was beating it to *Shrek 2*!'

The hysterical nature of the memory is enough to turn him a really wonderful shade of red, as he struggles to breathe.

★

It's way past kicking-out time when we stumble out onto the pavement. The sudden impact of fresh air makes the world spin a little faster.

Ronnie departed a while back, unable to comprehend the ramblings of four drunken people. Before he left, he reiterated that I could stay at his whenever I wanted, but I know of the two offers – litter-strewn stoner flat/lady-filled lovely house – which I prefer.

199

Seb looks like he's one bad decision away from recreating his days of LSD-fuelled car-top running, minus the LSD. So I stir it up. For funsies.

'Hey, Seb,' I say with a grin. 'Remember when you used to be cool? When you used to run across the tops of cars like a sexy Jason Bourne?'

Dave looks up at him with a sense of new-found respect and I know what's coming.

'What do you mean, "used to be cool"?' Seb bellows. 'I *am* cool.'

And in seconds he's on the roof of a nearby Volvo.

'I AM A GOLDEN GOD!'

Dave follows suit, as I knew he would.

'I LOVE THIS TOWN!'

They leap from car to car until the inevitable alarm lets out its piercing shriek and with uber-unfortunate timing a police car comes tearing around the corner.

Seb and Dave flee into the night and I turn nonchalantly in the opposite direction and start walking, the alcohol removing any sense of guilt I might have about my friends' current predicament.

'Should we follow them, check they're okay?' Lizzie asks.

'I really wouldn't worry about it. Dave's pretty fast and Seb's a smooth talker. They'll be fine. Just fine. Walk you home?'

She smiles and takes the arm I offer.

If I wasn't more than a little squiffy, I wouldn't ask this next question.

'Lizzie? When me and Ellie first started going out . . .'

'The pedestal thing, right?' she answers clairvoyantly.

I might get some T-shirts printed with *Nick the Predictable* on them.

'Right. You made a really testy crack about me putting Ellie on a pedestal and how it must be the greatest pedestal in the whole entire world.'

She stops walking and rubs her right thumb across her left wrist.

'I'm surprised it's taken you four years to ask, but yes, I liked you.'

She starts walking again.

'Really?'

This 'really' pisses her off a little and she gives me the same expression Seb offered when I told him about how awkward I felt being with Ellie in public.

She continues as if explaining the situation to a toddler. 'Yes. I really liked you. I don't mean I *really* liked you. I wasn't pining for the one that got away. But, yeah, why not. You fit the bill for a prospective mate.'

'A prospective mate? How romantic.'

'Look, dickhead,' she says with a smile. 'It was four years ago. Don't rub it in.'

'I wasn't. I promise. I'm just surprised, that's all. And flattered.'

'Well, you never were the quickest tool in the box when it comes to human behaviour.'

'If I was, I probably wouldn't be—'

She stops me both walking and talking.

'Homeless, jobless, ra-ra-ra.' She conducts this last bit of her sentence with a flick of the wrist. 'As a word of advice from one member of the sex to the opposite, this woe-is-me schtick ain't exactly intoxicating, if you know what I mean.'

'Sorry.'

She points up at the house we're outside, and for the first time all evening I have an Ellie flashback.

'This is me. Thanks for walking me home. You're a true gentleman.'

'Let's not forget prospective mate,' I joke.

She takes a step up her path and shuts the gate between us, a definitive physical obstacle to let me know I shouldn't be getting any funny ideas.

'You have my number, right?' she asks.

I nod.

'It may be far too soon for you, but any time you want to ask me out . . .'

She shrugs her shoulders, leaves the offer there and exits, no bear in pursuit.

26

5 November 2008 – 03.02 GMT
Obama 200
McCain 115
270 needed to win

The minor disagreement over the ballad of Mr Carrey and Ms Winslet had brought a sombre mood to the walk back to the house party.

I couldn't speak for Ellie, but I knew I had an uncomfortable, spiky-to-the-point-of-being-testy reaction to her 'that's kind of the point of the film, Nick' comment. I think it was the 'Nick'. It's amazing how few times people use your name in conversation. It felt a bit like a disconcerting power move. Or maybe it was just because I thought she'd put a little patronising sass on it. 'Nick' – with a heavy *keh*.

I wanted to bring it up. To let her know I wasn't being moody because she disagreed with me on a film-related matter. I wanted to do this. But I couldn't entirely convince myself that last statement was completely true.

Thankfully she offered an out in a rather unusual form.

'So, how many?'

I looked at her with just enough of a squint to say I wasn't one hundred per cent sure of the question. She looked back with one that said 'you are one hundred per cent sure of the question'.

'Is this because of the girl at the Chicken Shop?' I asked.

'No,' she answered, convincingly matter-of-fact.

'Okay then. Less than there are *Halloween* films, more than there are *Rocky* films,' I said, with neither pride nor remorse.

'Oh.'

I was suddenly unsure whether I'd answered the right question.

'You did mean how many people have I slept with?'

'God, no!'

She said it with such conviction that it took me a while to realise she was teasing me again. It took even longer for the red to drain from my face.

'And you?'

She stopped walking and bounced her head from side to side, each bounce, I assumed, one more lover to add.

'How many *Halloween* films are there?' she asked.

'Ten.'

'And how many *Rocky* films?'

'Six.'

'Put them together then.'

'Sixty!' I wailed.

She stepped back, partially out of offence and partially because the volume of my cry was loud enough to cause a light to come on in one of the nearby houses.

'Why did you times them!?' she shouted back. 'I said add! Sixteen. I've had sex with sixteen people!'

The window where the light came on suddenly opened and a frail octogenarian poked her head out and shouted, 'Good for you, dear, but it is rather late!'

I think Ellie's embarrassment came more from disturbing the nice old lady than the revelation of the number, but I wanted her to feel okay with revealing something so intimate and make sure she knew there was no judgement here.

'Sixteen is a good number. I mean, there have definitely been sixteen people I'd have liked to have slept with. If I was good-looking, like you, and had confidence, I could probably have got to twenty with few regrets.'

'Oh, there were some regrets.'

The conversation was heading in a direction I really didn't want it to, hints of past demons rearing their ugly heads.

'Well, I bet the regret is on their side for not treating you better.'

Her smile helped me know she was back in the present.

'You're sweet.'

'And that sweetness is why I'll be number seventeen.'

She punched me in the arm in the exact same spot as before. But she didn't deny it.

'So,' I asked, careful to not make too big a deal of the thing I knew was going to be a big deal. 'How many of the sixteen were you . . .'

I tried to find a less sugary way of saying it, but Ellie came to my rescue before I needed a thesaurus.

'In love with? I don't really know. I know I was crazy about Oliver. He was my first, y'know.'

I knew.

'I was fourteen. Which some might say is too young. "Some" being the law and my parents. But he was sweet and we were very much crazy about each other. Not many boys would hold your hand in our school. It was not the cool thing to do. But Oliver did.'

'What happened?'

'Nothing really. He went to a different college. That was enough. I cried and cried and cried and cried about it. Locked myself away to silently sob.'

'Why silently?'

'Didn't think it was fair on my folks. Like they still had bigger problems – well, the biggest problem – to cope with.'

Something about this beautiful creature having to go through that romantic pain alone, to protect her parents, made me feel like the worst human being in the world. Even when my nan got ill, like hospital-stays ill, when I was fifteen, I still devoted more time to my relationship struggles than her well-being.

Not for the first time in the evening, I remember convincing myself I did not deserve to be with someone this good.

27

'Hip, hip, hooray.'

Only Andrew the Accountant could make this asinine phrase sound any more vacuous.

'Hip, hip, hooray.'

God, I hate his stupid face.

'Hip, hip, hooray.'

Fuck, fuck, fuck off, more like.

I am surrounded by well-wishers wishing to wish my parents well as they abandon their only son to go off in their pursuit of snow-capped mountains and Sam Neill.

The second worst thing about events such as this is the location. They're always in hotels that haven't been updated since the eighties, featuring a bar that serves two different types of shitty lager, a tacky dance floor covered in a combination of said beverages, a 'disco' consisting of one red, one green, one blue and one yellow light, and carpets straight from *The Shining*.

They really put the fun into function room.

The first worst thing about events such as this is the repetition of questions I have to hear and answers I have to give. Maybe it wouldn't be so bad to say it over and over again if the answers were 'Great, thanks, just bought my own home', 'Yep, maybe we'll be the ones giving them a grandkid next' and 'Well, I should keep it hush-hush, but yes, they have green-lit my feature film. I believe the dumper truck full of money is arriving Thursday.' But trying to put a spin on the fact that I am failing in my aim for both job creation and procreation puts me at a loss for tantalising conversation.

Aunt Tess tries anyway.

'Nicky, my dear, lovely day, isn't it?'

I look out of the hotel bar's window at the grey, overcast sky and wonder what medication she's currently on and whether I can steal some.

'Yeah, real scorcher. How's Ed doing?'

'Edward's great, sends his apologies that he couldn't come. He's moving into—'

She stops herself.

'Things. He's moving things around a lot at the moment.'

Christ, I think. These pills must be the good stuff.

'And Kat?'

'Katherine, ah, she's grand. Just got a great promo—'

She halts her sentence again mid flight.

'Prom, prom, she's got herself a great Proms in the Park ticket.'

It quickly becomes apparent to me that a brief has been circulated to our nearest and dearest not to mention relationships, work or houses for fear that I might completely lose it, set fire to my clothes and run off screaming into the busy high street.

It could be fun – albeit mean fun – making Aunt Tess try and wriggle her way free of talking about three such big topics, but I don't have the energy for it. I've not been sleeping well. I've taken Ronnie up on his offer of a hemp roof above my head – on a temporary basis. His sofa bed is everything I dreamed it would be and less. Not that I'm not amazingly grateful to him for putting me up rent-free, seeing as my options were reduced to his house or the stairwell at the cinema.

Back when I was gainfully employed, I would sometimes daydream as to where I'd live in the semi-unlikely event I'd have to go on the run. I saw myself as a Bruce Banneresque drifter, moving from movie house to movie house using my in-depth cinematic knowledge to lie low in stairwells, back rows and disabled toilets, living off popcorn, nachos and the leftover contents of the slushie machine.

Aunt Tess is still backtracking as I ponder how long man could live off pick 'n' mix alone.

'And so really, while the jobs and houses and relationships are going fine, I'm not sure either of them is truly happy.'

It's such a British thing to do. To downplay the success of your own children to make someone else's feel less shitty.

I look to Gabby for help but she's currently having her stomach rubbed by everyone from our parents' travel agent to the couple who live at number 30, whose names I can never remember. The only downside to Gabby's pregnancy is that it's a constant reminder of how long Ellie and I have been separated. She's due in just under two months, which means it's been three months and two days since the point of no return.

With Gabby indisposed, I beckon my folks over to put an end to Aunt Tess's torment.

'Mum! Dad! Tess was just telling me about how great her kids are doing!'

I know this will fluster my aunt and I feel sort of bad about it, but at the same time I need her to stop.

'I haven't said anything about them doing well!' she protests.

'It's all right, Tess,' my dad assures her. 'Nick's winding you up.'

'No I'm not,' I offer sullenly in one syllable, like I've just been accused of taunting a fellow primary-schooler. 'And if I am, it's only because you've obviously been gobbing off to everyone about how lousy I'm doing.'

Dad huffs, making it abundantly clear he's in a real pisser of a mood with me.

'Well done, Nick. You figured out that we might have told a few people to be careful of what they say around you. What terrible parents we are to think of your feelings in this way.'

Tess gets out her shovel again.

'I'm sorry, I didn't mean to cause any tension. I didn't mean to say that my kids were doing any better than your kids. I mean, Gabby is doing great!'

'Yep, there's only one complete failure here!' I offer.

'Nick,' Mum says, rubbing my back in a signature Mum move, 'you're not a failure. And anyway, I've got some good news. You remember Jim and Paula, from number thirty?' She points them out and they wave in a creepily enthusiastic way. 'They have a job offer for you.'

'They want to harvest my organs?' I helpfully suggest.

'They've started up their own charity business and they need someone to help on the phones.'

She's so happy to be offering me this. But still . . .

'Oh, thanks, Mum,' I say, drenching everyone in sarcasm. 'I always dreamed of being a phone monkey. Do you really think I have it in me, though? Do you?'

'I just thought—'

I go on.

'Speaking words into a phone. Do I need to dial the numbers too? I'm not sure if I can manage that sort of responsibility. I could always ask Katherine and Edward and Gabriella for help.'

This causes Tess to flutter again.

'I didn't mean to upset him. I-I-I—'

'You didn't,' Dad says. 'He's just being a little brat.'

Mum plays peacemaker.

'Why don't we go to the bar and get you a refill, Tess?' she says, leading her away. But before she goes, she turns to my father and hisses, 'This is exactly what we talked about last night.'

She leaves me and Dad chewing our cheeks.

Because he's turned an angry shade of red, I look around for an out and see that Gabby's finally free. I beeline for her, hoping for a friendly face. What I get is an unfriendly one being stuffed with Chinese spring rolls.

'All right there, Hugh Laurie,' I jibe.

Gabby offers a snarl and slurps up a loose noodle while failing to acknowledge my witty putdown. So I explain it.

'Hugh Laurie played Dr Gregory House in the TV show *House*, also known as *House MD*, and you are—'

She picks up a handful of cheese puffs and through them says, 'As big as a house.'

I place the index finger of my left hand on my nose and swing my right arm to point at her, like she's won the star prize. I don't get so much as a flicker of a smile.

'Your references are getting more and more tenuous. And more and more annoying.'

'All right, cranky pants, do you need to eat something?'

She grabs me by my jacket and shakes me hard.

'I've eaten everything, Nick! They catered for fifty people and only thirty turned up. And still all the food is gone because I ate it. I ate twenty people's worth of food. And I'm still hungry.'

She lets go of me and over her shoulder I see Andrew tiptoeing towards us. This should be fun.

'Can I get you anything, my love?' he asks with nause-ating submission. I brace myself gleefully for what I hope will be an incredibly scathing retort from my sister, along the lines of 'How about a bag of dicks for you to suck, you pathetic wimp?'

But instead she gently strokes the side of his face and pecks his nose with little kisses.

'I could murder a kebab,' she replies, in such a soft, caring voice it makes me wonder where the ventriloquist is.

'Of course, my snookems. Anything for you, Nick?'

I shake my head and stare in horror at Gabby as Andrew runs off on his latest meat-based errand.

'My snookems?' I repeat, leaning heavy on the word.

'Don't you dare say a single bad word against that man. He is a god. Compared to him you are nothing but a wretched little dung beetle.'

'Easy.'

'Except dung beetles are useful, whereas what is actually the point of you?'

It's nice to know the real Gabby is there somewhere, but I'm not sure why I'm getting it all to myself. A new tray of food distracts her and so I return to Dad, who's standing alone clutching his pint, still flushed in the cheeks.

'What's crawled up everyone's bum?' I say.

'Do you really want to know? Do you want to know what's up my bum, Nicholas?'

Considering he's changed to a different colour of red, I'm not sure I do. But he continues anyway.

'What's up my bum is that I've dreamed about this bloody move all my bloody life and you know what I've been hearing from your mum these past two weeks? "We can't go now", "It wouldn't be right", "Nick needs us", "He'll never make it on his own."'

Typical Mum. Always laying on the drama. If she'd joined RADA, she'd have an Oscar by now.

My father continues, bursting my bubble by zeroing in on the thing I'm using to excuse my actions. 'I know you think she's just being overly dramatic. But she's not. She cares about you so much. We both do. But you're thirty bloody years old. You need to be able to look after yourself.'

'I can!' I protest, convincing no one.

'It's going to be so hard for her to go with you in this state. And that's what's killing us.'

It's not just the words that sting. I can picture the two of them now, in bed, him just wanting some peace, her fussing and worrying about me until her fussing and worrying gets to him too. Then, as soon as she's calmed down, he'll be the one to start questioning everything.

They don't deserve this.

As much as they wind me up, they've always done right by me. I feel like a 24-carat arsehole, and so I offer my dad a tiny expression of sorrow and, without a word, walk over to — shit, was it Jeff and Pamela? John and Patricia? — and hold out my hand.

'Hi.'

'Hello, young Nicholas, how are you?'

After exchanging pleasantries, I glean a few facts about the job that all seem to make it sound tolerable. I don't need experience. I will be allowed smoke breaks. The office is small, cosy and local relative to Ronnie's flat. And working for a charity offers 'job satisfaction'.

'Oh, and it starts Monday. How does that sound to you?'

It sounds, I think, like I'd better actually learn your names.

★

The rest of the evening is pleasant enough. Mum is positively giddy that I've accepted the job, no matter how many times I tell her it's just on a trial basis. Dad, meanwhile, is just relieved he won't have to cancel his plane tickets or sell a house he's only recently bought on, literally, the other side of the world.

I have another minor run-in with Gabby, whose hormones are still making her a total whackjob. She apologises profusely about the dung beetle comment and I can tell she really wants to get into a conversation about Ellie. Lots of needling questions without a definitive endpoint. I have a feeling she knows about Ellie's job offer, but I can't bring it up in case she doesn't.

I sneak out just before eleven.

Making my great escape, however, I bump into Margaret, Ellie's mum. It makes sense she'd be here. Our parents have been close for a while and often send each other invites to various gatherings. But it still surprises me that she actually said yes. These invites are usually caveated with 'They won't come, but it'd be rude not to invite them.'

'Hello, Nick.'

'Margaret.'

A shiver runs down my back. We haven't spoken since 'Margaret's drunken visit'. 'Margaret's drunken visit' that may or may not have shaped the entirety of the lead-up to me and Ellie ending.

'Margaret's drunken visit' that I know I'm still not ready to truly reflect on.

Yet.

'Are you leaving?' she asks.

'Yeah, early start for me,' I lie. Then, trying not to sound desperate, I blurt out, 'Is Ellie with you?'

'No, she's having a leaving meal of her own. She flies next week.'

'I know.'

'Tonight's just her and her dad.'

'Are you and him still not . . .'

She shakes her head.

'Are your parents inside?'

I nod.

'Okay, then. Best go say hello.'

She ducks to my left and I'm grateful there's no awkward hug.

*

I arrive 'home' to discover Ronnie passed out on the couch, also known as my bed. We have an understanding that if this happens – and it often does – I get his room. It's an okay compromise, but I feel more than a little funny about taking it in turns to share a fifty-year-old's bed with him.

When it came to the decision of where to live next, Lizzie's 'ask me out' speech made it almost impossible to say yes to her previous offer of accommodation. There is definitely a part of me open to the idea of getting to know her better. At some point. Prospective mates, indeed. But the phrase 'crapping where you eat' has never felt more apt.

So while I'm definitely drawn to the idea of Lizzie and me, a nagging voice inside says I need to see out at least one date with someone not on my Facebook feed first.

I get undressed to my pants and T-shirt, grab my laptop and get under the covers.

There are arguably too many dating sites.

A quick Google spits up the big guns: eHarmony, OkCupid, Match. I'm not sure about PlentyOfFish. I get the idea of the title – 'Don't be despondent, there's someone out there for everyone' – but it feels a bit like 'Check this out, we've got plenty of fish.' AdultFriendFinder? Nope, don't click on that. Guardian Soulmates? Bit on the nose, even for me.

I pick one of the big three.

Enter your email address: *whatsmymantra@hotmail.com.*

Choose a username: JonnyBigDick seems quite subtle. Oh, it's already taken. *Try JonnyBigDick12.* My God, there are eleven other JonnyBigDicks? I was just messing around. Maybe this isn't the best site for me if I'm competing with eleven guys who think JonnyBigDick isn't a joke name.

Right, stop talking yourself out of this. I need something clever, but not too clever. Something filmic, obviously, so I can whittle down the ones that don't get the reference.

LassoTheMoon.

That feels subtle enough.

Are you looking to date men or women? I think it might actually be easier if I pick the former, but . . .*Women.*

Age range? Let's not be creepy about this. *25–35?* Seems okay.

About you? Next question.

*About you?**

**This section requires completion.*

Fine. *I'm 30. I'm male* (as you can hopefully tell from the picture). *I live in Clapham Junction, near St John's* (if within a mile is near)*, with a former workmate* (fifty-year-old stoner).

217

I used to be a projectionist at the Royalty, I now work for a local charity (this job is paying off already!). *I love films and storytelling of all kinds, books, plays* (I even went to watch a whole one once), *etc.*

I'm looking for the right person to be with.

For some reason I think about how my parents have lasted this long.

I still believe in love.

28

5 November 2008 – 03.20 GMT
Obama 210
McCain 130
270 needed to win

After what she'd said about her childhood boyfriend holding her hand, all I could think about was doing the same. But even this tiny action – one that would come with low odds of rejection – was too big a bridge for me to cross.

We were a minute away from the street where Tom lived, and I knew that the more time passed without me summoning up the courage to ask Ellie out, the less likely I'd actually be to do it.

'So, yours?' she asked, interrupting my classic self-doubt.

'What's that?'

'Your first?'

'Can I pass on the first? Go straight to the second.'

The reason for me not wanting to go into my first at that

moment was because my first contained too many similarities to Chicken Shop Vicky, as she would henceforth be known. I really didn't want to paint another picture of strong alcohol and feeble fumbling. Truth be told, if it wasn't for the fermentation process, I'd probably have made it to my mid twenties with my virginity intact.

'Cathy. Or Cat, as she liked to be called. We met in the first week of uni. We'd both been to the same V Festival the summer before, and so, as you can imagine, my fate-o-meter went into overdrive.'

'You do seem a slave to Moira.'

'Who?'

'It's a Homer thing,' she explained.

'Like *The Simpsons*?'

'Like *The Odyssey*.'

'Right. Like *O Brother, Where Art Thou?*'

I gave a wink to show I knew more than I was pretending to, but I knew in my heart that I knew less than the wink suggested.

'So . . .' she sighed, trying to get me back on track.

'We lasted a couple of months. It was fun, but I don't think either of us thought it would make it past the first term.'

She offered a look to suggest I was holding back some crucial information. She was right and so I divulged.

'There was someone else that I liked. I know that sounds awful. Before you think of me as a complete and utter bastard, there turned out to be someone else that Cathy liked too. Before the Christmas holidays she'd broken up with me and asked him out. I heard they got married.'

220

'That doesn't sound much like a first love. Was the follow-up the real thing? The other girl you liked?'

'Oh no, that was a textbook unrequited. The list of unrequiteds runs long. To quote Groucho again, I'm not a huge fan of belonging to any club . . .

'. . . that would have someone like you as a member.'

Ellie looked sadder than she had in a long time and I congratulated myself on timing this particular bout of woe so well.

'So, who *was* your first love?' she asked.

I folded my arms and blew out air slowly from inflated cheeks, giving myself a little hug and a moment's hesitation. An instance to reflect before I doomed myself.

'I don't know. I mean, I've loved a lot of women.'

We were right outside Tom's house now. The noise from inside was loud enough to be heard from miles around.

'But we're talking about being *in* love. You can only be in love with someone,' Ellie said, 'if someone loves you back.'

29

'Ellie?' I ask. 'Are you awake?'

She replies, 'I'm here.'

She's lying next to me, but our backs are facing each other.

'Can I ask you how close I am?'

'To what?'

'To losing you?'

She doesn't answer. She never does.

★

I've had a variation of this dream every night since she told me her news. This means two things: 1) I'm still not over her, and 2) I need to stop listening to *Cherry Tree* by The National on loop.

Tonight's dream has an even more lucid quality, because today is departure day.

There will be no race to the gates of Gatwick and no surprise last-reel intervention. For two reasons. The first is because I'm never late and the second is because Ellie flat-out asked me to take her to the airport.

For a reason I still don't fully understand, I said yes.

★

The flight is at stupid o'clock in the morning, so we set off three hours prior to this. I worry about a range of different things on a day-to-day basis, but nothing makes me as anxious as missing scheduled transport.

Maybe it's why she picked me for this particular job.

Like the gentleman I occasionally pretend I am, I help her with her bags and place them in the boot of the rented car. All her possessions for her future life are in those two standard-sized cases.

'You didn't have to rent a car. We could have taken the train.'

I made a promise to myself that I won't journey down memory lane with her, but there's no avoiding mentioning our ill-fated trip to Cannes, and happier times.

'We don't have a great track record with public transport getting us places.'

She grins. 'We don't have a great track record with hire cars either.'

I hold my own grin back, instead fixating on the contents of the cases.

Has she packed any photos of me? Will a ghost of me look down on her new home? Will a photocopy of a happy me sit by her bed and watch over her as she sleeps?

The bags can't be holding much. They can't be holding Sir Isaac Teddington, the cheap stuffed toy I won at Winter Wonderland the day we attempted to tick off each item on my list of 'Mightiest Romcom Clichés'. They can't contain

223

the framed poster of *Cinema Paradiso* I bought us – and yes, I do mean us – when we moved into the flat together. I gave it to her in the 'divorce', but now it unquestionably sits in storage.

There is, however, definitely room for the – ahem – 'toys' we bought together one drunken Saturday night in Soho. But I can't decide whether I hope she's taking them or not. There's definitely not room for me. Unless she jettisons the entire contents and saws me in half.

I must have been staring at the bags a while because Ellie's now behind me checking her watch.

'We're fine,' I assure her. 'We've got two hours' journey time – including an hour leeway for heavy traffic – thirty minutes to get to the terminal and a further hour for check-in.'

Before we get in the car, she touches me on the arm.

'Nick,' she says, 'I really appreciate you taking me. There's no one I'd rather be with today.'

I melt for a moment as I can see how apprehensive she is about all of this.

Don't be a dick, I tell myself. Just for today. Don't be a dick.

She pulls out three CDRs from her coat pocket and tries on a big cheesy smile.

'I made road music.'

*

Every single song she's chosen kills me. Every single song is a Nick and Ellie number. There are songs from our first night together, songs from anniversaries, songs from gigs we went to together and songs from movies we shared. I wonder why she's being so cruel as Sam Beam sings about lovers dying in each other's arms.

The early start and the music choice are making a big dent in my 'don't be a dick' mantra. That she feels such a need to reminisce about good times is the icing on a shitty Victoria sponge. My bearish behaviour will seep through, firstly in the form of monosyllabic answers, and then in lengthy silences. As long as I don't snap, we'll make it to Gatwick.

'Do you remember the first time you met my folks? We were at their house and you pulled out the chair for me to be all romantic and I had no idea what you were doing and I ended up falling on my arse.'

'Yep.'

Instead of this three-letter contribution to the conversation, I want to scream, 'Why? Why are you doing this? Why am I even here for this?'

She tries again, but I bite my tongue.

'And that time you let Snuffles out and she ran into the road and—'

'Uh-huh.'

'Remem—'

I can't take it any more. I snap.

'Can we not do the "remember when" thing?'

She shifts in her seat, knees away from me, her body language more than making up for her silence.

'How's the job-hunting?'

On the back of my dour demeanour and hostile chit-chat, it's an absolute miracle of wonder that this question is asked in a nice manner and not soaked in venom.

'I had a trial week with my parents' friends' charity last week.'

'That's brilliant! I mean, good for you.'

She sounds genuinely pleased for me, but I guess it's just a relief that she doesn't have to feel guilty about leaving me at my absolute lowest. I'm one floor up from the dank basement of life.

'It's not working for the Associated Press or anything, but it's okay, it's a steady pay cheque.'

We share the smallest of smiles and look at each other. As I turn my attention back to the road, I can feel she's still looking at me.

'If you've got a solid wage, you can use your redundancy money to come visit me. See where those *Ghostbusters* did their busting? Visit Leon and Mathilda's Italian restaurant? Take a trip to Montauk?'

I shrug, and out of the corner of my eye I see her look away. I think about telling her that that restaurant has been torn down, but her fake invitation has me riled. Riled enough to offer something I've been holding back.

'I've got a date tomorrow night, actually.'

I look over and realise the word speechless has never been more apt. Her mouth is open and she's trying to form vowels and consonants, but they simply won't come.

'She seems nice. Her name's Mia. We're meeting at The Ferryman.'

'Our pub?' she squeals in a way that I know she instantly regrets.

I try not to appear smug.

'I think it was around a few years before we got together.'

She shakes her head and shuts her eyes and I wonder if she's going to cry and why the hell I'm choosing to hurt her this way. The date is true but I've completely invented the meeting location for maximum impact.

I can't make her love me again but I can make her hate me. Is that the plan? Is that where this is heading?

'What happened to your ten per cent rule? We were together four years!'

I can't help myself.

'Three years nine months actually.'

'Still, ten per cent of,' she does the simple maths quicker than me, 'forty-five months is four and a half months. It's been just over three since you had your emotional breakdown!'

What is she talking about? What's that supposed to mean, my emotional breakdown?

I present her with a guttural noise that's meant to signify she should proceed; instead she offers me disdain and a pretty hurtful laugh. Not that I can really protest at the jab with the mean shit I'm flinging.

'No, please,' I patronise, stretching out the word in another attempt to inflict pain, 'tell me all about my emotional breakdown.'

If she bites her lip any more, there'll be blood.

'So the last few months you've been fine, yeah? No problems at all with us?'

'I was happy,' I mumble.

She very nearly hits the roof, causing me to swerve a little. I get a honk for my driving.

'Happy! That was you being happy. I'd hate to see you

miserable, Nick. Moping around all day. Never doing anything. Never making plans. If I strapped a satnav to you for the last month we were together, I'd have seen a straight line from our house to the cinema, our house to the cinema. There's more to life, you know.'

'What about you?' I yell back. 'You were pretty bloody miserable too those last few months.'

'Oh, I'm sorry that my parents' break-up left me a bit glum.'

I forget that Ellie is the queen of sarcasm.

'You could have tried talking to me about it.'

She shakes her head.

'Believe me, I tried. But recently – and I do swear this is only recently, Nick – any offer of comfort from you is just like your ten per cent rule, completely full of shit.'

A wanker in a white Audi flies up behind me and flashes his full beams. I pull into the slow lane and switch off the music so we can spend the rest of the journey in silence, bar the dull hum of the M25.

*

I park up. We unload the car. I take one suitcase, she takes the other. We wait for the bus alongside a group on a stag do. If I had to guess, I'd say Magaluf. The one in the mankini must be the groom-to-be. I wonder as to their reaction if I were to just break down sobbing, begging for Ellie not to go.

I pray to God they don't notice us, and for once my prayer is answered.

*

228

'You got me here on time,' Ellie says.

'It's one of the few things I'm good at.'

For some reason known only to airport staff, once we're in the terminal, our car fight is forgotten. It's as if the glow of the departures board has a calming effect. Or perhaps it's the realisation that we are moments away from being three thousand miles apart.

'We've time to spare if you want to grab some tobacco at the duty-free,' she says with a slightly smug Sherlock look about her.

'How did you know?'

'That you were smoking again? Just a hunch. Confirmed by your last sentence.'

I forgot about that trick. She's so good at that trick.

'Do you know if your date smokes? Sorry, I shouldn't have asked that. I'm sorry. Please. Forget I said it.'

She's flustered, and Ellie rarely flusters. This does not bode well for either one of us keeping it together.

'You gonna watch the plane take off?' she asks.

I nod.

'Not gonna run down the gangway knocking over security guards, are you?'

I shake my head.

'Good. Because after 9/11 they will just shoot you.'

I smile as she takes her case from me.

'Well, Nick Marcet.'

'Ellie Brown.'

We both have the same wet eyes and crack in our voices.

'Oh shit. I nearly forgot,' she says as she swallows the

emotion and reaches into her pocket to pull out another CDR. This one is labelled *A Fresh Outlook*.

She continues, 'These are songs you haven't heard before. New songs. New bands. Unless of course you've discovered them in the last two months, in which case, well, here's a CD of some bands you recently discovered.' Her voice goes higher and higher as the tears stroll down her face.

'Thanks,' I say, wiping snot across my sleeve. 'Any standouts?'

'I think you'll like Kishi Bashi. He's a lot of fun.'

We're both barely intelligible to other human beings, but we understand each other's every word.

'Kishi Bashi, right,' I say.

'Yeah, he has an album, *151a*. It's really good.'

'I'll check it out if I' – I hold up the CD as a prop; it's already wet with salty splashback – 'like the song on here.'

To anyone watching us it would look as though one of us is dying. Maybe even both of us.

'Sack off your date and come with me,' she says.

'You know I don't like disappointing people,' I reply.

'Exactly,' she says, and we both laugh through the mucus.

She throws her arms around me. I close my eyes and I am no more.

When I finally open them, she's gone.

It could have been so different.

Third Intermission

When it came to life's surprises — the ones delivered on an insignif-
icant Tuesday when your guard was down — both the Boy and the
Girl would find themselves wanting. The Boy would do his best to
muddle through them but fail to give them the respect they deserved.
The Girl would grow heavy with the weight of them, unwilling,
and often unable, to share the load.

It started with a text.

Nick was standing in line at his second favourite cinema in Leicester Square when his phone buzzed. Rather than wait for Ellie and queue together, he'd made the call to get their seats, letting her know she could find him later. It was a move Ellie found increasingly irritating.

The text read, *I'm late.* Which seemed to Nick an oddly literal thing for her to write, considering he could tell the time and she wasn't where she'd said she'd be.

He wrote back, *I know. It starts in 5. I'm not missing the start. I missed the start of* Meet Joe Black *and didn't understand why Brad Pitt was being so weird.*

Immediately she replied with *You tell me that every time you think I'm going to be late. And I don't mean I'm late. I mean I'M LATE. Can you meet me at the Costa on the corner?*

★

Five minutes later, they were sitting in the corner of the coffee shop, hushed voices and hunched shoulders over two gargantuan Americanos.

'How late?' Nick asked, burning his lip on his drink.

'Over two weeks.'

Ellie alternated between chewing on the corner of the nail on her left little finger and the one on the right. Nick was trying his best not to display his excitement bubbling under the surface.

'It could be stress,' he said. 'I've heard stress can delay a period, and work has been tough for you recently. Quite a few late nights.'

She shot him a death stare and he knew what was coming.

'Work hasn't been tough. And I've worked late once in the last fortnight. If you want to have a conversation about my job, we can, but please can we sort the possible pregnancy thing first?'

Nick raised both hands in surrender, sipped at his coffee and burnt himself again.

'Just let it cool!' Ellie yelled loud enough for the other customers to turn and look at them.

Once the stares had faded, Nick put his hand over hers and whispered, 'I'll go get a test. You can do it in the ladies.'

Ellie took a deep breath and put her other hand on top

of his, making a hand sandwich. Then she removed both hands and tore at her cuticle with her teeth.

'Thank you.'

★

Alone in the corner shop, Nick let his mind wander. What did it mean if she was pregnant? Would he propose? Would it be a boy or a girl? Would it have her skin and his ears? Having never seen *Star Wars*, would Ellie cotton on if he tried to name the baby Leia or Han?

The possibility of being a father wasn't something Nick had considered. He and Ellie had been together two years and he was certain that she was the fabled 'One' he'd been looking for all this time. But a dad. Was he ready?

His best friend Seb was. He'd been in his mid twenties when he and Tracy got pregnant with Sally, now two. They hadn't batted an eyelid. Just got on with it. And sure, Nick thought, Seb wasn't quite as much fun as he used to be. He needed a pass to get out of an evening, and had knocked the drugs and booze on the head, but there was no doubt he was more content with life. Even if his lack of sleep left him as tightly wound as a miniature slinky.

Nick found the medicine aisle and scanned the shelves for a pregnancy test. Each one claimed to be '99% accurate'. He'd know soon enough. He picked up one that had 50 per cent off, reasoning that if they were all pretty much infallible he might as well save some pennies now.

He counted out change and handed it over at the counter with a proud grin.

★

Ellie still hadn't touched her coffee. She felt bad for shouting at Nick but was glad he wasn't there now. She needed time to think. Time to get her head together.

In this together head she compiled a list of pros and cons.

Pros. I love Nick. He'd make a great dad. Someday.

The cons list was longer. I'm not ready. I don't know if I ever will be. Nick's definitely not ready. Despite what I've just told him, work is stressful. But I love my job. This could change all that. We can't afford it. At all. London with a kid? No way. I'm not ready. I'm not ready.

She repeated this last phrase to herself as he re-entered the café. And that was when she saw his elation, that happy nervousness that sometimes defined him. She knew she'd have to act fast before he got too carried away, before he started to imagine this perfect family life that they'd never be able to live up to. He wouldn't be capable of imagining the sleepless nights, the fights that came with the exhaustion, the anxiety she was convinced he'd suffer trying to make everything 'just so' when a child was the epitome of volatility.

Instead, he'd fixate on holding his child for the first time. The first steps. Taking it to their first cinema trip.

She hated this role. Having to be the unromantic, level-headed one. The killjoy.

'Here you are,' Nick said cheerily.

'Nick.' She matched his eyeline and even moved her head to make sure he couldn't break contact. 'Before I do this. If it comes back positive, that doesn't mean we're having a kid. It just means we have some stuff to think about. And a pretty big decision to make. You okay with that?'

Nick nodded, but if you asked him honestly, he'd admit he shouldn't have.

★

The walk-in clinic was packed with the ailing and the infirm. The fact that it was a Sunday in Soho only made things worse, with the inclusion of those who had partied much too hard the night before. The thirty or so little plastic chairs – alternating red and blue – were all taken, so Ellie and Nick joined the perimeter of the great unseated.

The twenty-minute queue to get an appointment at some time in the next three hours had done little to help their mood. Their silent walk to the clinic, once the little plastic stick had confirmed Ellie's fears and Nick's hopes, was looming large. Ellie had decided it best to consult a medical expert to find out their options straight away. The fact that this was not a conversation had riled Nick to the point of complete dead air.

Now he pondered whether to ask Ellie if she'd like to play their fictional casting game, in which they selected members of the public to play shitter versions of famous characters, either from films, books or history.

It felt a little too much like he would be trying to distract himself for the benefit of himself, so he kept quiet.

'Crap Gordon Gekko just walked in,' Ellie said, with a half-smile.

The feeling of relief washed over Nick like a wave.

'Did you see Huw Edwards' much worse brother earlier?' he replied, safe in the knowledge he was definitely allowed to join in.

'I think that actually *was* Huw Edwards.'

'Oh. Christ. Either the BBC News make-up department is worth every penny of the licence fee, or he's in a bad way.'

Ellie made a 'yeesh' face.

'How long did she say it would be?' Nick asked.

'At least an hour. If you want, you could go for a wander. I'll be okay.'

'It's cool. I'm good here.'

He took her hand and scanned the room for another Shit Celebrity™ as a thirty-year-old Mick Jagger wannabe stepped out of the gents.

'That one's too easy,' Ellie said.

Their attention quickly moved to a young couple, younger than them, with a baby girl in their arms. Nick and Ellie could hear the infant wheezing from across the room, and variants of the same thought went through their minds, and those of countless others in the waiting room.

Please, let her be okay.

That thought, however, hadn't made its way into the brain of a middle-aged City boy wearing chinos and a shirt with rolled-up sleeves, who, when he saw the frightened parents take their rightful place ahead of him, loudly complained that he'd been waiting for ages.

Ellie was in no mood for this.

'Wind your neck in,' she snapped, much to the man's displeasure and the surprise of Nick, who had always made it his life's mission to avoid confrontation of any sort.

'What did you say?' came the angry reply, the man sitting up and forward for the first time; after spending most of his time slouched with his legs wide open, as if his crotch needed to see all the world had to offer.

'You heard her.' A booming male voice came from behind them. 'And while you're at it, you can stand up too. You've been in that chair all morning, huffing and puffing every time someone gets seen before you. There's elderly people and pregnant women who have been too polite to say anything. I'm not that polite.'

Nick and Ellie looked with awe as the hero of the hour hovered over the City boy, making it abundantly clear that if he didn't stand now he wouldn't be able to later.

Meekly, but with a pissy lament of 'This country', the villain moved and took his place in the corner of the room. Ellie and the hero exchanged complimentary nods as an octogenarian took the offer of the seat and a smattering of applause filled the room.

'Where did that come from? Wind your neck in?' Nick whispered, grinning.

'Weeeeell,' Ellie replied, 'the guy was a prick.'

Nick reached for her hand and wrapped his fingers in hers.

'Our baby is giving you superpowers.'

She closed her eyes and shook her head before throwing his hand off and storming out. City boy piped up again as Nick followed her out. Nick pretended he didn't hear him.

*

Outside in the wet spring air there was five feet between them but much more distance. His apologies hadn't been accepted and neither had her requests to be left alone. So

239

now they stood in a stand-off on either side of the double doors as patients entered and exited the building.

Eventually, after a lungful of calming cool air, she stepped towards him.

'Nick. I don't want to have a baby with you.'

He didn't respond and she stood her ground. She knew this scenario and well understood that the more she said, the more he'd have to work with and the more he could come back on. As cruel as the words might sound without a follow-up, it was the best way forward.

Eventually he responded. 'Ever?'

Ellie looked at him warmly and put her arms around his back, drawing him in.

'Just not now.'

It was his turn to pull away, to break their connection, and she could see by his expression that he had an angle ready. She waited patiently for the bus to hit.

'Okay. I get that right now might not be the best time. But this has happened now. The last thing I'm being is all sanctity-of-life, I get that it's just a few cells on from being nothing, but . . . but it isn't nothing.'

'I'm not getting into a debate about what it is and what it isn't. This isn't something I'm taking lightly. Nobody does. Nobody wants to have an—'

'What about Gabby?'

Ellie rubbed her temples, more to access some well of strength than anything else.

'What about Gabby?'

'You know she and Andrew have been trying . . .'

240

'Jesus, Nick. Are you kidding?'

'They could give it a great home.'

She felt like screaming. She felt like hitting him. There was an anger inside her she hadn't experienced before. A compelling desire to rip him apart and rip apart anyone else who had the audacity to presume to tell her what to do at this precise moment. Her blood flew around her veins and she could feel her forehead tightening.

Breathe, she told herself. Breathe and count.

In her head, she counted back from ten thousand. It was a technique she'd learnt in counselling as a child. Nine times out of ten it worked, and her senses soon returned, her pulse slowed.

'I'm going back in now,' she said, composed. 'I'll talk to the doctor about what the next stages are. If you want to join me, you can.'

Her offer was genuine but came with no physical placation. No hand on his. No soft, gentle stroke of an arm. Nick watched her walk back inside and berated himself privately, unsure of how he'd let his intentions be so misunderstood.

★

The junior physician's name badge said *Dr Hannah Swift*, and she had lived up to her surname in the taking of Ellie's information. Blood pressure (a little high but nothing to worry about), weight, height, family history. She'd asked Ellie to pee on a stick not dissimilar to the one she'd taken into the Costa coffee loos, and Ellie had obliged.

The stick sat in a little bowl on the desk while they talked. Nick sat to Ellie's left, participating only by listening. The quick-fire Q&A was as fast as what had gone before.

'When was your last period?'

'From the start or the end?'

'Whichever you can remember.'

'I think it ended around about the eighteenth of May?'

Both Nick and Ellie silently worked out the mathematics, and neither was particularly pleased to put the figure at around six weeks.

'Any soreness? Tenderness?'

Ellie shook her head as Dr Swift took a quick glance at the test. She did a double-take at the results and then looked back at Ellie.

'Is there something wrong?'

'No,' the doctor replied as she rooted around in a nearby drawer for a second stick and a second opinion.

'Would you mind giving it another go? Just to be sure.'

As Ellie stood to find the toilet, Nick handed her a bottle of water and she thanked him. It was the first exchange they'd had in over half an hour.

'Should I?' he said, motioning to the door Ellie had just walked out of.

'No, it's fine. You can stay. She'll only be a couple of minutes.'

Nick rested his head between his hands and surveyed the posters on the wall. As a man prone to differing degrees of hypochondria, he let himself imagine he was afflicted with each and every disease and illness the wall was warning him about. The possibility of a new life had left him contemplating his own. Not that these were new thoughts. The closer he got to ending his twenties, the more time he spent on his own mortality and what, if any, his purpose here was. He never got close to a conclusion.

'It's not planned,' he suddenly blurted out, to the surprise of both himself and the doctor. 'This. It's . . . it's all a bit of a shock.'

She turned from her computer and gave him her full attention.

'It's my experience that these things rarely are.'

'Except for the ones who are trying . . .'

'Isn't that how life works?'

'When you least expect it.'

Ellie returned with the third piece of plastic she'd urinated on that day and handed it to Dr Swift, who studied it with scepticism before asking, 'Do you have the box for the test you did earlier?'

Nick found the cardboard packaging from his bag – it was his plan to add it to their shoebox memories – and handed it over.

Within seconds Dr Swift made her assessment. 'You're not pregnant, Ms Brown.'

Ellie's entire body inflated, her shoulders lost their hunch and she let out an audible gasp of relief. For the first time that day her frown was banished. It took Nick seconds to let the frown back in the room.

'Those things are ninety-nine per cent accurate. What happened?'

Dr Swift held up the box and read from the side. 'Use before 22 April 2010. It's only a couple of months out of date, but sometimes that's all it takes. Over-the-counter tests work by using a chemical to pick up the hCG level in your bloodstream, but in an out-of-date test the chemical may be faulty.'

If Ellie grew in size at the sudden reversal, Nick shrank. This thing that hadn't really crossed his mind before was now all he could think of. The injustice of it all. What if they'd been really trying for a baby? What damage could this false information bring? As so often, he was focusing on the wrong thing.

'Thank you, Doctor,' Ellie said, standing.

Nick, usually a courteous young man, slunk out of the room after her, not saying a word.

★

The baby elephant in the room lasted until the following Sunday evening, when Nick rode upon it like Tarzan.

He and Ellie were nestled on the sofa, a blanket over their knees, watching a BBC nature documentary, when he turned to her and said, as emphatically as his hesitant nature would allow, 'I think we should try for a baby.'

Despite the fact that she was very much enjoying the sights and sounds of David Attenborough's dulcet tones over footage of elephants, Ellie picked up the remote control and pushed the red button. The screen went blank and she turned to him.

'Nick.'

'Just hear me out. I'm not saying we should start hanging

up ovulation charts and texting each other whenever you get a twinge . . .'

'What the hell is a twinge?'

'I'm just saying maybe we put the pills in the cupboard and wait for the chips to fall where they may.'

Having known this was coming at some point over the last seven days – and truth be told, she was impressed he'd held out this long – Ellie was well prepared for the following conversation.

She joked about him 'just wanting more sex' in as light-hearted a way as she could to put him at ease. She maintained physical contact and kept her body pointed towards him, predicting he'd interpret any hostile non-verbal communication as an attack on the foundation of their relationship. And she made it abundantly clear, in no uncertain terms, that no, she was not ready for a child.

It wasn't long before he acquiesced.

'Okay. I understand. Last week was just a roller coaster of stuff I hadn't even considered, and then when it started to look like . . .'

She offered a sympathetic nod.

'I just couldn't think of anything better than me and you having our own family. And I'm twenty-eight now—'

'If you say "and you're almost thirty", I may make it impossible for you to ever have children.' To back up her statement, she put her hand between his legs and grinned menacingly.

'I was going to say, I'm twenty-eight and finally starting to think about this sort of stuff. Don't you?'

She took her hand from his groin and placed it on the side of his face.

'I don't see a life to come in which I don't have a family,' she said. 'And I don't see a life to come without you.'

It was all he needed to hear and to know. If he gave it the right length of thought, he'd come to the realisation that what really worried him was the lack of a foreseeable future. Now that she had given him no doubt, he was content again.

He kissed her for it, warm and deeply.

'We could have a little practice,' he said, 'for when the time comes?'

The mischievous glint in his eye and the smirk at his own corny line was enough to melt her, and she climbed onto his lap. Because she loved him. She was *in* love with him. She was thankful she'd found someone who made her happy. Who she wanted to make happy.

And, she thought to herself, she could always catch Attenborough again on iPlayer.

The idea of a new life, a step into true adulthood, offered a lesson for the Boy to learn. But it was another one he missed. He still hadn't yet understood that the Girl — however susceptible to the occasional bout of regression — was not a girl. She was a woman. While he was still, very much, a boy.

End of Third Intermission

30

5 November 2008 – 03.51 GMT
Obama 210
McCain 130
270 needed to win

My confession was eating away at my self-belief.

Part of me wanted to step into a time-travelling fridge, go back ten minutes and make up a story about how my first love was a beautiful tattooist who took off to Mexico with my cousin. And how after this loss, I'd been in love a thousand times before and knew exactly what I was doing when it came to relationships. I was just unlucky, that was all.

Not clueless.

Just unlucky.

The paranoia ran deep. Was she acting oddly because of my disclosure? Or was I acting strangely because I was worried about her acting oddly? It was a vicious circle, twenty-seven years in the making.

'Shall we?' she asked, opening the gate in a spirited way, allowing me a brief respite from the most nagging of doubts.

We'd spent the last few hours in the fortress of our own solitude, and so it was with an abrupt force that the reality of other people re-entered our lives. I was lucky, in hindsight, that 'Hunky Bob', aka Nathaniel, was the first person we should have contact with.

As we walked up to the house, he was on his way out. He met our happy little dispositions with a sneer, and as he opened his mouth to speak, I hated him instantly.

'So there you are,' he offered by way of a snarl. 'I've been waiting all night to speak to you.'

Ellie looked over his shoulder at the front door, so tantalisingly close.

'There's really nothing left to say,' she replied.

I considered reaching for her hand, but I bottled it on the grounds that it might have come across like a possessive move.

'I really don't like the way things have been left between us,' he went on.

She glanced over at me, hoping to subtly indicate to him that this was neither the time nor the place for a heart-to-heart.

The subtlety was lost on him.

'Hey, friend, do you mind?'

I put my hands up in mock surrender, hoping to win cool points for my nonchalance versus his intensity.

I said to Ellie, 'I'll just have a quick smoke,' and walked back down the path, positioning myself ten metres from their conversation, easily close enough to hear even their hushed whispers.

'A smoker? Really?' he asked in as condescending a manner as I'd ever come across.

I could almost hear her rolling her eyes.

'Are you drunk?' she asked.

'You know I don't drink. And even more so given that tomorrow's the CrossFit finals. I told you about them. I don't think I'll smash the planking if I get myself squiffy the night before.'

He snorted at his own joke and it was all I could do not to yell out, 'You're a bloody planker all right.' A planker to think this wonder woman had any concern for his earthly troubles. While he worried about the physical, she was on a higher plane. He could never entertain her with his triathlons and chin-ups.

The music inside the house kicked up a notch and my audio zone was suddenly compromised. I could just about make out something to do with 'Tough Mother' and how he had already bought tickets for her. I took a sneaky glance over to discover she was not impressed by this information, and made a mental note not to ever listen to this band in her presence.

The next bit confused me further. 'Tough Mudder's the best. A real feat of human endurance.' Were they a hardcore metal outfit? Did he need to pronounce 'mother' like that? Was Ellie into extreme music? Was he? I doubted the answer to any of these questions was yes.

It was in the searching of Nathaniel's flaws that mine were highlighted. I didn't care that he was taller and better-looking and – let's be honest here – had the potential to be

251

a much more 'pin you up against the wall', 'throw you onto the bed' animalistic lover.

That didn't bother me. Much.

What bothered me was how sure I was he was governed by the same petty shit I was. That he was probably defined by the thing he loved. In his case, sweating. That he was undoubtedly guided by his penis. That he was desperate to have someone 'pretty' on his arm. That he was self-involved and anxious about how people viewed him. That he was man. And I was man. And neither of us would ever be as good as she deserved.

'And him?!' I heard him yell.

He pointed one of his big tree-trunk arms in my direction. I wondered if I could get close enough to put my cigarette out in his eye before he stomped on me.

'It's got nothing to do with him. I only met him tonight.'

My heart sank a little. But then she continued.

'But if you must know, in the few hours I've been with him, he's made me smile more and laugh more and feel better about myself than you did in two months.'

He scoffed and peered through the darkness at me.

'But . . . but look at his weedy little arms.'

I heard Ellie's exhalation of exasperation from my safety zone.

'Look,' she said, 'you don't like me. I don't like you. Why is it so hard for you to accept that we should go our separate ways?'

As he contemplated the answer, a silence fell between them. I'd had my back to them for eavesdropping purposes, but now I turned, wanting to see his face. He looked lost.

Her direct question and sympathetic tone had caught him off guard, and the truth came to him in a flash.

'I don't like losing,' he managed.

Then I heard the last words he'd probably ever hear her say.

'Let's just call it a draw then.'

She turned away and started to walk into the house. His mood seemed to thaw and I made my way up the path to join her.

He offered his hand and said, 'Nathaniel.'

I took it and said, 'Nick.'

Ellie glanced back to see what was going on, and so I held up my cigarette.

'I'll meet you inside, if you like. I'll just finish this.'

She smiled and nodded and left, and at that moment Nathaniel's demeanour rapidly changed. In a second, he went from passive to snarling. He leant close to my ear to whisper:

'You really think she likes you?'

I blew my smoke at him, knowing full well the move could get me pulverised.

'Who knows?'

He mock-laughed and then did a little unintended cough from the fumes.

'Fine. Waste your time. I'm just trying to be helpful. I've known her two months, and from what I've learnt, you wouldn't last a week.'

I fluttered my eyelashes.

'Okay,' I replied, my short answers designed to piss him off as much as possible.

I could see it was working, as he blustered, 'I'm not even bothered.'

I offered one final 'Okay' and turned to enter the house.

He hadn't squashed me into a small cube.

But the damage from his opening gambit was still done.

31

Sack off your date and come with me.

  Sack off your date and come with me.

  Sack off your date and come with me.

  Sack off your date and . . .

'You okay, Nick?' Paula asks, peering from behind her monitor.

'I'm tip-top, thanks, Paula.' I assure her, as I hit the delete key and expunge from existence the written ramblings of my inner Jack Torrance.

Jim plonks the fourth cup of tea he's made me this morning down on my desk. I have a caffeine headache but don't feel comfortable enough to turn down beverages yet.

My new workspace is almost as small as my old one. The closeness certainly has the familiarity of being unable to hide my current state of mind from my fellow workers. Four desks all banked together. One for Paula, one for Jim, one for me and one for a potential future employee.

'Up to anything enjoyable this evening?' Jim enquires.

'I have a date, actually,' I say. I don't know why I add the word 'actually', like people won't believe it if I don't.

'Ah, young love,' Jim says. 'Dinner and a show?'

'Dinner, not sure about the show. We'll see how dinner goes.'

My work phone rings for a callback and I'm grateful of the distraction. As lovely as Jim and Paula are, and they are quite lovely, I know that any in-depth discussion of this too-soon date could easily talk me out of it.

I launch into my script over the phone.

'Hi, my name's Nick Marcet and I called earlier on behalf of Christian Aid.'

The rest of my conversation points are laid out in front of me on two sheets of A4 paper. The trick is to make it seem like each word is spontaneous, even though it's meticulously worded to tease the most money out of potential donors. It may be for a good cause, but there's something sinister about the preprogrammed nature of it all. Something unbecoming about the trigger words designed to elicit sympathy.

Anyway. It works.

I hang up the phone.

'Another twenty pounds a month,' I tell Jim and Paula with a little pride, knowing they'll clap like seals. I think they're genuine in their love for this job and so I play along, becoming a caricature of a happy employee because I need the pay cheque and there are worse jobs out there.

'Excellent work, Nick. You're doing great,' Paula says.

She doesn't realise this is the first thing I've excelled at in a while, and the realisation of that is more than a little depressing.

'It's your scripts, really,' I offer. 'You should write me one for my date tonight!'

And we all laugh.

In a way that makes me die inside.

My Dinner with Mia

A one–act play by Nick Marcet

A young couple have just been seated at a trendy gastro pub in south London. Drinks and food have been ordered. The place is expensive but not white-tablecloth expensive. The food, when it arrives, is served not on plates but on chopping boards, however impractical this may be.

NICK (30), curly brown hair and puppy-dog eyes, sits opposite her (possibly early twenties), jet-black hair in a Louise Brooks bob, the deep red lipstick a striking extra touch.

There should just be two people at their table, but they are joined in a few moments by an uninvited third.

NICK: I think one of us is supposed to say something like 'This is a bit weird, isn't it?'

MIA: What is?

NICK: Just, y'know, the whole internet dating thing.

Mia offers a tiny shake of the head and a shrug.

MIA: Online dating makes about a hundred and twenty million pounds a year, and that's just in the UK, so . . . no I don't know if I'd call it weird, exactly.

257

NICK: Do you work in business, then?

MIA: No. I just read. I thought your ad was pretty clever, the little interjections about the truth.

NICK: I didn't realise I'd left them in.

MIA: That's funny. See, I could tell you had some smarts.

Nick plays with the edge of the tablecloth.

NICK: So, Mia. That's a nice name. Do people make lots of jokes about you being missing in action?

MIA: Nope.

NICK: Well, it's just, Mia is . . . Never mind.

Our third diner enters. She is a figment of Nick's imagination that only he can see. She is lit by a spotlight, but only when she speaks.

IMAGINARY ELLIE: Are you gonna start singing Emmy the Great songs to her now? 'Her name was either Mia or M.I.A . . .' Is that sort of what made you pick her?

Nick ignores the unwelcome presence and continues talking to Mia.

NICK: Do you go on a lot of these?

MIA: Is that supposed to be a compliment or an insult?

NICK: No. Neither. It's just, this is my first.

MIA: Date?!

NICK: Internet date. I've been out with people before, a few, actually.

IMAGINARY ELLIE: Ooooh. A few. Nice brag.

NICK: Where are those drinks, huh?

Nick looks around for the waiter.

MIA: How come you've never done internet dating before?

NICK: It wasn't really that big a thing when I was last single.

I mean, I knew of it and knew people who'd done it, but I suppose I thought I was above it. In a way. That's not to say it's lame or . . . It's just four years ago it wasn't the done thing, I suppose. Erm. Yeah, so, I was in a relationship for four years.

MIA: Riiight.

IMAGINARY ELLIE: Oh look, she elongates her words like I do. It's meant to be.

The waiter arrives with the drinks. Nick downs his before the waiter has a chance to get away.

NICK: Sorry, just mega thirsty. Can I get another?

IMAGINARY ELLIE: She's cute. A bit young. Didn't you set an age limit on your profile?

MIA: That's some quick drinking. So, how long have you been split up?

NICK: It was ages ago.

IMAGINARY ELLIE: Not even ten per cent. But sure, Nick.

MIA: I wouldn't just be a rebound fuck then.

Nick almost chokes on his drink and Imaginary Ellie shifts uncomfortably in her imaginary seat. Mia appears excited by Nick's embarrassment.

MIA: You look so uneasy. Does your generation not talk about sex?

NICK: What do you mean, my generation? How old are you?

MIA: Old enough.

Mia takes a big gulp of her drink.

MIA: You see, my generation eats a—

Nick erupts into a fake coughing fit to drown out Mia's comment, then excuses his outburst to the middle-aged couple at the next

*table who almost overheard her remark. Nick stares at Imaginary
Ellie, more than a little scared.*

MIA: Lighten up. I'm just fucking with you.

She follows this up by mouthing, 'Or am I?'

MIA: But seriously, you do like sex, right? I don't want to
be wasting my time.

NICK: Yes, I like sex. But I'm looking for something a little
bit more . . . y'know.

MIA: Like kinky shit?

IMAGINARY ELLIE: Is she for real?

NICK (*to Imaginary Ellie*): Are you?

MIA: Am I what?

NICK: Nothing. I was talking to someone . . . I meant, I'm
looking for something more. Like I wrote in my ad, I
still believe in—

MIA: Ha! I thought that was a joke. Like an ironic statement
or something to take the piss out of all those sad old
romantics looking for their 'one true love'.

IMAGINARY ELLIE: I think I might go. This is pretty devastating to watch.

NICK: You don't believe in all that?

MIA: What, romance and teddy bears and walks in the rain?
No, not really. Do you?

NICK: I used to.

IMAGINARY ELLIE: Oh Nick.

NICK: So why do internet dating? Why not just go to a club?

MIA: No thanks. They're just full of pissed-up horny bastards.
I don't mind you being pissed up and horny, it's just nice
to witness the progression, you know what I mean?

NICK: So what made you choose me?

MIA: I dunno. Like I said, your ad was different. And your photo. You are pretty fit.

NICK: Really? Thanks. I guess.

The waiter arrives with the food.

NICK: Thanks. Looks great.

Nick begins to cut up his food, but bits fly off the edge of the chopping board.

NICK: What's wrong with plates? I mean, they seemed to be doing a pretty good job for a few thousand years.

MIA: What's that?

Nick looks up to see Mia on her phone.

NICK: Don't worry about it.

Nick puts down his cutlery. The couple sit in silence for a moment.

NICK: Look, I'm not sure if I'm ready for this. I don't mind if you want to leave.

MIA: Okay. We can go back to mine if you like? I think we could have a lot of fun.

Nick's eyes widen as he chokes on his food, gasping for breath. He swallows just in time. After he composes himself, he looks over to see if she's serious.

MIA: Like I said, you're pretty fit.

IMAGINARY ELLIE: You're on your own, Romeo.

And like that, Imaginary Ellie is gone.

End scene.

There's an alternative reality in which I immediately take Mia up on her very generous offer of uninhibited, no-holds-barred, mind-blowing sex. But I don't want that. I mean, one part of me does, but that timeline is not for me. I have nothing against anyone who enjoys a one-night stand, but my own past experience has proved that that way lies dollops of self-hatred and confusion and mess.

Also, there's a pretty big part of me that thinks this entire dinner is being filmed and that I'm going to be the lead on the next series of *To Catch a Predator*.

'Gabby,' I whisper.

'Why are you whispering?' my sister replies.

'Because I'm in a toilet.'

'Why are you in a toilet?'

'I'm on a date.'

'Why are you on a date? I thought you had a ten per cent rule?'

I almost drop the phone into the toilet bowl.

'Can everyone give me a break about the ten per cent rule?'

The toilet next to me flushes and I realise whispering is doing me no favours.

'I need your help, Gabby. My date is being crazy forward. She's basically asked me back to hers for sex and we haven't even had pudding yet.'

'Pudding. Who still says pudding?'

My sister's ability to wind me up has never been, and never will be, matched by anyone. And in this particular instance my gears are being ground to nothing.

'Gabby!'

'What? What do you want me to say? Have sex with her. Don't have sex with her. It's really up to you.'

'I'm pretty sure it would be a terrible idea.'

'Then say no!'

Her screech causes so much feedback on my phone that I have to give my ear a little rub with my open palm.

'But what if she's the last person who ever wants to sleep with me?'

'Nick.' There's a softness to her voice now. Either that or I've got tinnitus from her screaming at me.

She continues, 'My sisterly advice is that you are not ready for this yet. Go back out there, eat your pudding and bid her a fond farewell.'

This feels like great advice, and for a second I actually convince myself I'll take it.

'Thanks, Gabby.'

'No worries, pudding boy.'

She hangs up before I can come up with a pithy retort.

Right, I think to myself. I'm obviously not going to take Gabby's advice and do the grown-up thing. Because if Mia makes one more suggestive comment, my willpower isn't powerful enough to resist.

What are my options? Escape through the kitchen à la *La Femme Nikita*? It's a strong move but riddled with potential accidents of the third-degree-burn kind. The ventilation shaft, like John McClane and countless others? I don't think I have the upper-body strength for that.

Then I see it. The open window. This should be no problem.

It's a good job I still have my phone in my hand when I realise I haven't paid for the meal. Skipping out and leaving Mia to stump up for my half-eaten pie doesn't seem fair.

263

I dial the restaurant's number.

'Hi, yes . . . This may seem a bit odd, but can I pay for my meal over the phone . . . No, no problem with the service, it's just I had to leave early and . . . Great, thanks . . . The long number across the top? 5550 6700 0923 1121 . . . April 2013 . . . 195. Can I leave a tip? . . . How does twenty per cent sound? Actually, make it thirty . . . Yes, thank you . . . Actually, before you go, could you do me one big favour? . . . Great . . . Could you send someone down to help me out of your toilet window? I seem to have got myself a little stuck.'

32

5 November 2008 – 04.01 GMT
Obama 273
McCain 141
270 needed to win

The cheer that erupted when I walked through the door was deafening. And for the shortest of moments I was sure it was meant for me and Ellie, a hooray to celebrate our new-found togetherness.

'Yeah! Way to go, Nick and Ellie!'

'Nick, our hero! You communicated effectively with someone you're attracted to!'

'You did it, dude, you managed not to freak out all evening long!'

My answer to the last one was: oh so nearly.

In the short space of time between opening the front door and entering the living room, I even convinced myself that Tom had arranged this euphoric reception specially to make me feel like the king of the world. Then I remembered he would never do anything nice like that if he knew people would find out. And then I remembered what the point of this party was and what people were actually cheering for.

The ticker tape below David Dimbleby's chin read *VICTORY FOR OBAMA*. California's fifty-five electoral votes had turned the map blue.

The two Americans – the ones who had a legitimate reason to be celebrating this hard – had taken control of the sound booth (Tom's laptop and speakers) and were blasting out some Springsteen. The crowd was hollering back 'Working on a Dream' in the most off-key way possible. I had the feeling Tom would delete that from his iTunes library quite quickly tomorrow morning.

Ellie was waiting for me just inside the living room.

'Fucking hell,' I yelled, eloquent as always.

'I know!' she whooped back. 'This is a really good party and you made me miss it.' She gave me her best shit-eating grin as she waved to a friend across the room.

'I have to say hello to someone, but DON'T GO ANYWHERE.'

As she left my side, the hole was instantly and rather spookily filled with Tom, sipping from a bottle of Jameson.

'All right there, Nick?' he asked, both of our eyes on Ellie and her friend.

'McNulty,' I said back, eye-checking his booze.

'I see myself as more of an Omar type.'

'Course you do. Good party. Did we miss anything while we were gone?'

Tom surveyed his kingdom, filled with shiny, happy people. I could see his cold heart thawing.

'Just a load of hope-filled sycophants whose optimism will turn to abject misery in four years when Obama fails to live up to any of the promises he made and they vote in Jeb Bush.'

'Ha. You said Bush.'

'I knew there was a reason we were friends.'

He passed me his bottle and I took a mini swig. Clear minds would be needed from this moment on.

'So, Ellie Brown?'

I nodded casually.

'You can't pull off the casual nod, Nick,' Tom informed me. 'You're not a casual person.'

'What am I then, you big Irish drunk?'

'You're one of them, aren't you,' he said, gesticulating wildly to the room. 'One of the hopers. One of the dreamers. One of those "things with feathers". Except for you it's not about an idealistic world or unworkable, over-simplistic international relations. For you it's as simple as one day a boy will meet a girl and all will be well.'

I nodded, this time less casually, because between the front door and here I'd made a decision. A stupid, stubborn decision. But it was my decision, nevertheless.

I'd like to say that Tree-Trunk Neck's words hadn't affected me. The truth was, while sticks and stones might break my bones, it was words that tore me apart. And his words had cemented an instinct I'd been fighting since I'd watched Ellie let him down far more gently than he deserved.

While it was the most painless break-up I'd ever witnessed,

I didn't want it to be me some day. And I was sure it would be. I could not be good enough for her. I didn't believe it was better to have loved and lost if you never found someone better.

My decision then. That future didn't have to be mine.

I could keep tonight special. Perfect, almost.

I could walk away at any time.

33

Needless to say, I did not see Mia again.

She did, however, see me, being helped backwards through a sixty-centimetre by thirty-centimetre window. She laughed possibly harder than I'd ever seen anyone laugh and I was quite pleased I'd at least been able to give her this gift. She could dine out on it for months.

There was one dicey moment in Windowgate where the sticky-uppy bit of the window lodged firmly in my belly button and I was sure I'd end up disembowelling myself on the bathroom floor and thus claiming the number one spot on the Darwin Awards all-time funniest deaths list.

Ultimately, the only thing bruised was my ego, and there wasn't much of that left to bruise.

*

I made a rule: if I'm ready to start dating, I won't check Ellie's Facebook page to see what she's up to in New York. That rule lasted a whole day.

She updated her location to *New York, New York* two weeks ago, but still hasn't posted a status since she landed. Her last was the day before we went to the airport, when she wrote: *Until we meet again, Mrs England.*

But – and here's the big update – she has three new friends. Two female.

And one male.

I worked out that one of the females went to the same school as Ellie and moved to New York a few years ago. It makes sense they'd connect. The other woman is an account manager for Associated Press. New workmate. That too checks out.

But Brad Bright? Who the fuck are you? Why is your account set to private? Why can't I find out anything about you other than your superhero name? What are you hiding, Brad?

I'm staring at my phone trying to ascertain key information from his tiny, blurry profile picture – which is piss-wankingly arty – when Gabby calls, giving me a fright due to the proximity of my face to the screen.

I compose myself and open with 'All right, Arbuckle?'

To which Gabby instantly replies, 'When this baby comes out of me, I'm going to beat you to death with its placenta, then we'll see how many more fat jokes you make.'

Her inflection on 'fat jokes' gives me pause.

'You know, if I thought they actually upset you, I wouldn't make another,' I say as a check-in.

A warmth seeps into her voice.

'Of course, you big softie. But that's nice of you to say.'

'I am nice. Now, to what do I owe the pleasure?'

The warmth is replaced with sketchiness.

'Nothing. Just wanted a chat with my little bro.'

There's a long pause as Gabby tries to work out how to steer the conversation in the direction she wants. The pause is long enough for me to pull open my laptop and bring up Brad Bright's profile again, all lens flare and blue sky.

The pause doesn't end, so I say, 'Come on, Gabby, out with it.'

And out it comes.

'I spoke to Ellie. Last night. *She* called me, in case you think this is a betrayal.'

I don't give even the briefest of expected pauses.

'It's fine,' I say, with such indifference I almost convince myself. 'You guys were pretty good friends. I wouldn't want you not to speak.'

'That's very grown-up of you.'

The surprise in her voice makes this a competitor for back-handed compliment of the week.

'So, who's this Brad Bright guy then?' I spit out.

'Who?'

'Ellie's new boyfriend.'

'She doesn't have a new boyfriend.'

This is good enough for me. Gabby has never been a bullshitter, and for that matter, neither has Ellie. But I'm not yet ready to lower my guard, because I know Gabby has an ulterior motive for her call. What it is, I have no idea.

'How did the rest of your date go the other night? Did you get out with your pants still on?'

'More or less,' I say, omitting the toilet window ending

271

for fear of that becoming the go-to story of every family gathering for the next twenty years.

'So you didn't . . .' She fake-clears her throat as a way to imply the words 'have sex with her', a coy move for someone with a docker's vocabulary.

Is that what this is? A fact-finding phone call for Ellie? My hackles are up again.

'No. I didn't. You can tell your friend that next time you speak to her.'

'You know it's possible for two women to have a conversation with each other without it being about a man?' Gabby retorts.

A lengthy silence follows, which I can only presume is because Gabby's trying to work out a way to undercut her last comment by saying they did talk about me. Because let's face it, if they didn't, why is she calling me now to tell me they spoke?

'Okay,' she finally admits. 'Your name came up. A couple of times.'

Before she can get to what she wants to talk about, I feel my stomach tighten and the hurt and shame and regret of the last year rises up inside me and I just want off of this call and to stick on a DVD and shove pizza and Pringles into my face with the wild abandon of a latter-day Orson Welles.

'She says she misses you.'

'Then she should have fought for me.'

'You didn't exactly make it easy.'

'Yeah, I forgot I was the one that moved out first and then flew three thousand miles away.'

And the award for greatest use of righteous indignation in a telephone call goes to . . .

'Are you still not going to take any responsibility for how you've been this year? I don't know what happened in that head of yours, but—'

'That's right. You don't.'

'So tell me!'

I go silent long enough for Gabby to let out a long, frustrated sigh. I use it as my cue to put an end to a conversation I was never in the mood for in the first place.

'Next time you speak with her, tell her I said hi and I'm really happy for her and Brad.'

I flip the phone shut without saying goodbye in the way people do in movies but never do in real life.

Then I flip it open again.

And text Lizzie.

34

5 November 2008 – 04.09 GMT
Obama – 273
McCain – 141
270 needed to win

Tom was growing impatient. 'I'll ask again. So, Ellie Brown?'

I took my time responding; it was, after all, a complex question with a multitude of different answers. I'd started to make a list of reasons to justify the One Perfect Night plan.

1) Who am I kidding?

Like Nathaniel said, 'You really think she likes you?' I mean, she might do a bit – the kiss, the jokes – but not enough to see us as equals, to see someone she could actually be with. Which brought me to point number two.

2) I foolishly told her I'd never been in love.

This seemed like the most legitimate of points. And the one I thought Tom would be able to sympathise with. That little revelation meant she'd always view me as someone who was naive about relationships. She'd put every little communication hiccough down to my inexperience and eventually it'd be too much for her.

3) She mentioned how she wanted to move to New York.

Even at the time, I knew this third reason was clutching at straws. But who was I to stand in the way of her dream? What if we did start seeing each other and then she flew away after a couple of months? I didn't think I could take that kind of rejection.

If I told Tom the truth – I had three reasons why I couldn't see a future that didn't end in tears – he'd frogmarch me over to her and force me to make arrangements to see her again. Which would totally go against the One Perfect Night plan.

I settled on the middle ground between truth and lie.

'She's very cool. But I think she's just getting out of something with some guy.'

'She isn't,' Tom replied, directly. 'I mean, she went out with a guy – his name's Nathaniel and he's a bit of a poser – but she never had any feelings for him. It was her decision to end it and she's certainly over it. So, you like her, then?'

This combative questioning was unnerving.

'Yeah, like I said, she's pretty cool. I just don't know if . . .'

'If she likes you? Haven't you just spent the best part of the night with her? Didn't she just tell you not to go anywhere?'

What was his game?

'I'm not sure we have that much in common, though.'

'Yeah, you do. She loves movies, has great taste in music. She's smart, funny. Super-talented and driven.'

'Well then, we don't have that in common.'

I quickly began to realise there was more to Tom and Ellie than met the eye. He had an insight into her world I hadn't expected him to have. I felt a bit like Han Solo on Endor when Leia started banging on about how much she cared for Luke. Please let Ellie be his undiscovered sister, I thought. No. It didn't matter. I was never seeing her again after tonight.

'So,' I prodded carefully. 'You and Ellie?'

'You're as subtle as a sledgehammer and only slightly smarter. No, Nick, I do not fancy Ellie.'

It was almost time for another *phew*.

'Then why the interest?'

He turned to face me and took a long sip of his whisky.

'I know you think of me as this hard-hearted, cynical Tory whose only goal in life is to return England to the Victorian age, when poor people worked in factories and rich people lived in mansions.'

'I don't think that, Tom.'

I did sort of think that.

'But when it comes to my friends, I only want the best for them. And you, young Nicholas Nickleby, are my friend.'

The jubilant atmosphere must have got to him. He was one step away from a hug, and I'd never seen him physically embrace another person in my entire life.

He continued, 'When my sister first told me about Ellie, I thought of you. When I met her, I thought I was meeting the other half of you. I invited her here tonight hoping that you'd have the courage to speak to her. Which, unbelievably, you did. I'd sown the seeds of your "you-ness" but I

276

don't think I'd fully prepared them for how "you" you can be. Because right now, as you stare with puppy-dog-eyed devotion at a girl you like, who unless I'm mistaken – and I'm never mistaken – likes you back, you seem to be looking for the best way to sabotage things. Am I right?'

I stayed silent, annoyed and impressed at how right he was. In turn, he became even more serious, resting his hands on my shoulders and looking me earnestly in the eye.

'Whatever you're planning on doing or planning on not doing. Don't.' He paused and tried to sober up enough to make this advice seem irrefutable. 'Or do. Do.'

I nodded, even though I was sure he was wrong and I was right.

The One Perfect Night plan was still a go.

'For now, my friend,' I said, 'I just have to hope this party never ends.'

He shook his head and stepped back.

'And when that doesn't work?'

His fatalism was not going to get me down, however correct it was.

'You think you'll throw another one in four years' time?'

35

I will admit, the timing of my drinks with Lizzie could have been better.

While not exactly the date of what would have been mine and Ellie's four-year anniversary – that was two days ago – the occasion is just as monumental. Because tonight is the night of the 2012 presidential election.

The night is young, though, and there's a long time before any of the results will start coming in. The TV in the corner of the pub isn't yet doing rolling coverage, and for that I'm thankful. Tom is, of course, having another party, in the hope that America will, in his words – definitely not mine – 'undo the damage they've done with their silly throw of the dice'. So yes, my decision to ask Lizzie for a drink tonight of all nights is largely due to wanting a distraction.

But.

It is equally due to the fact that I've been thinking about Lizzie a lot recently. I have to move on, and the Mia fiasco has taught me that internet dating might not be the best move for someone in my condition.

Lizzie – and I don't mean this to be an insult – is a safe pair of hands. She has said she likes me, so the large part of my brain that hates me can shut up for an evening. We share very similar interests, so conversation should be a doddle. Finally, as she comes through the door, I'm reminded that she is objectively an attractive, smart, cool and switched-on woman, and that I should be very grateful she has asked me to ask her out.

I stand and we awkwardly hug. A little more matey than datey.

'How have you been?' I ask.

'Good. Work is weird but we're—'

I hold up my index finger and she stops talking, aware of what's coming.

'Rule number one. No previous work talk. I'm not sure my tender heart could take it. Rule number two—'

She interjects, 'No previous relationships talk.'

We shake hands and grin.

'Wait,' Lizzie asks. 'Does no work talk mean no film talk?'

'God, no!' I exclaim. 'I wouldn't have a clue how to get through a day, let alone a date, without talking movies.'

At this she beams.

'Great. Because last night I saw a film you are going to adore!'

*

Despite the witty repartee and extremely enjoyable company, my eyes keep drifting to the TV behind Lizzie's head, and on the third time of asking she calls it out.

'Is there a football match on?'

She turns and clocks what's been taking my attention.

'Oh, right, the election.'

Then the penny drops.

'Right. The election. You and Ellie . . .'

I put my hands up in surrender.

'I know. I know. The timing is really weird, but if I can confess something . . .'

She nods.

'This is a much nicer distraction than I would have thought possible. I think I really needed it tonight.'

She places her hand over mine and offers a compassionate 'It's all right' before standing and picking up our empties.

'Let's distract you properly then. Same again?'

As Lizzie makes her way to the bar, I take out my phone and see four messages from Seb. Not wanting him to get too carried away with the idea of me and Lizzie, we decided not to tell anyone about our date – including Seb – who is now doing his best to persuade me to come to Tom's election party with poorly spelt messages such as *There ain't no party like a NckNick party.*

'Lining up your next date?' Lizzie asks as she hands me my fourth drink.

'Yeah, I'm such a player. No, it's Seb. Trying to persuade me to join him at the party.'

Lizzie sips a little nervously at her drink and we share our first uncomfortable silence.

'I absolutely wasn't planning on going,' I state for the record. 'But. We can. If you want?'

Her eyebrows rise in surprise and she starts nodding enthusiastically but without actually stating an opinion. It's like she's gone mute and I'm having to decipher her desire through the movement of her head.

'You would like to go?' I ask gingerly.

Her head makes tiny, fast movements from side to side, but this time with contradictory words falling from her mouth.

'Yes. I mean sure. Yeah,' she replies. 'If you want to?'

If you were to put a gun to my head and ask me to tell you categorically whether Lizzie wants to go to the party or not, there would be a fifty-fifty chance of my brains being splattered up the pub wall.

I try one last time.

'Honestly, it's completely up to you. I'm happy to—'

'Great. Then so am I.'

That settles it. We're going to the one place I absolutely don't want to go.

*

Ben Folds is singing about how weird it is to be back here. And he's one hundred per cent correct.

It's not the first time I've been to Tom's since November 2008. Because he was a mutual friend, and played such a pivotal role in our eventual coupling, Ellie and I were invited over for many special occasions, including Christmas drinks, the occasional summer BBQ and the 2010 general election. The last was a big win for Team Tom and the Libertarians.

Tonight, however, feels the worst kind of weird.

Compared to 2008, this party is lacklustre at best. There

are half as many people in attendance as four years ago, and a quarter of the buzz. Maybe it's because it can't ever be as historic as Obama's first, maybe it's because the whole night seems to be such a foregone conclusion. Romney's '47 per cent' comment, in which he managed to write off just under half of all the people who could vote for him, seemed to most commentators enough to make him a dead candidate walking.

And also, he's really, truly boring. It's often said that America votes for the guy you'd most like to have a beer with, regardless of policy. Mormon Romney isn't anyone's idea of a drinking buddy.

My drinking buddy, Lizzie, is way more fun than Mitt Romney.

I'd like to think that my arrival sparks a bit of life into the party, but it's all Lizzie. Within five minutes of our arrival she's already endeared herself to Tom by giving him a legitimate debate about church and state, and started a game of beer pong with a bunch of Tom's weed friends.

But still. But still.

I know Ellie's in America, but I'm convinced I'll see her here, the place where it all began. Tom and Seb see me constantly checking the door from the other side of the room and make it their duty to intervene before Lizzie notices my wandering eye.

'I like her,' Tom says, just the right side of lecherous.

'Yeah,' I reply. 'She's very likeable.'

They exchange a look of concern that they make no attempt to mask.

'Don't get carried away,' I tell them. 'We're just seeing where it might lead. And yes, of course I realise that this is the weirdest place for a first date, but she wanted to come. At least I think she did.'

We watch on as Lizzie bounces another ping-pong ball into a red cup to a chorus of cheers. She accepts the applause and makes her way back to the three of us, two beers in her hands.

'I won you a beer,' she says, passing me one of them.

'I thought the idea of beer pong was to get your opponents to drink?' I ask.

'It is. But that seems like a stupid way to play. So I made up my own rules in which you get more beer if you score more.'

Everyone nods, suitably impressed.

'This isn't quite like 2008, is it?' Seb says, without realising he's saying the exact wrong thing.

I gloss over it. 'I still remember your reaction to Obama's speech, Tom.'

'Shut it,' Tom says.

'What's this?' Seb asks.

I look at Tom and see him reddening.

'Nothing.' I grin.

The grin is quickly eradicated when I spot a familiar face. Nathaniel.

It makes sense that he's here, but his face is still an unwelcome one, a ghost of elections past.

'Fancy a smoke?' I ask Lizzie.

*

As Lizzie is kissing me in the back garden of Tom's house, metres from where Ellie and I helped a girl with spew in her shoe, it hits me like an ACME load.

I can see our entire relationship.

It begins with good films and great sex and reminiscing like we did tonight about shared happy times. She'll be understanding of the fact that I've just got out of a long-term relationship and give me the time I need to deal with that. I'll move in almost straight away, because circumstances dictate I must. As the early months go by, she'll start to become bitter that the ghost of Ellie is hovering *Rebecca*-like over our heads. But she'll ultimately accept my false declarations that I've moved on.

Then there's the middle section, where we comfortably segue into the day-to-day pleasantries of being with someone we like just enough. The cinema will become a constant reminder that we do have a lot in common, the thing we tell ourselves is proof that this is right, even when part of us knows it isn't. I'll meet her friends and I'll consciously try to get them to like me – because I must be liked – while subconsciously I'll try to alienate them, in the hope that my not being the perfect prospective friend-in-law is enough to drive a wedge between us.

In the end, there will just be misery. Because I know I'll try to make it work. Because I'll do anything to not be the bad guy. And by doing so, I'll inevitably become him. With each day that goes by, I'll become more and more like Michael Myers. The next Darth Vader. Harry Lime, Nurse Ratchett and Tommy DeVito all rolled into one.

She'll ask me if I'm happy, and I'll say, 'Sure.'

She'll ask me if I love her, and I'll say, 'Of course.'

I'll lie about how I feel until the day she says something

like 'Don't you think we should start thinking about being a family?' or 'Can you imagine what we'll be like as an old couple?' and I'll finally, quietly mouth, 'No.'

Did Ellie leave because she couldn't handle the pain of pretending to love someone?

I pull my head back and look, as Lizzie's smiling, happy face sees my expression and turns to one of worry.

'I can't,' I say.

Her new expression is strange. If I had to define it, I'd say it was a mixture of hurt rejection and smug satisfaction. Like she knew this was coming but took a shot anyway. She shakes it off and steadies herself. Projecting an aura of being cold and composed.

'I'd rehearsed a speech ready for this moment, if it happened,' she says. 'But it feels a bit self-indulgent, if I'm honest. I could give you the edited highlights if you like?'

I nod.

'I knew this would be a gamble. That it would be too soon or feel too wrong or too whatever. But I thought it was worth a shot because, like I said, I like you. You fit the bill . . .'

'. . . for a prospective mate.'

'The fear I had was that I might never be able to make it special enough. Big enough. That short of employing Burt Bacharach to serenade us through our early courtship, you'd always struggle to justify the normality of two friends hooking up. You'd never be able to persuade a brain and heart that wants total romance. Any minor blip, any fluctuation from the Hollywood narrative and . . .'

I look at my feet and then back at Lizzie.

285

I need her to know this isn't any failing on her part, but I'm pretty sure she doesn't want or warrant a half-hearted 'It's not you, it's me' speech. This wording will be crucial.

'You know, none of this is you,' I say. 'I accept full responsibility for my failings as a human being. Nothing that you've said is wrong. I am trying.'

'But your system is just still so full of Ellie.'

'I don't know if it ever won't be.'

She offers a sympathetic smile, takes my hand and interlocks my fingers with hers.

'That, Mr Marcet, is up to you.'

A shadow moves across the window above us, and I'm pretty sure it's Seb stalking us to make sure all is okay.

It isn't okay. We both know it never would have been. Now that it's done, there's a relative okayness in that.

'How about we move past prospective mates and just try for proper mates for a while?' Lizzie offers.

'That sounds like a very good idea,' I agree.

*

Lizzie makes her excuses and ducks out early. I'm pleased she does.

Even though we ended things on far more amicable terms than I thought I was capable of, it was still pretty awkward. Seb and Tom both tried to make her feel at ease, but she decided to go before the first state was declared.

Now she's left, I have one mission on my mind. To get as paralytically drunk as I possibly can. Because I have the hand–eye coordination of a Cyclops with the shakes, I decide the beer pong game is a good place to start. I approach two strangers with dyed red and green hair respectively – I think it's a nu-punk thing – and ask them, 'Who's up for a game?'

'All right, Grandad, we'll play you.'

'Grandad?' I reply incredulously. 'Fuck off. How old are you?'

They reply in unison, 'Nineteen.'

Their first shot hits the target and I drink.

'Then how do you know Tom?'

I shoot and miss.

Again in unison, 'We sell him weed.'

'So how old are you?' Green Hair asks, as Red Hair makes another shot and I'm forced to neck a further half-pint of lukewarm beer.

'Thirty.'

My ball bounces off the rim of a cup and hits a couple on a nearby sofa making out. They don't even flinch.

Red continues, 'So you totally could be a grandad. Think about it. If you had sex when you were fifteen and then your son had sex when *he* was fifteen . . .'

He would have a point if I'd lost my virginity anywhere near my fifteenth birthday, but I'm not going to point out how wrong he is.

'Smoke, Grandad?' Green asks, pulling out a joint of Camberwell Carrot proportions.

'Don't mind if I do,' I say, realising once these words have left my mouth that I'm more than a few sheets to the wind.

As I'm about to inhale, Tom arrives in the nick of time to snatch the psychotropic substance from my fingers.

'You two, scram,' he shouts. Red and Green do as they're instructed.

'Hey! Quit harshing my buzz,' I say in my best dude-speak.

Tom's face is the dictionary definition of schoolmasterish.

'When was the last time you smoked weed, Nick?'

I shrug. 'Dunno, about five years ago.'

'Then you are ill-equipped to handle the recreational drugs of the new generation.'

'Can I have some gin at least?'

He scolds me like an errant dog.

'No. You know how you get on gin.'

★

It's easy to shake the host of a house party, and about five minutes after I find the gin, I find a new group of friends – a bunch of politiphiles sitting in front of the TV. I don't recognise any of them so consider it safe to join. I do this with a simple nod of the head.

The nod is returned and I take my seat between a guy in a Radiohead T-shirt who looks like a young Steve Buscemi, and a girl with a Welsh accent who clearly models herself on Lena Dunham.

'This is great, isn't it?'

My opening pronouncement is met with half-smiles and a great British discomfort.

'I mean, this guy.' I point to the screen as footage of Obama meeting and greeting the voters of America plays out. 'He's amazing.'

Welsh Lena tries to help me out.

'He really has done some extraordinary things in just four short years.'

Mini Buscemi joins in. 'Imagine what more he could have done without the Republicans stopping him at every turn.'

I slap him on the leg in a far too familiar way and take his indignation up a level.

'God, you're right. The fuckers. Why can't they just let him be him? Sticking their noses in. Ruining something that could have been really great.'

A sober me would know my exuberance is over-the-top, but drunk me thinks I'm a massive winner.

'Save my seat,' I say to my new friends. 'There's something I need to do quickly.'

*

I swear to God I know that Richard is the last person I should be messaging. I was just scrolling through old messages from Ellie and I came to one that had her dad's number in it. I can't even remember why she sent it to me. I think her phone had died and she wanted to keep in contact. Ready access to my phone is a big mistake in my present condition. Forget fingerprint identification; the next iPhone should come with a breathalyser.

I've sent six messages and I'm halfway through my seventh when Tom and Seb appear around the corner together. That I'm sending angry messages to Ellie's father rather than to Ellie should tell me something. But I'm in no state to say what that something is.

The first thing Seb does is take my phone away from me. This is immediately followed by Tom snatching away my drink and sniffing it to ascertain its potency.

'This is gin! I warned you about the gin! You're not good on gin, Nick.'

'But it makes me feel like I'm in *Nineteen Eighty-Four*,' I slur.

'Why would that be a good thing?'

'Who have you been messaging, Nick?' Seb asks, trying to both get the conversation back on track and limit the damage I've done.

'Doesn't matter, does it? I've sent 'em. Too late, my friend. The joke is on you.'

I snatch my phone back and peg it away from them as fast as I can.

*

Back in the house, under the warm glow of the TV and David Dimbleby, I rejoin Welsh Lena Dunham and the young Mr Pink. My reappearance isn't met with the applause I was hoping for, and the gin bottle I'm carrying is eyed suspiciously.

'So, where were we?'

Silence.

'Gin? Anyone?'

I offer my bottle and it's politely declined.

'That was it. We were talking about the Republicans being absolute shits. Do you remember 2008?'

They offer polite nods.

'God, that was amazing wasn't it? All that hope. All that potential.'

I drink from the bottle, the glass I was carrying long gone.

'He was so young then. So much of his life ahead of him. Something great in front of him. Something really amazing.'

Welsh Lena and Young Steve are now looking at me with completely different eyes. Where once there was irritation and discomfort, there is now concern and compassion.

'Are you okay?' Young Steve asks.

'I'm good. It's all good. He just needs a second chance, doesn't he? To make it right. To fulfil that promise,' I take another swig, leaving snot and tears on the lip of the bottle.

'Gin?' I offer again.

'No, you're all right, mate.'

Welsh Lena waves to beckon someone over. Out of the corner of my eye I see Tom and Seb striding towards me.

'Give us the bottle, Nick.'

I make a meal of standing up and extend my right arm to hold them back as I bring my left arm and the bottle up to my mouth. Give me a little oblivion.

By the time they've prised the drink away from me, there's only backwash left.

That old familiar feeling of the floor giving way takes over. The walls and ceiling no longer mesh. I hear the next sentence out of my mouth before I've said it. Before everything goes black.

'I might have made a mistake.'

36

5 November 2008 – 04.21 GMT
Obama 273
McCain 141
Barack Hussein Obama projected to win the presidency

The TV camera cut to Sarah Palin and the revellers booed like they were at a panto. The hipster in the beanie hat (indoors, with the heating on, I mean) said, 'It was a shame that she had to be the first ever female vice-presidential candidate,' and Tom nearly exploded at the misinformation, giving chase to him around the house chanting 'Geraldine Ferraro' over and over again like he was Al Pacino in *Dog Day Afternoon*.

Dave from work – who I hadn't seen all night because I had spent my time with The Most Amazing Woman in the World™ – was standing beside me.

'Who's that?' he asked, without a hint of irony.

I wondered how in-depth my response should be seeing how a) little of any information I passed over would be retained, and b) I was too distracted with trying to see where Ellie had gone. Had she had a change of heart and run after Captain Beefcake? Had she been abducted by a crocodile? Had she decided that this night was perfect as it was and therefore she was going to bail on me?

Nah. Only an idiot would come up with a plan like that.

'That's Sarah Palin,' I said.

A light bulb went on above his head and I momentarily considered I might have underestimated Dave's knowledge of current affairs.

'Right, of course. *Nailin' Palin*,' he said, referring to a topical and reasonably well-put-together skin flick. 'Have you seen it? *Nailin' Palin*?' he asked.

Just as I was about to answer truthfully, Ellie popped up beside me.

'Have you, Nick?' she asked, all teeth and mock fluttering eyelashes.

I gulped, shuffled my feet and made some indistinct sounds that were open to interpretation until she finally let me off the hook by saying, 'I have. The resemblance is uncanny.'

Keep trying, Ellie, I thought. My mind is made up. Like 2Pac.

Damn, I'm cool.

'So, enough about satirical spank material. I was just chatting to my friend' – she pointed to a fashionable twenty-something with big, frizzy eighties hair – 'and she says that the Prince Charles is showing *Cinema Paradiso* on Sunday.'

I remember clearly how she left little pauses between every other word of the next sentence.

'Do you . . . want to . . . go with . . . me?'

Remember the plan, Nick. Remember the One Perfect Night plan.

'Err,' I said.

'Err' was not what she expected to hear.

'Sorry,' she leapt in quickly. 'That was probably way forward. Forget it. I didn't mean to.'

The situation had become so obviously uncomfortable that even someone as unobservant as Dave cottoned on to what was happening.

What *was* happening, though?

I couldn't very well say yes to her invitation. I mean, I was sort of being an arsehole by just disappearing, but I'd be more of an arsehole if I arranged a date and then never saw her again by standing her up. But this 'err'. This 'err' was just brutal.

'No, I mean, that definitely sounds like something I could do. Would do. But I'd have to check I'm not working. First.'

'You're not,' Dave piped up.

'What's that?' I asked.

'You're not working. It's Lizzie on the mid and me on the close Sunday.'

I watched Ellie become hopeful once more and I wanted to punch Dave for making me be the one who had to dash it all again.

'So, Sunday?' she asked.

'Can I get back to you on that? I just know there's something I'm forgetting.' I was about as convincing as Heather Graham's cockney accent in *From Hell*.

'Sure,' she said, trying for carefree. 'I'm just going to go for a quick smoke. Join me if you want. Or don't. Your call.'

I presented her with the most awkward double thumbs-up as she walked out through the kitchen. Dave turned to look at me.

'Dude. What are you doing?'

Shut up, Dave, I thought to myself. I have a plan. A plan to protect myself. A plan to keep things perfect. It's a perfect plan.

37

At the hospital, two nurses and one doctor are bemused and amused by my request for directions to the maternity ward. I know I'm not bleeding because I keep dabbing my hand to my cheek, but I'm guessing by their reactions that the bruise around my eye has started to swell and I wonder if they think I have concussion.

I don't remember hitting the coffee table with my face and I certainly don't remember lying sparked out on Tom's living room floor. I do remember coming to with a packet of frozen peas on my face.

I feel awful. And not just because the booze is still sloshing about my stomach and my head is pounding from my Glasgow kiss of Tom's IKEA furniture. I feel awful because when I sobered up and checked my phone, I had five missed calls from Andrew and six from Gabby.

Gabby went into labour at exactly 23.21, and less than three hours later, Freddie Dylan Marcet was born. Of course the baby got her last name; it was a minor miracle that

Andrew never had to change his by deed poll after their wedding.

Mother and baby were both doing well, Andrew informed me, but they wanted to keep them in overnight anyway. I was invited to come and visit as soon as I wanted. I chose right away.

'Nice shiner,' the lady on the desk says. 'You sure you're in the right place?'

'Pretty sure,' I reply. 'Gabby Marcet?'

The receptionist raises her eyebrows.

'Did she give you that?'

'No, she's my sister.'

'It's just, well, she's got a tongue on her, hasn't she?'

I nod in sympathy and grin to myself at the thought of Gabby shouting swears loud enough to wake the coma patients on the top floor.

'Down the hall, first room on the right, last bed on the left.'

Despite her and Andrew's ridiculous wealth, Gabby still refuses to go private. Even during their failed attempts to conceive, she believed wholeheartedly that the NHS would come to her rescue, repeatedly saying, 'Why should I get care that others can't afford?'

I share her principles now, but would I if I actually had money? Who knows?

I find the room, and there they are, nearest the window. I see an image that I know I'll keep with me until my mind eventually turns to mush. Huddled together on the bed, this perfect family unit. Gabby, Andrew and what I assume is Freddie. I assume because without getting closer, honestly it could just be a bunched-up towel wrapped around a bunch of other towels. But the way they're looking at this thing.

Total and utter devotion.

And then they look at each other. And I get it. I finally do. After all these years.

I don't want to spoil the moment, so I just stand and watch for a while, until a cranky midwife the shape of a bowling pin pushes me into the room.

'You make a good window but a terrible door,' she says inexplicably as she barges past. I wonder what clashes she and Gabby have gone through as they finally look up from their firstborn and wave me over.

'Hey,' I say in a hushed tone.

'Hey,' they both reply, replicating my resonance.

'Jesus, what the hell happened to your face?' Gabby asks, again keeping the volume at a respectable level.

'Should we see the other guy?' Andrew tries. God, he does try.

'Good one. Anyway, how's this guy? Hey, Freddie, it's your Uncle Knick-Knack.'

His eyes are tightly shut and his little monkey hands are clasped together. It's a shame, but Gabby's soppy personality I witnessed from the door has already disappeared. I wonder which version Andrew gets to see when they're alone.

'Get us two coffees, Andrew,' she commands, and he jumps to attention, reciting our preferences off by heart.

Gabby shuffles up the bed and pulls across a little plastic cot on wheels, lowering Freddie in like she's auditioning for a remake of *The Hurt Locker*.

298

She peers closer at my injury and winces, 'So, what the fuck happened to your face?'

'Had a date with a nice girl. Took her to a party that I shouldn't have. Got so drunk I passed out. Had my fall broken by a helpful table. How was your night?'

'Some black shit came out of my vagina about seven, which was the worst possible thing that could happen because it meant the baby had shat himself inside me, which they're not supposed to do. Got in the car. Drove here. Well, Andrew drove to begin with, but he was being a pussy waiting for red lights and pedestrians, so I took over.'

'Vin Diesel's got nothing on you.'

She mimes a tiny bow and winces.

'Which turned out to be the right thing to do, because little Freddie here came out almost instantly.'

'I'd say you had the better night then.'

She looks over at her sleeping angel and smiles.

'Yeah.' The smile disappears and she looks at me with utter contempt. 'Christ, you're a moron.'

The sudden turn takes me back a little, but I reason it must be something pregnancy-related that I don't understand.

'Why did you hang up on me the other day?'

'Because. Because I was pissed off Ellie called you. Why *did* she call you?' I ask, having wanted to ask for the last ten days.

'Because she's fucking awesome and nice and she knew I was due soon and wanted to wish me luck.'

That's right. Two women can have a conversation without it being about a man. It's not all about me. Still, I counter with a little petulance anyway. 'Maybe you should have had a baby with her instead.'

'Instead of boring Andrew, you mean? I know what you think of him,' she says.

I hang my head for the umpteenth time tonight.

'Thought of him,' I offer. 'I saw it when I walked through the door. What you mean to him. What he means to you. I'm sorry if I give him too hard a time.'

'Don't be. You wouldn't give him a hard time if I didn't. And he wouldn't put up with it if he didn't like it. People are simple.'

She cocks her head. The contempt she showed before is now a thing of the past, replaced instead with curiosity.

'Can I ask you something?' she says, cocking her head to the other side.

I nod.

'Do you like being unhappy?'

It takes a while, but I let out a meek 'No.'

Maybe that's not the question I need to ask myself, but it's damn close.

I ask, 'When I took her to the airport, Ellie said I had a breakdown. I didn't, did I?'

'You sort of did.' Even in our hushed tones Gabby says this with a softness that lulls me. 'But everyone breaks down. Everyone does, from time to time. It's when you reassess everything. What shit means to you. What matters. It was such a damn fucking shame that everything else went tits up so soon after.'

'I still don't think it was a breakdown,' I argue.

'What did you do in April?'

'I don't know.' I rack my brain to try and figure out what she's getting at. 'I worked a bit. Nothing special.'

'And what did you do the April before that and the April before that and the first April you and Ellie were together?'

The realisation is fast and painful.

'Oh Christ.'

I had completely forgotten the tapes to Lucas. The ritual we had every year. The promise I made to get out the camera. To leave the flat. To let Ellie record her messages to her brother and feel better.

'Why didn't she say something?'

'How could she? "Hey, Nick, you know that heartbreakingly nice gesture you did for me? Well, you forgot this year." She'd never want to make you feel bad.'

She wouldn't.

'Like I said on the phone, something in you just switched off earlier this year. You came to ours with Ellie, it was around March, and there was something missing. Something changed. You just collapsed inwards. Like a . . .'

'Like a dying star?'

'Like a fucking twat. I know things have been tough lately. You loved that job, and it was a fucking shock to me too when our parents decided to fuck off halfway around the world. Especially when I've got that' – she points at her darling sleeping child – 'fucking parasite to try and keep alive. But you switched off before all that. I just don't know why.'

I'm desperate to tell her there were other factors, outside influences, but I know now isn't the time or place. And even

301

the mitigating circumstances don't stop her being right. I like how right she is. I don't know why I didn't rely on her rightness before now.

'Ellie told me she invited you to America.'

'She didn't mean it . . .'

'Christ, Nick!' The sudden raised voice makes Freddie twitch, but he settles himself, allowing his mother to lay the sarcasm on thick. 'Of course, she was just calling your bluff. Playing a prank. And when you arrived at the airport, bags all packed, she'd laugh in your face.' Sarcasm complete.

'She might.'

The withering look Gabby gives me next makes me fear for her son.

'Well, it seems like you've moved on anyway. What with your date and all.'

I haven't told Gabby about Lizzie, so she must mean Mia.

'Did you let her down gently?'

Because I've forgotten to get Gabby and Freddie a present, I think I might as well give them the following.

'I climbed through the restaurant's toilet window. But I got stuck halfway and the staff had to help me free.'

A smile crosses Gabby's face. Followed by a little chuckle. Then a hearty laugh and a snort and full-blown guffawing. She's taking such delight in my suffering it's enough to wake Freddie and a couple of other babies on the ward. Evil glances are given by the other mums, and returned, as Gabby picks Freddie up and puts him on her boob. He bounces up and down as she continues to laugh.

'It really wasn't funny.' I grin at her grin. 'Let me guess, hearing that is the highlight of your day?'

She finally settles, wipes away a tear and says, 'It might just be.'

I make sure Gabby can see me looking at Freddie.

'Did you hear that, Freddie? Two hours old and she's already putting my misery above your happiness. She'll be a terrible mother.'

Gabby helps Freddie find his food with one hand and holds mine with the other.

'You'll be all right,' she says.

'I love you,' I say.

'I know.'

★

Before I leave the hospital, I find a seat outside the ward and drink the coffee Andrew bought for me. On the TV, Obama is giving his victory speech. He looks implausibly older in these four short years, the specks of grey in his hair, the already long face somehow longer. He speaks of an optimistic future, the promise of the country's founding, how as a nation people aren't as cynical as the media would have them believe. He talks of how America is greater than 'the sum of our individual ambitions . . . more than a collection of red states and blue states'.

It's an impressive speech. Better than the last one even, but last time around it was so much easier to believe in. So much has happened between Obama '08 and Obama '12.

As a British outsider, I see so much anger. From both

sides. Angry comedians shouting angrily about how wrong and angry the angry commentators are. And angry commentators shouting angrily about how angry and wrong the angry comedians are.

With so much bad blood, how can they possibly 'seize this future together'? Hope and change seem a distant memory. And to misquote Dylan, I was so much younger then. I'm older than that now.

But with age comes wisdom, right?

Gabby's diagnosis of my shutting-up shop earlier this year brings with it an avalanche of recriminations and filtered-out memories.

I haven't added to the *Reasons We're No Longer Together* list since Ellie flew away over six weeks ago.

I think of the truest way to write this.

#5 I SHUT DOWN.

Like a form of relationship narcolepsy, I switched my feelings off and coasted. I didn't listen when she made it clear she was unhappy. I didn't try when I needed to. And I forgot about those damn tapes that meant so much to her. I might not be able to pinpoint where the other things on the list started to go wrong, where they started to eat away at the future of us.

But this moment, the catalyst for the great switch-off, this I do remember.

And so, for the final time, I'm ready to tell our story. Truthfully.

Fourth Intermission

The Girl knew that change was a part of life. The Boy feared it with every fibre of his being. His reluctance to bend to what life threw at him would invariably lead him to break, bringing with it more change than he could possibly deal with.

The news that Ellie's parents were separating, after three decades of marriage, blindsided everyone who knew them. Ellie most especially. She replayed the meal at which they announced their split when she returned home.

'I felt like I was twelve. Like, this is the sort of thing that happens when you're growing up. Not when you're thirty-one.'

She spoke clearly but dispassionately. As though she was retelling the plot of a book she was reading. Plenty of 'then he said' and 'then she said'. She was blinking a lot too, still trying to make sense of it.

'I half expected a "this isn't your fault" speech, but thankfully it was all about them. About how they'd been unhappy together for a while now. How they were of an age at which they both wanted more than the other could offer.'

She stopped talking and Nick did his best to figure out what would be helpful in this situation. He landed on sharing in her shock.

'I'm amazed,' he said. 'I just thought that was it for them. In it for the long haul. Like if this was a computer game, they were so close to "completing married life". Why stop playing now?'

He wasn't sure if Ellie was listening, if she was taking in any of his pearls of wisdom. Not wanting to push it, he offered her tea instead.

'No thanks. I think I'll find it hard enough to sleep anyway.'

She kissed him on the cheek.

'Thanks for listening, Nick. Sorry it's so late.'

That night in bed she held on to him tighter than normal.

★

The week following the big announcement, Ellie's mother, Margaret, journeyed down to London to meet up with a friend who she described as 'a fellow divorcee', even though she and Richard had only marked off seven days from their separation calendar.

Ellie had said she could stay at theirs if she wanted and been met with 'If I don't get lucky out on the town!' – a line of dialogue no daughter ever wants to hear from her parent.

Thankfully for Ellie, Margaret was back at their flat, safe and sound, by midnight, though more than a little under the influence. Ellie was in the bathroom, so when the doorbell rang, Nick went to answer it. He was met with a hug, a double cheek kiss and the peculiar scent of vermouth and too much perfume.

'Hi, Margaret, how are you?' he asked.

She hung her coat and bag up as if she'd been living with them for years and led the way down the hall.

'Call me Mags, Nick. I love it when you call me Mags.'

'Okay, Mags, can I get you a drink?'

'Got any vermouth?'

Ellie met them in the living room and shot Nick a look that said 'Please choose your words more carefully when offering her a beverage.'

'No, Mum, we don't have any vermouth. But I think coffee would be a good idea.'

Nick nodded and left them to it, although such was the space in their flat he could hear the entirety of their conversation.

'Oh Ellie, I feel so free.'

Margaret pulled off a graceful twirl to accompany the word 'free' and slumped onto the couch.

'I imagine you feel quite drunk too,' Ellie responded.

'Don't be a downer, Ellie. This is good for both of us. For all of us. Your dad's a good man, but he's not the man I married. Goodbye, old pants!' She giggled loudly.

'Don't call him names!'

'No, I mean it literally. I will never have to stare at his old-man pants again.'

There was joy in her voice like she was tipsy, but the

actual words betrayed the fact that she was well and truly sloshed. Ellie assessed her and came to the conclusion that she had spent too much of her life convinced adults had it all figured out. It was unsettling to see someone thirty years her senior fall apart.

Nick took his time over the coffee, knowing that if he went back into the living room he'd become part of the discussion and have to give opinions and take sides. He predicted there was no way on earth that would end well for him.

Alone with her mother, Ellie tried to coax out more answers to the question that still so confused her. Why, after everything they'd been through? Why now?

'Are you saying you'd stay together if Dad bought new underwear? Because I'm sure Nick could take him shopping.'

'You're talking like this was all my idea, Ellie. It wasn't. It was a mutual decision. Mutual boredom.'

These words hurt Ellie, and Nick, hearing them through the wall, needed to offer his support. He settled on the pretence of not knowing how Margaret took her coffee to make his entrance.

'Milk? Sugar?'

He prayed she wouldn't come out with a 'sweet enough, Nick' flirtation, but before she could answer, Ellie barked, 'Black!' at him and added a large water to the order. She did this in such a way that Nick immediately thought it best to retreat back to the safety of the kitchen.

'I feel like our job is done now,' Margaret continued. 'We did the thing we were meant to do. We raised you. You're all grown up now.'

To contradict her point Ellie sullenly observed, 'So it's all my fault? Me growing up has caused you to separate?'

'No. No, you're twisting my words.'

Margaret lowered her voice. Or at least she lowered it in the way drunk people do, where they dial it down for a second before forgetting why and raising it back to the previous volume moments later.

'You don't know what it's like, my darling.'

'Then tell me, Mum.'

'Nick's . . . Nick's so good for you, Ellie. Can't I have someone look at me the way he looks at you?'

Her voice carried and Nick thought to himself, 'Why am I being brought into this? I'm supposed to be safe in the kitchen. Don't make your daughter's boyfriend one of the reasons you're leaving your husband. And please, God, tell me you didn't tell Richard that. He hates me enough as it is.'

Ellie replied aggressively, 'You don't think after thirty-odd years of being married to Nick his old pants will piss me off too?'

Nick made a note in his phone. *Buy new pants.* And another to *Google latest trends in pants. Make sure you're keeping up with the times.*

As he thought about his pants, he could hear Margaret attempting to drop the decibel level again, this time with such great effect he had to move to the edge of the kitchen to hear her.

'You were smart,' she began. And Nick thought how nice it was when proud parents got all gushy about their kids.

That was until she finished her point.

'You were so smart, Ellie. With Nick. So smart. You aimed . . . low.'

The words crushed him.

'Mum!' There was rage in Ellie's voice despite her hushed tone.

'He can't hear me. It's fine. But you are. You are. So smart. You could have had anyone. But picking him, you know he'll always idolise you.'

'Mum, seriously.'

There are times when you can ride something out by saying, 'It's the booze talking.' But this remedy only lasts for as long as you can keep out the thought, 'What people say when they're drunk is what they really mean.'

A silence enveloped the flat.

Nick waited for the conversation to pick up again before he brought Margaret her drinks. He knew that if he went in too early the awkward silence would be brought up again later, when he and Ellie were alone. If he timed this wrong, he'd have to lie about what he had heard.

'One coffee, black. And one large water.'

★

They talked about London and work and anything they could think of that was uncontroversial until the drinks were drunk. Then Ellie showed Margaret to their room. When she reappeared, Nick gave her the sofa and took the floor.

As they lay, she held his hand from her higher ground.

'How much of that did you hear?'

'Just your mum saying how great I am,' he lied, as he'd

known he would. 'How she wishes someone would look at her the way I look at you. Although as nice as that was to hear, it did make me incredibly sad.'

Ellie stayed silent.

'Why? Did she say anything else?'

'No,' Ellie lied back. Although her lie was arguably a little whiter. 'Nothing of note. Just drunken ramblings.'

'Are you okay?' Nick asked.

'No.'

'Can I help?'

'You can come up here and give me a cuddle.'

He did as he was asked.

'You'll be okay,' he whispered. 'And they will be too. Given time.'

*

In the morning, Ellie left for work before Margaret was awake, leaving Nick the unenviable task of dealing with an in-law nursing a hangover and remorse.

He considered inventing a reason to bail, perhaps an emergency at work. But two reasons kept him around. First, he hated to be seen as a bad host. Second, he didn't want to give Margaret the chance to snoop around their flat and find more reasons to judge him unworthy.

He made himself a double espresso because he hadn't slept. Because this woman's words had kept him awake most of the night.

'You were smart, Ellie. You aimed . . . low.'

All those fears, the ones he'd had years ago – even on that

first night – the fears that had lain dormant, they spewed forth now. He wasn't good enough for her. Someone had finally had the balls to say it.

Before last night, he would have placed a considerable sum of money on it being Richard, Ellie's dad. But Richard just made his contempt clear through non-verbal communication, like even taking the time to tell Nick he wasn't worthy of his daughter was offering him too much respect.

Now it was out there. It couldn't be taken back. And while the sickness swirled in his stomach, there came with it a strange sense of validation. Validation of the part of him that had always doubted himself. The part that never felt comfortable with a happiness he was sure he didn't deserve.

*

Ellie sat at her desk, unable to concentrate. Her inbox was filling up slowly but with the kind of messages she could easily ignore. Recent cutbacks had left her doing the job of three people, and she found herself increasingly tied to a desk, performing administrative tasks. She missed the distraction of being out of the office, capturing the picture that would tell a thousand words.

But she was grateful to have the job. Lesser and greater publications than hers had switched to freelance photographers or – as was becoming depressingly familiar – were using 'citizen journalists' to provide free, inferior work.

Knowing the inevitability of redundancies, Ellie had made herself as useful as possible. Colleagues came and went, decrying

314

all change and bemoaning the fact that things were not what they used to be. Their attitude, sadly, made her think of Nick.

She wanted to fight these thoughts.

But she was tired. She was tired of listening to the voices of doubt. The ones that said things had been stagnant for too long. That he had no drive, no ambition, no direction. That she was feeling that way about herself. Apathy by osmosis.

She was angry with the voices, too. She knew it was not her job to change him. To fix him. Whatever these voices said. Fixing someone was a game. A way to make yourself feel better, more powerful. For her it was an odious concept that went against her ethical – but never religious – doctrine of 'do unto others'. Previous partners had tried to fix her, and she had resented them totally until they reached their inevitable catastrophic conclusions.

But Ellie wanted Nick to change. And therein lay the rub.

She opened another internal email. It was Martina's birthday and she'd brought cakes into the kitchen. Ellie consigned the message to the digital rubbish bin and returned to that pervasive thought.

'You aimed low.'

It wasn't true.

Nick was kind, he was considerate. But lately he had not been happy, and this unhappiness was growing worse. Three and a half years they had been a part of each other's lives, and Ellie could chart on a graph Nick's descent from euphoria to ennui.

That first day, which he would often recount, that was

his peak. His mountain summit of joy. But even that, she knew, had been reworded to the point of fiction.

She'd tried to convince herself his lack of a life's course would be fine for her if only he was content. She knew this was a fallacy. Was it because she cared for him so much that she saw this potential in him? Had she fooled herself into thinking there was more to him?

'You aimed low.'

It wasn't true.

★

Nick was on his phone, reading an article about the domino effect of divorce on other couples, when Ellie's mother awoke. It was around noon and she was sheepish in her salutation.

She and Nick both adopted the opposite positions of authority.

'Morning, Nick. Has Ellie . . .'

'Gone to work? Yeah. A few hours ago.'

She noticed the time on the clock and her eyes went cartoon wide.

'Is it . . .'

'Yep, noon, pretty late, huh?'

Finishing her sentences was born out of both Nick's pity and a pitiful way of seeking revenge. This adult/child dynamic they'd settled upon was unignorable.

'I hope I didn't do or say anything silly last night,' Margaret offered tentatively.

Nothing that won't have long-term effects on mine and Ellie's future happiness, Nick thought.

'Coffee?' he asked.

'Nick,' she said, suddenly taking on the demeanour of the responsible one. 'Ellie's going to have trouble with all this. I know I was a bit . . . silly last night, but Richard and I both think the world of you and . . .'

Nick bit his lip and let her continue.

'. . . when we were discussing us not being together, one thing we knew was that Ellie would be okay, because she has you. In many ways, we see you as being the one to take care of her now.'

She stood up and attempted to hug Nick as she left, but he gave nothing back. Then she disappeared, leaving him alone with the two thoughts he'd do battle with for the next few months.

One, he needed to make sure Ellie was okay.

And two, there was a good chance – if her mother's drunken declaration was anything to go by – that long term there were far better people for the job.

★

Maybe buying the ring was a stupid idea.

It had felt right at the time. The sales assistant, with his 1920s moustache and red braces, had certainly made it seem like a good idea. He'd asked Nick questions about where he and Ellie had met and listened to his plans for where he might propose. He'd even suggested a few wedding ideas. When Nick asked if the ring could be returned, he'd smiled and said he was sure there'd be no need for that. Before going on to inform him that they offered store credit.

In hindsight, Nick would be the first to admit, finding out if marriage was something Ellie actually wanted should have preceded spunking his credit card balance on a tiny, shiny rock. A final dice roll of heart over head.

★

Ellie's mood had worsened in the month since 'the drunken visit', and her dad's far-too-fast move to London only sent her spiralling down a hole of questioning how long her parents' marriage had been falling apart. Questioning that extended to 'How did I not see this coming?' and 'How much am I to blame?' in equal doses.

When Nick suggested they raid 'Nick and Ellie's adventure fund' – current total, one hundred and fifty-three pounds and fifty-three pence – and stay somewhere for a romantic night and a fancy meal, he was met with a zero on the enthusiasm-o-meter.

'How about just a meal then?' he tried.

'I'm really not in the mood.'

'We could go see a band?'

'Can't we just stay in?'

'And do what?'

She pushed air through her closed lips.

'I don't know. Open a bottle of wine. Watch some TV.'

'Sure,' he said, wondering if after half a bottle of red he'd accidentally pop the question between *University Challenge* and *Only Connect*.

Slumping on the sofa, Ellie took the remote and started

hopping around the channels. Nick opened the cheap super-market wine and poured two glasses.

'Look, *Four Weddings and a Funeral* is on,' he said. 'If they don't make a sequel in the next ten years called *Four Funerals and a Wedding*, I'll eat Hugh Grant's hair.'

She grimaced and offered to switch over to it with the same eagerness one would associate with cleaning a grill.

'If there's nothing better . . .

They settled into their usual positions, her legs on top of his, all four elevated on a footstool. As Hugh Grant took one to the jaw in the name of honesty and true love, Nick began fishing.

'Would you punch me in the face at our wedding?'

'Our wedding?' Ellie scoffed.

Nick sat up so quickly he sloshed wine onto his legs and the sofa, causing Ellie to jump to her feet too.

'Why did you scoff like that?' he asked.

Ellie stared down at the stain. 'Are you going to clear that up?'

Nick was fixed in his position.

'Do you not see us getting married?'

She looked between him and the liquid seeping into the fabric before throwing her arms in the air and exclaiming, 'Fine. I'll do it.'

She took off into the kitchen and started running hot water and Fairy into a plastic bowl. She grabbed the kitchen roll and returned to find Nick standing with his hand out.

'Give it here.'

She shook her head and dabbed at the wine.

'If you're not willing to do it yourself, I don't need your half-arsed attempt to help.'

His voice rose with frustration. 'What's that supposed to mean? And why won't you answer the question?'

She scrubbed harder at the stain, her hand a blur.

'What question? Would I like to marry you? Is that what you're asking me? Are you proposing, Nick? Great timing!'

'What if I was?'

Nick grabbed the remote and hit the off button, knowing in that moment that her mum's words had had as much of an impact on her as they'd had on him.

'What if you were? Well, I'd ask a few questions, I suppose.' Her tone was getting angrier, like she'd been waiting for her chance to explode. 'Questions like, what does our future look like to you? Sitting on that couch watching movies every night you're not working? And as for work, what does that look like in a year's time? You'll just keep on at the cinema until you get less than half a shift a week?'

'I like my job! What's wrong with actually liking what you do?'

Ellie, resigned to the fact that the sofa was beyond saving, threw the clumped-up paper towels into the bowl. Soapy water slopped over the edges onto the carpet.

'It's not wrong. It's just finite. You're the only one who doesn't seem to see it. It would be nice if the man I planned to spend the rest of my life with had a Plan B. When was the last time you wrote something?'

It was Nick's turn to stamp his feet and have a strop.

'I'm not a good writer.'

'Says every writer!'

'Says every fucking rejection letter.'

'Fine. Don't write. Become a sky-diving instructor or a flipping orchid collector, just find something that makes you happy.'

'I have you! You make me happy!'

'BUT THAT'S NOT YOUR JOB!'

The eruption brought with it the first moment of silence between them. Both of them felt that sickness in their gut, the sickness that said this wasn't just a row. Everything they said from now on would be permanent. It was a feeling that could rein in the anger, that could curb the emotion, or they could choose to ignore the feeling and persist. Ellie chose to persist.

'I can't love you like you want me to, Nick.'

He would blame the sound of his heart breaking to explain why he didn't hear what she'd really said.

'You don't love me?' he asked.

The answer was still yes, she did, but she wouldn't answer for fear of confusing him.

She steadied herself, ready for what she knew had to come next. She said, 'I know the words you want me to say, but I can't say them. I won't read from that script any more.'

She rubbed her eyes and continued.

'I know you're scared . . .'

'Of what?' Nick asked bitterly.

'Of so many things. Scared of trying. Scared of failing. Scared of rejection and everything that comes with it. Scared of being alone. Scared of a life where you don't know what the next words out of someone's mouth will be.'

321

She knew he was listening. She didn't know if he really heard her.

'So what *are* the next words?'

Ellie shook her head.

'I don't know.'

It would take the Boy months to really see why the Girl was gone. Months to see it was an act of kindness as much as it was self-preservation. There was a path they could blindly walk down until the cliff edge was in view. She had steered them away. Given them a chance at a future. When the Boy finally understood, he lamented the lesson learnt too late.

End of Fourth Intermission

38

5 November 2008 – 04.34 GMT
Obama 333
McCain 145
Senator John McCain concedes

The devil said, 'There's no time like the present.' The angel begged for fifteen more minutes. For one final conversation. Just a few more moments in Ellie's company.

I started off watching John McCain give his concession as my way of postponing my exit. But I'm a sucker for a good speech, and despite his earlier casting as Chief Villain, he nailed this one. One line in particular, in which he gracefully told the crowd the loss was his fault and not theirs, genuinely moved me. I'm not sure anyone on the right has ever done that. But then he sang Palin's praises and became *persona non grata* in the Marcetverse again. On the other side of the room I saw Dave speaking to Tom, and Tom was instantly not best pleased.

He marched over to me.

'Can I have a word?'

'I was just watch—'

Before I could get to the closing part of my sentence, Tom had my ear between his finger and thumb and was dragging me into the vacant hallway.

'Come here, Francine,' he scolded me.

'It's not what it looks like,' I replied.

'What it looks like is Dave tells me the really nice girl you spent the night talking to has asked you out on a date, and rather than say "Yes, of course, I'd love to" you've made up some bullshit excuse and left her hanging.'

It turned out it was a little what it looked like.

I knew Tom was a logical sort and so I attempted to wow him with reason.

'Look. I like her. I do. A lot. But it's like . . . it's like *The Phantom Menace*.'

He was not impressed by the start of the analogy.

I carried on regardless. 'You remember how excited, how head-over-heels, pant-wettingly excited you were in 1999 when you first saw the trailer for *The Phantom Menace*?'

He nodded.

'And you also remember how soul-destroyingly heart-broken you were when the credits rolled and you realised that it was a massive bag of crap and you wished you'd just gone to see *The Matrix* again.'

'Sorry, who's *The Matrix* in this metaphor?'

I stopped to try and work it out.

'Nobody's *The Matrix*. *The Matrix* isn't the point. The

point is I felt excited about something again for the first time in a long time. It's a nice feeling to have. But you know me, I'll only fuck it up later. Or she'll see the error of her ways and run a mile. If I leave it as it is, I can have one perfect, amazing, "tell the grandkids about it" night.'

I could tell Tom was trying so hard to see things from my, admittedly strange, perspective. But he just couldn't.

'There's a problem with this master plan, Nick. If you always think like this, if you say no to every good thing that comes along for fear of spoiling it or fear of it going tits up, then you'll never have grandkids to tell stories to. About this night or any other.'

I'd heard him out. I'd considered his point of view and he'd considered mine. We were at an impasse, but I felt the need to reassure my friend that this was a significant occasion and a one-off, rather than some dangerous trend that would leave me alone at fifty with nothing but Lego reconstructions of famous film sets.

'Tonight's been pretty unique. How often can you say that?' I asked.

He replied flatly. 'Every night. You can say that every night. Because every single night is unique, Nick.'

'Okay, tonight was special. It was . . .'

He eyes pleaded with me not to say it.

'. . . like a film.'

It was then he realised he wouldn't be able to change my mind. No clever words would sway me. He knew me well enough and so he handed me my coat and hat from the banister behind him. All the while shaking his damn head.

'If she asks . . .' I said.

'Which she will,' he countered.

'. . . just tell her I had the best night of my life tonight.'

I opened the front door and made my way into the cold morning air, the best party I'd ever been to behind me.

Tom called out one final time. 'You shouldn't make monumental decisions based on the inferior work of George Lucas. You have to remember his good stuff, Nick! Remember his good stuff!'

I'd had worse advice yelled at me in the early hours of the morning. But this was my decision. And no one would talk me out of it.

I knew my worth.

39

My hangover still hurts.

It's been two days since the 2012 election and the news is already speculating on 2016. The smart money seems to be on a Clinton/Bush rematch, with this round to be played by Hillary and Jeb.

I know I have apologies to dole out to those who witnessed the debacle at Tom's. I can access fragments of memory about what I said or did, and one that is crystal clear is that Seb deserves thanks for looking after me.

As I'm strolling up the path to Seb's house, Tracy, his wife, comes marching down it. Eyes and cheeks red from rage and snot.

'Your friend is a fucking arsehole,' she aggressively informs me, not stopping for a second to say hello.

On first meeting Tracy, you might be a little taken aback that this primary school teacher – who also tutors piano, sings in the community choir and exclusively wears flowery summer dresses – could have the mouth of a sailor in a

Mamet script. But when she is primed to blow, Tracy is a hamper of explosives.

More tears meet me as I enter the house.

I move towards the noise, inwardly marvelling again at Seb's journey from grotty apartment above an Indian restaurant in Brixton to this actual house with an actual garden in south London.

The shitty part of the story is that he had to lose both parents to afford even the requisite 10 per cent for a place like this. Even with mine gone to New Oz, I'm not sure I could come back from a double blow like that. And I know he'd go back to Brixton in a heartbeat if it meant his kids had their grandparents around.

The house, though, is only a small piece of his character arc. The defining parts are the two rugrats, Sally and Stevie, who are currently making his abode sound like the seventh circle of hell, with the wailing in Dolby Surround.

I haven't visited Seb anywhere near enough since he's been a parent. Part of me never made peace with him having kids and moving on from our extended teenage years. Opting out from our arrested development. Seeing him now – one arm trying to keep his four-year-old at the table as she screams for toast and the other pushing a pram back and forth – I wonder how many times a day he questions his choices.

'Hey, buddy,' I say. 'How can I help?'

He doesn't comment on my black eye, just issues instructions on where to find the bread as Stevie, now ten months old, uses every ounce of strength to fight free from his four-wheel prison. I remove two unused but slightly charred nappies from the toaster and look over to see a giggling Sally. I replace them with bread and march over to her.

'Rooooaaaarrrrrggggggh,' I cry, making the most of my one good trick – a pretty nailed-on impression of a velociraptor. Sally's giggles turn to full-blown belly chuckles. As I stomp around the kitchen, teeth bared, the chuckles become infectious, and Stevie joins in with such commitment he laughs himself to sleep in under thirty seconds.

'Apology accepted,' Seb says.

'Wha' happened to you eye?' Sally asks, jabbing it with her tiny index finger.

'Ow. Please don't do that again, Sally,' I say, rubbing my eyeball. 'What happened to me eye? Erm.'

'Clean version please, Uncle Nick,' Seb instructs me.

'I didn't eat my broccoli for a whole week and it just turned this colour.'

Sally looks to her father for confirmation and is met with a shrug.

Now that the tears are dry, I manage to eke out of Seb a little of what happened before I showed up. It was the usual lack-of-sleep-induced arguments about comparative resentment and freedom. Seb feels trapped having to work a job that doesn't fulfil him any more. Tracy feels useless that she can't find a job that will pay well enough to even cover the childcare costs.

'If we could just say to one another, I feel shi . . .' Seb stops himself and looks at his innocent daughter '. . . pooey for you, instead of trying to one-up each other's problems, we'd probably be okay.'

331

I nod.

'But whenever we get into it, it just feels like we're doing our best to take the other one down. All hint of reason goes down the f . . . flipping pan.'

'Mummy,' Sally pipes up, and we turn in unison to see Tracy standing in the doorway, face dry and no longer blotchy.

'Can you say you feel pooey for me now?' she asks.

Seb looks at her with love, affection and just the right amount of remorse.

'I can.'

Things are looking up, but there's still a tension in the room I don't fancy being in the middle of.

'Swings now,' Sally demands.

Seb and Tracy look at each other, resigned. Another job in the list of never-ending jobs appearing in front of them.

'I'll take the kids,' I say with total commitment.

The parents of said kids stare at me like I've just offered to sell their offspring on eBay.

'Come on! One's asleep and the other wants to go to the park. I'm an actual bona fide uncle now. I need the practice.'

The last line doesn't instil confidence, but after a little cajoling from Sally, Tracy and Seb reluctantly agree to my proposal.

'If he wakes and isn't happy, you bring them straight home,' Tracy says.

'Nappies and a change of clothes are in here. Drinks, snacks and toys are in here.' Seb hands me two huge bags like I'm about to do a tour of Afghanistan.

'Cool,' I say, halfway out of the door. 'And one last question. Which is your favourite? Just in case there's a zombie attack and I can only save one.'

★

Despite the time of year, the sun is out over London and the park is full of parents and their children making the most of the daylight before it's gone for good, sucked up by the winter blues.

Stevie's still sound asleep, so I position him next to the swings and put Sally in one. Worried that I might send her sixty feet into the air, I select the ones that are probably meant for much smaller children, the ones with the little bars across them, and am met with no resistance. I push her higher and higher, and each time she lets out a little 'squee'. Her simple and pure happiness reminds me of the line in *Knocked Up*, where new dad Paul Rudd says something about wishing he liked anything as much as his kids like bubbles.

I don't feel like I have that level of pleasure in me any more. But I could see myself enjoying it second-hand through my own kids.

A random playground parent (RPP) comes and takes the swing next to me for her two-year-old. I'm scared she's going to comment on Sally being too big for her swing, but she doesn't. She just smiles at me and gives an upwards head nod. I wonder if this is how parents interact and so I offer one back.

'She's adorable,' RPP says.

'Thanks,' I say, taking credit for someone else's DNA. I

point to her own daughter's weird pig bobble hat. 'I like the hat.'

She says something back about her kid being a big fan of pepper, which I don't quite understand, but I give a little forced laugh to cover my tracks regardless.

'It's great when one of them's asleep, isn't it?' she asks rhetorically.

'Better when they both are, am I right?' I throw back.

This gets a full-on chuckle from RPP and I wonder for a fleeting moment if this is flirting. Am I flirting with a mum? She's very good-looking and has nice soft eyes. She has hair like Ellie and for God's sake can I please have ten minutes where I don't think about Ellie?

Good-looking RPP's child suddenly starts bawling, and I wonder if she's telepathically linked to my misery.

'Better get her home for a nap,' she says, and disappears before either asking me for my phone number or suggesting I help raise her daughter.

Probably for the best, I think. The Ellie hair thing would have been a constant bummer. Once I'm alone again, the strange thought that I could steal these two children enters my head. I run with it to find out what the ending would be. It involves a hail of gunfire and a very disappointed Seb.

'Horsey now,' Sally says, snapping me out of my day-dream.

I lift her out of the swing and place her on a wobbly plastic horse thing. As she careens from side to side, I run around her pretending to smack two coconuts together. This provokes more hysterical laughter and I think again how much I'd enjoy having an audience like this all the time. As I pretend to fall over and collapse onto the floor her laughter reaches its crescendo and she dismounts her horse.

She offers me help getting to my feet, although I must say it feels like I'm doing most of the heavy lifting. Once I'm upright, she cocks her head to the side and looks at me strangely.

'I like you, Uncle Nick. You make me laugh.'

I thank her for the compliment and ask if she's seen any good films lately.

She bounces up and down with excitement. 'Me and Mummy watched *Lion, Witch and Wardrobe*!'

'Cartoon, animatronic or CGI Aslan?'

She looks at me as if I'm mad, and she has a point.

'I got sad when Aslan was poorly,' she says.

'Yeah, that bit's tough.'

'But Mummy said, "It'll be all right in the end. If it's not all right, it's not the end."'

She grins a tiny-toothed grin and runs off up a slide as I am suddenly filled with a hope I haven't felt in a long time. A feeling that maybe she's right. Maybe it will be all right. It's hard to describe, but it's like a determination has taken hold. A determination for what, I'm still not sure.

Sally comes back and asks why I'm sad.

I give her a hug and say, 'I'm not,' and then wipe my nose on my coat. 'Just a little hay fever.'

'But there's no hay.'

She's right. There isn't. But there is something of a plan

beginning to form. I need to finish my apology tour first. I need to see someone who can give me the approval I crave to make sure I'm doing the right thing.

And I need to give Seb his kids back.

★

Back at Chez Seb, my best friend and his wife are beaming like Cheshire cats. Sally runs at her dad like a bullet train and he scoops her up, throwing her high into the air. This reminds me again how nice their house is. These wonderful high ceilings. If he tried that trick in Ronnie's flat, he'd be calling A&E and a plasterer.

He puts his daughter down and she runs off to play, with a sing-song 'Bye, Uncle Nick!'

Seb pats me on the back and I inspect their beaming faces.

'You guys look happy.'

They take each other's hand and say in chorus, 'We reconnected.'

I smirk. 'You mean you had sex.'

Without taking their eyes off each other, they repeat my line. 'Yeah, we had sex.'

Stevie wakes and Tracy takes him off for a feed, but not before she kisses me on the cheek and whispers, 'Thank you' in my ear. I'll be honest, as nice a gesture as it is, I do wonder where her lips have just been.

'I feel like a million bucks,' Seb says when his wife and kids are out of earshot. 'Thanks again, dude.'

'Any time,' I reply, feeling a little on the million-bucks side myself. Seb immediately picks up on this.

336

'Did something happen at the park? Did you meet a random yummy mummy?'

'I did, yeah, but that's not why I'm happy. You'll have to thank your daughter for her wise counsel. She's like a miniature Tom Hagen. She's helped me make a real breakthrough with something.'

'That's wonderfully vague.'

I shake my head. 'I'll tell you more when I know.'

★

When I arrive home, there are two letters on my mat. Actual letters. With stamps and everything. Neither of them is a bill or a late payment fine or a bank statement. Both of them are addressed to me by name and written in ink.

Just call me Vicomte de Valmont.

The first letter is from the Edinburgh Film Consortium, an organisation I first heard about from reading this letter. After a brief opening about finding my details through a Mr Sebastian Kendal (it takes me about twenty seconds to realise they mean Seb), they get to the crux of the missive.

It's an invite to work – in a freelance capacity – for Scotland's fourth largest film festival. Scotland, I later learn, has four film festivals. They need someone who can work a 35 mm projector and who'd be willing to work over Christmas and New Year. Seb recommended me, clearly – and rightfully – assuming I'd be pretty lonely for the week between 25 December and 1 January, what with my parents kayaking in Auckland, Gabby preoccupied with a small person on her boobs and Ellie a ghost of Christmases past.

I'd even told him that my new employers had invited me round for Christmas Day and how – while the gesture was nice – if I said yes it would be the lowlight of what was already a frankly awful year. There was an awkward moment in which I think he thought I was angling for an invite to his, but I quickly put that to bed by saying I was enjoying my solitude again.

It wasn't an outright lie. Since I've stopped working at the cinema, I don't really have a lot of 'me' time. My days are usually occupied by work, sleep, catching up with friends or hanging out with Ronnie.

Whereas I'm desperate for company during the evenings – and yes, at night – I miss how being a projectionist let me be by myself during the day. It was a strange occupation to be surrounded by people but with little or no interaction with anyone.

Will I go back to it? Even for just one week?

The pay is poor, and even without family it's still hard to be away from home at Christmas. But if I say yes, I'll be back lacing up film in a month's time. I'll think on it. For now, on to the second letter.

I don't need to open this one to know whence it came.

The Statue of Liberty stamp is a big clue.

When I do open it, out drops a USB stick. Not so late-eighteenth-century Paris after all.

But there's a handwritten note too.

It simply reads:

WATCH ME.

40

5 November 2008 – 04.44 GMT
Obama 338
McCain 155
Barack Hussein Obama is president-elect

No one could talk me out of it. No one.

Except, of course, her.

I was halfway down the road, my head telling me I'd done the right thing, my heart telling me I'd never get over it.

And then I heard her call out.

'Hey!'

I didn't have a clever line or witty retort for this moment. I genuinely thought I'd made a clean getaway.

'Can I take a photo?' she asked, holding up her camera. 'Something to remember you by in case I can't find you on Facebook. Or in case I wake up tomorrow and think, what did that jerk who ran out on me without saying a word look like?'

The happy person I'd spent the night with was melancholy and subdued, and I knew this was my doing.

Quickly, I thought, come up with an excuse.

'So sorry, I, erm, I started to get a bit of a, erm, head-ache . . .'

Me and my erms.

'You're a terrible liar, Nick Marcet. But you really had me convinced that you were a good person.'

I couldn't fathom whether the warm words were to make me feel better, to cool her feeling of rejection or to persuade me to stay.

She continued, 'But just so you know, what you're doing now is not what a good person would do. Leaving someone who likes you, who's made it clear that they like you, without a word, it makes them wonder what they did wrong. Makes them wonder what's wrong with them.'

I felt every type of awful.

'It's not you,' I blurted out.

'Not helping,' she replied.

Even without the benefit of hindsight, I knew the next line was a punt.

'It's like *The Phantom Menace* . . .'

All the muscles in her face conveyed the 'What?!' so her mouth didn't have to. I persevered.

'You remember when you saw *The Phantom Menace* back in 1999?'

'No,' she said. 'I don't really like *Star Wars* films and everyone said it was a bit rubbish.'

While I'd missed the point entirely, I felt validated.

'See!' I was animated now. 'There's something we'll already fight about.'

'What are you talking about?!' she yelled, matching my fervour but from a completely different angle.

The street was cold and I could see our breath meeting as I fashioned my master speech, the one that would make her understand.

'I had a great time tonight,' I said.

Her head nodded with a mixture of affirmation and shivering.

'I did too. That's why I'm freezing my bits off out here with you when I could be warm inside watching history unfurl.'

'But, I mean, I had a really great time. A spectacular, once-in-a-lifetime time. You know how often I dream of going to a party and meeting someone as amazing as you? You made me smile the minute I saw you. You made me laugh within ten. You made me feel like the lead role and not just some background extra. You're gorgeous and clever and obviously super-talented, and you're so cool and also really uncool in just the right amounts.'

Her cheeks, already crimson from the cold, blushed redder with each compliment.

'And you're so, I don't know, playful. Yeah, playful.'

She snorted at this.

'I think it's the right word. And your eyes. I could get lost in your eyes for the rest of my life, and I know the more I get to know you, the more I'll fall. And then one day, I'll mess it up. I don't know how or why, but I will. And knowing everything I know now, everything I've learnt in just one night, I know that losing you will be awful.'

Her assessment of my conclusion was short and sweet.

'That's all really nice, Nick. But it's fucking nuts.'

And then she started to laugh. At me. Maybe a little with me, but mostly at me. The way she did this was fascinating. No one likes being laughed at. It's not supposed to be a nice feeling. But once she started, I just broke out into the widest, daftest grin.

And it was all because she was still here.

I'd convinced myself she was a distant memory as I walked out of that house. I'd never been surer of anything than I was that I'd never see her again. But there she was. Looking at me like I was *mucho loco*. After a while, she chose a serious expression to wear.

'I like you, Nick.'

'I like you, Ellie.'

She put her hands on the sides of my head and kissed me.

'I don't know why you're so sure you'll mess this up,' she said. 'But I'm sort of looking forward to finding out how you do.'

She winked at me and grabbed my hand. Typical Ellie, I thought. Always taking the lead.

'It's just what I do,' I lamented, skilfully bringing the mood down again. 'I don't think it's possible for me not to.'

But she wasn't having any of it.

'Maybe. But a black man with the middle name Hussein just got elected president of the United States, so I think anything's possible.'

I waited until we were outside the house to stop her, brush my fingers through her hair and kiss her again. I also had a pressing question I needed answering as soon as humanly possible.

'Do you really not like *Star Wars*?'

41

The decision to watch the videos takes a long time. I can honestly say I never intended or expected to see any of them, but there's something fateful about loading the USB stick and seeing the four files. Something inevitable.

Each file has a name and the date of taping: 2009, 2010, 2011. One is cryptically labelled *BONUS*.

I open the first, *Ellie to Lucas – 10 April 2009*.

I see her face. She's in my old house, the one before we had our own place. She looks like I remember her from our first night. That skin. Those eyes. The only difference from 2008 Ellie is the red hair's fighting a losing battle with her natural brown.

A few months later, it would never return.

I press play.

Hey, Lucas. Little bro. Sproglet. What am I going to say? This is very much going to be about me, isn't it? I miss you. There. That's a start. A pretty sad start but a start nonetheless.

Mum and Dad miss you too. Okay. Happy stuff. Lighter stuff. What would we talk about? I live in London now. It's busy. Lots of busy people. Sorry. I don't really know who I'm speaking to. I didn't lay out any ground rules. Am I speaking to you as a five-year-old or you as a twenty-five-year-old? I should have thought this through first. I'll try the latter.

The screen goes blank and my heart skips a beat. Then, as quickly as she's gone, she reappears.

Hey, brother. 'Sup? Miss you. Life in London is pretty good. Coming up to one year now. Work is okay. I take lots of pictures of people holding things. It seems to be a local news thing. Hold this Roman coin you found in your back garden up for the camera, please. Hold this cake you baked for Prince William up to the camera, please. Hold this bill from Virgin Media that says you ordered pornography – even though your husband insists he didn't and is now in far too deep to just admit he did – up to the camera, please. The look on his face. Oh Lucas, it was sublime.

I'm not sure if I'd actually talk to you about this next part, but I like to think we'd be a cool close sibling pair. So here goes. I met someone. A guy. About six months ago now. It was his idea for me to do this tape. He's very, very sweet like that. His name is Nick. We're very much in love.

I think a lot about what I'd have been like around your girlfriends. Or boyfriends. Would I have been wildly protective? Would I have set you up with my friends? Would you have come to me for advice? Would I have come to you? Maybe that's what this can be. My forum for asking your advice. I never consider myself an only child. Because I had you. It felt important to let you know that. I know the rest has been waffle, but if I just find one important thing to say, it's probably worth it. Right? Right. Okay. That's me done for now.

See you soon. Love you.

Part of me wants to savour these, spread them out over days and keep her with me for a little longer. The other part of me wants to mainline them like they're the *Godfather* trilogy. You can never stop at Part 1. Even for all the faults of Part 3, it has to be watched. I know which part of me will win. It already has, as I press play on the next one: *Ellie to Lucas – 10 April 2010.*

She's in our flat now. 2010 Ellie has shorter hair, the red is no more. She's wearing one of my gig T-shirts (Regina Spektor's Far Tour from the previous summer), so she can't have been up long. I always loved how she'd wear my clothes to bed, especially my tatty ones, and make them look magical.

She's super-happy today. She has props in the form of a notepad. She glances at it before she addresses the camera.

Hey, Lucas. I'm much more prepared this year. I made a checklist of things I want to let you know about. So rather than the rambling nonsense of last year, we have five bullet-pointed items. Are you ready? Good.

Bullet point number one. The quote unquote career is still going well, although I now work freelance rather than just for the Clapham Gazette. *I've been covering a fair few gigs recently, which is awesome because I usually get to meet the bands and singers and they're super-happy to have a professional taking their picture rather than some blurry snapshot from a cameraphone. I like my job most days now.*

Something I didn't tell you last time. I take photos because of you. It was all I had of you for some time. I'm ashamed to say I'd forget your face sometimes, but Mum and Dad took enough photos to fix that. I could get lost in them. So, there's that.

Bullet point number two. Mum and Dad. Dad gave us a scare this year. A nasty case of pneumonia after the new year. I don't like hospitals – for obvious reasons – and seeing him in bed all day was awful. He said it was like prison, which made me laugh because, really, Dad in prison? Try as I might, I can't conjure up an image of him with tats, bench-pressing in the yard. Once he had the all-clear, things were back to normal (i.e. Mum complaining that the grass was getting long) soon after.

Bullet point three. An update on Manchester United. I'm afraid they did not win the league this year. But apparently the Manchester derby was one of the finest ever, with a man named Michael Owen scoring a goal in the ninety-sixth minute. Which I'm informed is quite late to be scoring a goal. I would not know if this is true, as I'm allergic to the footballs. I go through this fact-finding mission just for you. With help from Nick, which brings me to . . .

Bullet point number four. Nick is still as wonderful a human person as ever. He says to say hi from him. He's decided he's finally going to be an Oscar-winning screenwriter, but he seems to spend more time watching Oscar-winning films than

347

actually writing. He calls it research. I'm sure it is. We moved in together a few months ago. It's a very small flat above a florist. This is useful because, as I told you when you were four, boys are very, very smelly. The flowers help combat this. But even at Nick's most odorous, it's worth putting up with the smell for all the good times. There are many good times.

Bullet point number five. This has a heavy title: 'Losing You'. It's not meant to be all sad. I was. All sad. For quite some time. I was angry next. For even longer. Ours was a happy home before – and after, there was just a gap. We all went to different therapy sessions to help and they told us lots of things about moving on, and I don't know, maybe it got through eventually. Mum and Dad were constantly being told they had to put me first, which was awful advice to overhear. It made me feel crappy, like they had to forget about you and focus on me when that wasn't what I wanted at all. I wanted us to talk about you. For years we didn't. And for years I was really, really miserable. Like I said, that misery turned to anger and I think I'm lucky to be okay now. A few wrong choices and I think the trifecta of cool job, brilliant boyfriend and happy home would have been hard to come by.

It came down to a choice. I'm happy I chose love.

I miss you. I hope you like this tape. I know I like making them.

Love you, Lucas. See you next year.

Before the must-see next one, I try to figure out the purpose of all of this, the purpose of her sending me these recordings, the purpose of me choosing to watch them. Why are we putting ourselves through this? What lesson is there to be learnt? Nostalgia isn't what it used to be.

And now I remember. There's a man I need to see about a thing.

★

The last time I saw Richard, I didn't actually see him. I just heard his voice through the intercom as he refused to let me in to return Ellie's bike helmet. This time, however, upon hearing that his daughter's ex-boyfriend is outside his fancy Battersea apartment, he decides to buzz me in.

When I reach his floor, I take a moment to compose myself. Why am I here? What am I hoping to get out of this? Couldn't I just have texted an apology for the texts I sent? I knock and he opens the door.

He doesn't invite me in, or even acknowledge my presence; he simply turns his back on the open door, leaving me to step inside and close it. I'll be honest. It's a pretty gangster move for a guy in his sixties.

As I meekly make my way across the hallway's black and white tiles, I see the back of Richard's legs turning into a room. My mind wanders and I consider the possibility that he may have just let me in so he can murder me and claim self-defence. He'll tell the police he had no idea who I was, that he thought I was a burglar, which was why he beat me to death with a non-stick frying pan.

His back is still to me and he pours himself a glass of wine. I reckon the glass and the wine both cost more than I made today. He doesn't offer me a drink.

349

'I'm impressed,' he says, giving with one hand. 'I didn't think you'd have the courage to say you're sorry in person.'

'What makes you think I'm here to say sorry?'

He sips and shrugs, although the sip is more like a chug.

'Actually,' I say, 'I am sorry. And I am very much here to say that.' I know that if I delay by even a moment the apology, which he deserves, I'll bottle it.

He pulls out his phone and scrolls, reading the messages I sent moments before I passed out blind drunk at Tom's party.

'You're sorry for saying "Because you couldn't make your wife happy . . ."'

I wince as he continues to read, covered in the shamiest layer of shame. It's like he's playing a video of me in choir in primary school and my trousers have just been pulled down and I've wet myself.

'". . . you're to blame for mine and Ellie's misery."'

'Yes. That. I'm very sorry for that.'

He opens another message.

'And for calling me a "humane paraquat"?'

'That's supposed to be a "human paraquat". But yes. That too.'

'What's a para—'

I cut him off. 'It really doesn't matter. What matters is I shouldn't have said any of it. I was in a very bad place and looking for someone to blame. For some reason, that person was you. Will you accept my apology?'

He finishes his drink and pours himself another, pondering my question. After a moment, he smiles and his arm extends, just a little, as if the wine is slowly making its way to me. I smile back and reach out a hand to accept the olive branch, just as he snaps it back.

'No. I don't accept your apology.'

'Why?' I whine.

'I have thirty years of grovelling experience on you, Nick. And that was quarter-arsed at best.' He sits for the first time. Looking simultaneously up at me and down on me. 'Anyway, why do you even want my forgiveness? You and Ellie are over. You saw to that.'

'What's that supposed to mean?' I ask, knowing full well what it was supposed to mean. But not knowing how he'd figured it out.

'Ellie's mother wasn't the only woman I was ever with,' he explains. 'We didn't meet until I was twenty-seven. I don't know why it's so difficult for your generation to consider the fact that we had multiple partners over the course of our twenties. Probably because so many of you think solipsistically.'

He studies my reaction and spells it out. 'You think the world doesn't exist when you're not around.'

'I know what solipsism is,' I retort, with a little added petulance.

'Explained in a film, was it?'

Touché, Mr Brown. Touché.

'So, thrill me with your acumen. Why did Ellie and I split up?'

'I didn't say I knew why. I just know what you did. I've done it myself. I probably did it to my wife too.'

'Ex-wife.'

'Yes, thank you, Nick.'

351

He composes himself, takes another glug of Merlot.

'You understand that if you want to break up with someone you love, you don't fight with them. You don't cause arguments – or even worse, cheat on them – you don't do any of that, because that stirs up emotions and then you might realise what you mean to them and them to you. No. To really end things, you just slowly fade away . . .'

Richard looks over at a picture of his family, the four of them, happy.

'That's how you disappear completely.'

I move over to the bottle of wine and pour myself a glass. Richard doesn't give me, or it, a second glance.

'So why did you do it?' I ask. Half of me is hoping his answer might help me. The other half genuinely wants to know, in case there's something I can do.

'There wasn't just one reason. It's never usually that simple. Especially after so much time. You?'

I scratch at the back of my head and rub my neck. I suddenly feel very small.

'Because she deserves to be happy and I wasn't good enough for her.'

He stares me straight in the eye for the first time.

'I don't like you, Nick. I'm glad you're not a part of my life any more. You make weird jokes which you always seem smug about. You're vague in a way that's incredibly off-putting. At almost thirty years of age you still dress like a teenager. You say things like, "Thrill me with your acumen", thinking people won't know you've stolen it from *Silence of the Lambs*, even though the line is actually "Enthral me".'

Shit, I think. He's right.

'For all these reasons, I don't like you, Nick.'

He stops his judgement for a moment and the pity returns.

'But my daughter did.'

It might just be the nicest thing he's ever said to me, and I feel like crying all over his expensive Persian rug.

'Thanks, Richard,' I say. 'I'd better go. There's a video I need to watch.'

As he walks me out of the room, he mutters, 'And there's that vagueness again.'

'Maybe it was one of my smug jokes.'

I return the look of pity he offered me moments ago.

'Are you going to be all right?' I ask.

He shakes his head. 'If I say no, are you going to make a list of films we could watch together to help sort me out?'

He sees the look of enthusiasm in my eyes and I see the fear in his.

'If you want me to.'

'Goodbye, Nick.'

★

Back at the flat, Ronnie is out and so I have the time and space to watch the third video. It's the one labelled *BONUS* that I'm desperate to get to, but knowing Ellie, there's a reason why she wants me to watch these other ones first.

I click on *Ellie to Lucas – 10 April 2011*, and like magic she's here with me again. To the uninitiated she looks like she did in 2010. A jumper replacing the T-shirt. The hair the same, just tied up. Those ears on show. But there is something more this

353

time. Something I can't quite figure out. Something behind the eyes. A self-assurance I missed at the time.

I hit play.

It's me. Speaking from the other side.

This one will be present tense. I think in previous years we've covered grounds both new and old, but today we'll be firmly in the here and now. Agreed? Agreed. Well, I'll try at least. The past does have a certain allure after all.

Mum and Dad are well. He's suddenly taken an interest in gardening, so after years of being forced to mow the lawn and weed the borders, he's now enjoying it. He even has a little vegetable patch, although everything in it grows in the most peculiar direction. Still, he's proud of his wonky carrots, so we leave him be. Mum's retiring next year and I'm sure she'll have some advice on straightening them. How they'll get on when they're around each other twenty-four-seven is anyone's guess.

Work has its up and its downs. Feast or famine is the life of a freelancer, or so they say. I'm considering going back to full-time employment, as much as I loathe the idea. It's nice that Nick has a steady-ish job, although I'm not sure it's as future-proof as he likes to believe.

He showed me an old film last week. He does this sometimes. I used to get a bit moody with it, like he was pushing his taste on me, but I know now it's just him wanting to bring me his loves. It's okay when the film is good – and last week's was. Anyway, part of it is set in heaven and there's a line in which the lead character contemplates what the afterlife is like: 'I think it starts where this one leaves off, with all our earthly problems solved but with greater ones worth solving.' I liked that. I thought of you when he said it. I wondered if, where you are, you're curious as to my earthly problems. Anyway, I don't have many problems. I know how lucky I am and I'm grateful for it all.

But I do worry about Nick sometimes. Sometimes he goes places. I don't mean like the pub. I mean he just gets lost in his thoughts. Someone will say something and I'll see him staring into space working out what it all means, like there's some deeper meaning to a joke or a throwaway comment. He takes things so much to heart. I guess a lot of us do, but I notice it with him more than I've noticed it with anyone else. It's not a fault, I just sort of wish I could keep him here in the present. I want to yell at him, 'Wake up, Nick.' Selfish of me, I guess.

I wonder what the future holds for us. We've talked about children, but never marriage. I still feel like a kid myself a lot of the time. Next year I'll be thirty. Don't tell anyone.

C'est la vie, mon ami.

Okay, bye.

The abrupt ending is like a punch in the face. Although having actually been punched in the face recently by a coffee table, maybe the analogy is inaccurate. That one knocked me out. This one is having a different effect.

Both Gabby and Ellie have diagnosed me and they're rarely wrong.

Is there a cure?

For added torment, I skip back to the moment Ellie says, 'Wake up, Nick.' I play it over and over like she's Pinkie Brown and this is the end of *Brighton Rock*.

It's not. But here on my own, I'm allowed to pretend.

42

5 November 2008 – 05.35 GMT
Obama 338
McCain 155
Barack Hussein Obama is president-elect

The camera was trained on an empty podium in Grant Park, Chicago as 'Higher and Higher' by Jackie Wilson played out. As historic an event as this was, to me that song is so synonymous with *Ghostbusters 2*, all I could think about was Bill Murray and company as Obama greeted the crowd with a rock-star-ish 'Hello, Chicago.'

'Shut up. Everyone shut the hell up!' yelled the brasher of the two American guests.

And everyone did. Including Tom, who stood, arms folded, ready to make a quip or snide remark to undercut the feeling of unity.

The president-elect opened his address with a reference to just how unbelievable his accomplishment was. 'If there is anyone out there who still doubts that America is a place where all things are possible, who still wonders if the dream of our founders is alive in our time, who still questions the power of our democracy, tonight is your answer.'

While the Americans whooped and hollered, there was a knowing nod rippling through the British contingent. Namely the other 95 per cent of the house.

Maybe it was a case of everyone present – Tom excepted – wanting Obama to be their leader, but I felt there was something peculiarly British about him using the opening of his speech to point out just how absolutely nuts this was. 'America is a place' was a little jingoistic for sure, but the subtext was 'Okay, everyone, this has actually happened.'

A small group a few years younger than the rest were playing drinking games with the speech. Much to the annoyance of Americans One and Two. One player was taking shots of Southern Comfort every time Obama said the word 'change'. He was unconscious before the end of the speech.

For me, it was one simple line: 'What we've already achieved gives us hope for what we can and must achieve tomorrow.' Even though it wasn't meant for two comfortable twenty-somethings in south London, Ellie and I locked eyes and our hands found each other. The moment was broken by someone shrieking with laughter and pointing at Tom. 'Are you . . . are you crying?' they accused him, despite having wet cheeks themselves.

'He has feelings!' another yelled. And Tom was quickly in the middle of a huge bundle of hugs.

'Get off me, you fucking liberals,' he shouted, gasping for air.

As the bundle disbanded, ruffling his hair as they went, I looked over to Tom, who was pushing tears back into his eyes.

'It is pretty good, I suppose,' he grudgingly confessed.

I let go of Ellie's hand to throw my arms around him. She watched on, grinning, as he playfully pushed me off too.

The familiar sign-off of 'God Bless the United States of America' heralded the end of the speech, but more Springsteen signified that the night was far from over. I put my arms around Ellie's shoulders and we swayed in time to the music.

In that room, at that moment, there was no cynicism, no doubt. Nobody was saying anybody couldn't do anything. There was hope.

43

My original plan was to watch the final video at Ronnie's. But today he and some friends are having their yearly Yuletide bake off. So instead, I packed up my laptop and Ellie's USB stick and started to walk.

I wasn't exactly sure where I was going, but I was enjoying the Christmas lights making even the gloomier parts of London that little bit brighter. My internal navigator took me past a number of mine and Ellie's haunts. The pub where we had our second date. The venue where we saw Frightened Rabbit play *The Midnight Organ Fight* in full. The bench she'd sit on to meet me after work.

And now I'm here, staring up at the building I've been in a thousand times before.

★

'That's quite a favour during opening hours,' Seb says. 'How long's the file?'

'Less than five minutes,' I reply.

He checks his little slip of paper with the film start times on it. The only analogue remnant in his all-new digital world.

'Screen 2's free,' he says, pointing to a blinking panel of dials and LEDs.

'More machine now than man,' I quip.

'They were always machines, Nick.'

He pulls out the port window that separates the projection booth from the auditorium and feeds through a long grey cable. He attaches one end to the digital projector.

'Thanks for the Edinburgh hook-up,' I say.

'No problem. I know it's only temporary, but you think you'll take it?'

'I'm not sure. I want to, but it feels . . . I dunno, we'll see.'

He doesn't push for an answer; instead he fires up the digital projector by tapping in a few bits of code.

'Have you named her?' I ask.

Seb shakes his head.

'Can I call her Brigitte, the Maschinenmensch? For an old friend?'

He places an affectionate hand on my shoulder. 'Do what you like, just get out of here by quarter to. Deal?'

I salute him and make my way down the back of Screen 2. I plug in the other end of the long grey cable and my laptop screen saver fills the auditorium screen. I open *BONUS* and click play.

Ellie's face is smiling back at me from forty feet, looking just like it did when I said goodbye to her at the airport. And also completely different. Maybe this time I'll work out why.

Hey, Nick – bet you thought I'd suffix that with a 'the Dick', right? Well, I'm thirty-one soon, and as The Korgis – and latterly Beck – said, 'Everybody's gotta learn sometime', and by learn, I mean grow up. New York is big. And tall. Bet you didn't know that.

Americans like work, and as a wannabe American, I guess I do too now. I wouldn't say I was oversold the job, maybe I had a case of the Nicks in fantasising what it would be like – more historic events, less making folders of pictures of cats – but it has been a little mundane at times. Therefore, after five weeks out here, I have very little to wow you with that isn't work-related. Although I did share a lift with Michael Sheen the other day! He was making the woman he was with laugh a lot. I thought of you.

I thought of you again when I went to the cinema by myself last week. I know, right? Four years together and I never contemplated it. Always balking when you recommended I go to a movie you'd already seen. 'But who will I go with?' I'd fret. And you'd be all 'Just go on your own,' and I'd be like 'No, only losers go to the cinema alone!' and you'd be all pretend offended.

The day came and it was okay. Kind of fun, actually. You'll be pleased to hear you were right. It's easier to say that now.

The film I watched was called Ruby Sparks *and had the mute guy from* Little Miss Sunshine *in it and a girl whose name was Zoe something. You know I'm not good with names. I won't give away too much because you might want to see it, but it was about a lonely guy who's down on his luck with love and he's a writer and so he writes about his dream woman and she comes to life. It probably sounds a bit like* Weird Science. *But it's really nothing like* Weird Science.

I don't mean this in a loaded way, but you really should watch it. I'd love to know what you think of the guy and the ending and . . . well, I don't want to give away too much. It came out way back in June, but this cool little indie cinema was playing it as a rerun. Has it come out in the UK yet? That felt weird to write.

I hope Gabby and little Freddie are doing okay. I never thought Gabby would become a Facebook mum, recording every moment and sharing it online, but judging by the frequency of her posts, I regret to inform you she has indeed. I assume you're still bypassing all social media? I chat to Gabby quite a bit on there and, well, one of the many reasons I wanted to film this for you was to say she told me you felt awful about forgetting Lucas Day this year.

Please. Don't.

Those videos, that idea, it was the single most lovely thing anyone has ever done for me. They reminded me how much I loved him and made me feel close to him for the first time in years. I know you always said they weren't meant for anyone but me, but I thought they could be useful to you. Or to me. Anyway, I hope you've watched them. I wanted you to.

Now for a harder bit. I know it's wrong of me to say this, but I always thought if we went through a bad patch, you'd be the one to pull us through it. I'm so sorry for leaving that up to you. It wasn't fair. Or right. I will always regret that.

Finally, I don't want you to think Gabby and I only talk about you – this is obviously just for you so I'm not going to mention all the other things we talk about — but she also mentioned you thought my invites to come to New York with me weren't genuine. They were, Nick. Of course they were. And they still are.

I don't know how to convince you of that, if you don't want to be convinced.

I know it's a long trip, but if you ever wanted to come, it'd be great to see you.

I miss you.

And like that, she's gone. But not before I finally figure out what the difference was in her eyes. It was her growing. Seeing multiple versions of Ellie, from four years ago through to now, I see the way she made it out the other side.

We were both kids for so long. Way past the time we shouldn't have been.

It's easy to argue over the intent of the written word. A short email can easily be misinterpreted. A text even more so. This, however, there's something real about it. I feel the words more. And in these words, I feel Ellie. I feel that she's lonely and I feel her love for me. And I wish, I wish so much that I could separate those two things to find out which is more powerful.

*

Less than twenty-four hours later, I've drafted a letter to Ellie. I say drafted; what I mean is I've written it out fourteen times. Sometimes I omit details of my boring job. Other times I include them. A couple of versions have a recap of *Obama Election Night II: The Twattening*, in which I detail my every cringeworthy move. One even reveals the full extent of the date with Mia. Window and all.

This last version, the one I'm holding in my hand, is the right one to send.

Making Ellie feel good is essentially the purpose of the entire document, and so I've included a passage where I let her know that solo cinema won't last long if she doesn't want it to. That once she's over the ten per cent rule – invented by a genius, I add – she'll have every guy from Brooklyn to the Bronx beating down her door. And on that ten per cent rule, I tell her, I now have irrefutable proof that it is the absolute bare minimum of time needed.

I use the letter to apologise too. To say sorry for the 'narcolepsy', as Gabby calls it. I tell her that while I hope she knows, if she doesn't, I'm so happy for her and her new job. That I think she's amazing and it's good that good things happen to good people.

I let her know that alongside the ten per cent rule, there's a three-month rule for any new job, and so if she's not happy after three months, she should find something new. Wherever it might take her. She'll learn everything she needs to know within those twelve weeks, and if it's not for her, like she told me on several occasions, life's too short to waste it being unhappy.

The hardest part of the letter to write was the response to the video. I even thought of filming one in return in which I talked about how great she was, but it always came out like I was trying to get her back.

I can't do that in a letter.

If she was just here again. If she was just down the road . . .

I thank her again for the invite. State for the record that I now know the offer is genuine. Even make a joke that as I have her address, I might just turn up on her doorstep one day with a hot dog and a baseball cap.

My reply mentions that I've been writing again, and so I thank her for the pen and pad she hid away for me. I tell her I've had more rejections but one production company said my stuff has potential. They gave me notes to make it better. The old Nick would have thrown his toys out of the pram and refused to change a word. Now I take comfort in the realisation that a script isn't anything unless people want to make it into something.

I hope she won't mind, but I wrote a bit about us. Changed the names to protect the guilty. I tell her that I wrote about our first Christmas. About our ill-fated trip to Cannes. About the pregnancy that wasn't and the fight that was.

I've typed them up, I tell her, saved them to my laptop and emailed them to myself so they won't get lost. But I think she should have the originals. I tucked them into the envelope before I left the house.

What I don't include in the letter – because I don't think it will help her – is where I'm at now. With myself. That's something I can only reveal to her in person. Gabby was so close to asking the right question in the hospital. She asked, 'Do you like being unhappy?' but what she should have asked was 'Do you like yourself, Nick?' Too much of the time the answer is no.

And that's the truth I've been avoiding.

Ellie and I didn't end because we started too strong. We didn't end because life conspired against us. We didn't end because everything eventually does. And we didn't end because her parents put the seed of doubt into us.

It was none of these reasons and all of them.

Relationships end when people stop putting the effort in. And for lots of stupid little reasons – and one big one – I stopped putting the effort in.

We ended because of me. Because of decisions I made. Because, like I said to her dad, she deserves to be happy. Just like that first night, when I tried to run away and she persuaded me not to. I wanted to run away because I was scared, yes, but also because I truly believed I didn't deserve her. The magic of Ellie was that when she was fully there, she never made me doubt myself. With her, the answer to the question was yes.

She made me like myself.

For one short period of time when she needed me to look after myself, when she needed help, I wasn't there. I was thinking of myself and how I'd feel if she left. How scared I was to be on my own again and how I was desperate for it to not be her decision. I protected myself the only way I knew how. By switching off. To do what I did was selfish, cruel and blind. A monumentally stupid act of self-sabotage. But here I stand. I am sad. I am free. Free from the doubt that I'm not deserving of her love.

Here's the final lesson to be learnt. Because if decades of watching movies has taught me anything, there is always a lesson to be learnt.

In this story — my story — it doesn't matter what Ellie's mum said. Or what Ellie's dad thinks. Or the looks we got in restaurants. Or how I feel too much of the time about myself. What matters is what the people who matter think. And on the whole, they see a better picture of me.

As for Ellie? It was never up to me whether I thought I was good enough for her.

It was up to her.

*

Arriving at the post office to buy the little envelopes with the red, blue and white border, I stretch out my cramping hand in the freezing air. It's pretty sore from writing multiple versions of what turned out to be very similar letters. I always knew what I needed to say, I just wanted to get it right.

Christmas is coming, the geese are getting fat and the queue for stamps is longer than Santa's naughty list. A blinking board tells me the current exchange rate is 1 GBP = 1.59 USD. I'm also holding my reply about the projectionist's position in Edinburgh. I only ever drafted one. I know where I'll be spending Christmas. I know that when New Year comes around, this year I'll make my resolutions stick. For the first time in a long time, I know where I'm going.

44

5 November 2008 – 06.45 GMT
Obama 338
McCain 155
Barack Hussein Obama is president-elect

'Smile,' Ellie said, and as I turned, I took a faceful of blinding flash. It left that little white spot when I blinked. She shook the Polaroid and explained how each of these was roughly a quid, and so she rarely used this camera except for special occasions.

'I like the immediacy of them, though,' she said, as the image came into focus. 'And this one? This one's a keeper.'

She showed me the picture and I was happy with the result. I rarely thought I looked good, but the way she was watching me gave me confidence. If a girl like that could look that way at a boy like me . . .

'A keeper? It's too early to be jumping to conclusions like that,' I said.

'You're probably right. I'll give it a year.'

'How about four? We could meet here again at the next election. Fall in lo—' I corrected myself. 'Get to know each other a second time.'

Looking around at our fellow revellers, it didn't seem like a bad plan to do it all over again. There were lots of happy, lovely people here.

The party was winding down and a few familiar faces were heading for the exit. One young couple holding hands were immediately recognisable. He was the poor unfortunate who'd been given the word 'change' in the short-lived drinking game. He'd made a speedy recovery. She, Ellie and I noticed simultaneously, was only wearing one shoe.

Ellie pointed to the girl's bare foot as they walked out of the front door.

'Is that . . .?'

'I think it might be,' I replied, as we followed them out to watch them navigate the garden steps. The sun was just about ready for the new day.

'Fair play to them,' Ellie said.

'How long do you give them?' I asked.

'Oh, this is the start of something special for those two,' she said with surety. 'I'm talking marriage, kids, the full catastrophe.'

We looked on as the drunken couple reached the end of the path. They stopped, kissed, and then turned their backs on each other to vomit in perfect synchronicity. Afterwards they walked off in completely different directions.

'So.' Ellie turned to me. 'You sure you don't want to leave it at one special night?'

I pretended to contemplate the question with an elongated 'err' that fully justified her punching me in the arm. I'd need to get used to those punches, I thought. Or stop making bad jokes.

'Someone told me they're showing *Cinema Paradiso* at the Prince Charles on Sunday,' I said with a wink.

'Oh really?' she replied, seeing my wink and raising me an eyebrow. 'And who was this someone?'

'I don't think you know her. I mean, she's pretty special. Funny, gorgeous, talented. The kind of person you don't meet very often. But when you do, you make every moment count.'

I paused.

'On second thoughts, I'm not really sure I have much to offer her.'

She blinked twice.

'You should have a little more faith in yourself.'

45

My best day with Ellie involved a house party hosted by a libertarian, a shoe filled with vomit, an angry ex-lover outside a Chicken Cottage, a joke I can't remember, a view I'll never forget, and the unapologetic wonder of potential.

If the first letter I drafted to Ellie was an email, it would have been sent and I wouldn't be here. I wonder how many bad decisions have been made that could have been avoided if not for instant communication. When I got to the counter at the post office, I knew it was time. Time to – in the words of Ewan McGregor in the worst of all the *Star Wars* films – rethink my life.

I've come to a decision on the two big questions I have to answer. With the first, as much as I would love to turn back time, I can't. It was a huge part of my life, but it's over now. In the past, where it belongs. And so I delivered a 'no' to the good people of the Edinburgh film festival, declining their invitation to be a projectionist again.

I'm all about forward steps now. I have more patience

for them now. I have more patience for a lot of things. I've finally branched out. Even though I'd only been in the job with Jim and Paula for a couple of months, they were happy to write me a fantastic reference and put me in touch with some of their friends in faraway places. Sometimes it pays to do things that don't appear perfect, to get to where you need to go. Ellie taught me that.

She taught me a lot.

She also taught me that love is changeable. It's exciting and it's boring. It's head over heels and it's dependable. It's happy and it's sad. Sometimes it's like the movies. And mostly it's not. And I deserve every type of it as much as the next guy.

I'm not supposed to be half of a whole.

One and one makes two.

The key is to pay attention.

Pay attention to your family. To the people you work with. Pay attention to the one who shares your sofa. The one who shares your bed. Pay attention.

Pay attention to the safety instructions. They might just save your life.

★

I'm struggling to decide between watching *The Bourne Legacy*, which had iffy reviews, or rewatching *In Bruges*.

In Bruges was one of the first films Ellie and I watched together. I know it shouldn't have, but it mattered to me that we both liked it. I really adored the ending. It was one of the few films where the credits ran at the perfect moment. No more. No less.

I might just watch some TV shows instead, or listen to music. I'm really loving the Kishi Bashi album Ellie told me about. The second track, 'Manchester', is sublime, with just the kind of self-obsessed lyrics I can't get enough of. It even includes lines about wanting to be in a movie.

The third track, 'Bright Whites', is probably the most infectious piece of pop I've heard in a decade. It makes me happy and reminds me that I like being happy. And thanks to my friends and family and the people around me, I know that I can be.

I suppose I could watch another film, but it feels wrong to me to watch something meant for the big screen on a monitor mounted to the back of someone else's chair. But then it also feels wrong to be hurtling through the sky in a metal tube at 39,000 feet.

This decision, though, this decision feels right.

Acknowledgements

This book wouldn't be here if it wasn't for the following people and you'd just be staring at your hands.

First and most importantly, the biggest thank you goes to my partner, Nina. There are a million quotes I could steal to sum up what you mean to me (most of them said by Billy Crystal). Instead, I'll just say, you made this possible and you make every day better. Here's to the next ten years.

To Oscar and Isaac. I was only pretending to be a writer before you came along. You give me a reason to write every day.

To Hayley Steed, my Wonder Agent. Have I ever said, "Thank you"? Well, here's another three. Thank you, thank you, thank you. My advice to any aspiring authors is, get yourself an agent who looks at your words like Hayley looks at mine. And to the amazing team at the Madeleine Milburn Agency. I don't know how you do it, but you really do.

To my brilliant editor, Jess Whitlum-Cooper, who has so far been right about everything. Long may that continue.

And to all at Headline who made this experience an absolute delight.

To my mum and dad, Julie and Keith. And to my brother and sister, Gareth and Hannah. I am who I am because of you. This could be taken as a wonderful way to blame you for my shortcomings, but is meant as a thank you for all you've done and continue to do.

To my first, best reader, Jake Marcet. You not only let me steal your surname but called me a "Wonderful Shitass" when you read the first draft. That was all the affirmation I needed to keep going.

To my next-in-line readers Suzanne Sharman, Lewis Swift, Rob Perry and Sarah Courtauld. For helping me when I wasn't sure if Jake's praise was solely due to him seeing his own surname in print.

As George Bailey must remember, "No Man is a Failure Who Has Friends". I'm lucky to have the ones I have. Get yourself all the choc ices.

To all at the National Centre For Writing, starting with whoever picked the first few chapters of this book out of their submissions pile and passed it on for the Escalator Scheme. A big thank you to my Escalator mentor Benjamin Johncock, for your time and words of advice. To Laura Stimson, for organising every aspect of the scheme and to Cathy Rentzenbrink, for a single breakfast that made me feel like a writer. And of course, a big shout out to my fellow Escalatees. Thankfully you're now my friends and not just these amazing writers that make me feel slightly intimidated by their ridiculously great work.

Like many dreaming of publication, I had to pay the bills with an office job and was lucky to spend the past few years with the great Studio Team of Discovery House. Inside the Studio Team was the ever-supportive Copy Team of Rich Skelton, Rob Perry and Becky Done. A special thanks to my lunchtime writing buddy and first editor, Hannah Harper. Balloon room forever. Or, until just after one thirty.

Finally, I'd like to thank all the UCI/Odeon alumni who, in big or little ways, influenced this book, especially the booth team of Mark, Joe, Lewis, Rob, Tony, Jodie, Andy, Matt, Jon, The Johns, Clara, Roger and Chris. My last thank you is to Amanda, who in many ways started all this by giving me a job all those years ago. I hope I love my new job as much as I loved working with you all, when I was a little squirt.

KEEP IN TOUCH
WITH OWEN NICHOLLS

© Christopher Blythe

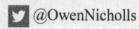 @OwenNicholls

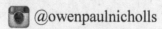 @owenpaulnicholls